The Arliss

A Novel by Ann Bakshis

Copyright © 2019 by Ann Bakshis

This book is a work of fiction. The names, characters, places, and incidents are products of the writer's imagination or have been used fictitiously and are not to be construed as real. Any resemblance to persons, living and dead, actual event, locales or organizations is entirely coincidental.

All rights reserved. No part of this book may be used or reproduced in any manner whatsoever without written permission from the author.

Published by Ponahakeola Press, 2019

Typeset in Garamond and Andale Mono

Dedicated in loving memory of my 'work husband' Doug.

I can't imagine a life without you in it.

Your big heart and contagious laugh will be greatly missed.

Rest well, gentle giant.

TABLE OF CONTENTS

One	5
Two	16
Three	27
Four	46
Five	51
Six	69
Seven	79
Eight	92
Nine	102
Ten	116
Eleven	127
Twelve	138
Thirteen	149
Fourteen	161
Fifteen	171
Sixteen	186
Seventeen	200
Eighteen	212

One

One… two… three. One… two… three.

I hold my breath as I try to psych myself into moving.

One… two… three… go!

Nothing. I'm frozen in place, too afraid to look out between the cracks of the debris on top of me. Terrified at what the world beyond my cover looks like. I don't remember what happened or how I even got here. I only know that my name is Sara, I'm covered in dirt and dust, and my legs are starting to spasm from being crammed into such a small space.

I can do this… I can do this.

I lean forward, position the metal sheet that is covering me between my shoulder blades, and push upward. The metal scrapes against other objects, but it does move… slowly. It takes several tries, and when I do free myself I quickly wish I hadn't.

The scene in front of me is a type of destruction I've never seen before, or at least I think that's true. Buildings of brick and metal lay in rubble on the ground. Those that are still standing have large portions missing, exposing their interiors to the bright red sky and harsh orange sun. Flames shoot high into the air from ruptured gas lines that poke up through the fragmented ground. Vehicles lay toppled and partially disintegrated along a strip of asphalt that must've once been a road. Ash-colored clouds wisp across the sky like brushstrokes. The air is slightly acidic, but surprisingly tolerable. I lift myself further out of the hole I'm in and start to cough as I disturb more dust around me.

I'm not sure if I was in a building or next to one, but beside the large metal sheet there are blistered bricks and melted glass. I glance down at my feet and notice that my heavy black boots have red splotches on them, but I'm not wounded as far as I can tell. My dark green pants have a rip in the knee, but there isn't a corresponding injury behind it. Wrapped around both thighs are large caliber guns nestled in their holsters. My arms are bare, with the exception of thick, black leather bands around each wrist. My shirt consists of a black tank top, which is tucked into the pants and fastened with a brown belt. Apart from the rip in the pants there doesn't appear to be a scratch on me, which I find disturbing considering where I'm crawling out from.

I hesitate to leave my spot as I have no idea where the hell I am. I don't see any signs of life, only a few body fragments that look fresh, strewn about next to the hole. I feel like I should be freaking out at the sight of them, but I'm not and it bothers me. I take another look around before climbing my way across the brick, concrete, and metal rods that litter the area. I plan the placement of my feet very carefully so not to injure myself and it takes a good five minutes to make it to an open spot in the road.

The harshness of the sun is starting to hurt my eyes, so much so that I have to squint just so I can see. I don't know which direction to go, so I start walking away from the sun as it continues to climb higher in the sky. I glance into vehicles as I pass, trying to see if any of them contain something I can use to shield my eyes. I finally find a torn ball cap stuck under the backseat of one of the thousands of vehicles that line the desolate road. I pull my straight auburn hair behind my head and shove it through the opening in the back of the cap, making a ponytail. The bill of the cap does help, but not a whole hell of a lot.

The landscape eventually gives way to brown grass and rusted fences. I catch a glimpse of the occasional house in the distance, but they're in the same condition as the area I just left. Fires burn at the base of a mountain range to my left. Something tells me those should've died down long ago. So why are they still roaring at full strength?

It's close to an hour before I come upon a gas station that's partially intact. The bell above the door rings when I open it, but no one responds. I'd have been shocked if someone did. I cross to the back of the store where three cold-storage units still stand. The glass is broken on all of them, which makes it easier to reach inside and remove several bottles of water. I have no idea if they're any good, or contaminated with whatever destroyed the area, but my throat hurts so much at the moment that I don't really care.

Though warm, the water in the bottle tastes fresh and unpolluted. I polish off two more before going behind the register to grab a bag to carry more. I should take some snacks while I'm at it, but nothing looks appealing. I know I'm being picky, given my current circumstance, but a little voice in the back of my head is screaming at me to only take the water. I return to the front door where I notice a rack of sunglasses leaning close to the windows. I grab the one good pair and slip them on as I go back outside and continue heading in the direction I had been. It doesn't take long for my throat to dry out, so I'm forced to drink one of the bottles I was hoping to save for later.

Hours must have passed, yet I feel like I'm getting nowhere. The scenery hasn't changed, except the mountain range is now directly in front of me. The fires have diminished, but ash and smoke still cling to the air. My legs are growing tired, and my stomach begs to be fed. I don't want to sit down without proper cover now that the sun has moved straight above and my skin is starting to turn a blistering shade of red. I eventually come upon a small clutch of homes wrapped around a cul-de-sac, its lone road extending to the one I'm currently on. The houses look to be intact, but upon closer inspection many have holes in their roofs, windows missing, and trees trying to creep up through derelict driveways. These were obviously abandoned years ago.

I step through a cracked doorway and enter into a living room with moldy floorboards, rotted bookcases, and one couch tipped on its side. I step deeper inside until I'm in the kitchen, which has a chipped terracotta floor, discolored countertops, and rusted appliances. I check the rest of the house, mainly to make sure there isn't anyone or anything hiding, but all I find is the same dilapidated furnishings throughout. I return to the living room, straighten the couch, and sit. My eyelids grow very heavy and it's taking all my strength to keep them open, but I find I'm losing the battle so I lean on my side and fall asleep.

My heart races as I run. I know what I'm doing… at least I think I do. They'll forgive me—eventually maybe, but not right away. I can't live in a world knowing what I know. How can anyone, yet I'm keeping the secret to myself. No one would believe me if I told them anyway, so I might as well let the truth die with me. It'll be better for everyone... especially those I love.

The bomb should be launching soon. I just hope I reach the city before it does. I'd rather be crushed to death than incinerated, which could still occur depending on where the bomb is aimed. My squad is in the lookouts today, so they'll see me die. I can't help that… I need to leave this world for good and there isn't anything or anyone that's going to stop me.

The city looms ahead, its tall buildings shining in the harsh sunlight of our shattered atmosphere. My feet hit the curb separating the debris-covered plaza from the cracked road, causing me to trip and fall on broken glass, slicing a deep cut into my knee and scraping my hands. I quickly get back up and head deeper into the city, but it's too late. The bomb has arrived, striking the burnt earth a mile in front of me, just outside the city's limits. The force of the impact shoves me backwards and into a plate-glass window, cutting off chunks of my arms and ripping off my ear. As I crawl out of the building, the superheated gases hit me and disintegrates me to dust.

A harsh noise jars me awake. I'm startled by the darkness that's suddenly enveloped me, as well as the nightmare I just had. I feel something heavy in my hand and that's when I notice the gun, which I have aimed into the void that now surrounds me. I don't remember taking it out of the holster, so it must've been an instinctive response. But what would've caused it: the nightmare or the noise? A scraping sound echoes around me, only this time it's much closer. I stand and slowly make my way towards the back of the house, holding my gun firmly in front of me. The noise is replaced by a low growl, which is now behind me. I spin around, but because of the darkness I can't clearly distinguish between the void and whatever is in front of me. The growling escalates, causing me to back into a wall. The thing charges and I fire the weapon multiple times. Silence takes over, but only for a brief moment.

"Sara!" someone shouts from a distance.

I step over whatever the thing is I killed and go back to the living room, but I don't lower my weapon.

"Sara!" My name rings out, but much closer this time.

I stop a few feet from the front door, when I notice through the bay window a light bobbing towards the house. The door bursts open, the light blinds me, and I haphazardly fire my weapon.

"Stop shooting!" a male voice yells.

"Then lower the light," I say as my finger caresses the trigger.

He lowers the light, but I don't recognize the face. The man, who had dropped to the floor when I fired, appears to be in his mid-twenties with a thin nose, short sandy-colored hair, and a strong jaw.

"We've been looking everywhere for you," he says, a little more relaxed this time as he stands.

I continue to stare at him, my gun at arm's length.

"We thought you'd been killed when we saw the blast."

My brain is working vigorously, trying to put a name to the face, but nothing will come. Nothing about him seems familiar, yet he knows me.

"Keegan!" a deep voice calls from several yards away.

"In here," the man replies.

Three people enter the house, not one of them familiar to me. The first one in is a man in his mid-thirties, my height, with an olive complexion and wavy, shoulder-length black hair. The next man is in his teens, possibly sixteen or seventeen, with a significantly scarred face, is very thin, and with curly blond hair. The last person to join us is much older than the rest. He's tall, bald, heavily muscled, and has a deep gouge over his right eye, which extends to the bottom of his cheek.

"Sara," the older man begins as he puts a hand up and slowly reaches for my gun. "We're not going to hurt you. I just need you to lower your weapon."

"Who are you?" I ask through gritted teeth as I try to hide the tremble in my voice.

"What do you mean, who are we?" the man they called Keegan asks, with an astonished look on his face.

"Maybe the blast fucked up her head," the man with the olive skin says, chuckling.

"It should've killed her," the older man responds in a serious tone. He looks around the room, then gestures to Keegan to move his light over towards the kitchen. Lying on the floor is a large wolf with thick black fur and white foam covering a good portion of his muzzle. "Jules and Cody, go check the outside perimeter. Keegan, check the rest of the house."

The three do as they're instructed without asking questions. The older man turns his attention back towards me, his arm now lowered.

"What do you remember?" he asks after several minutes.

"Nothing," I hesitantly respond.

"But you know your name?" he asks with a quizzical look.

"Yes, but that's all."

He glares at me, probably not believing anything I just said. I wish I did remember more, then perhaps I wouldn't be in this mess. The clothing the four men are wearing is the same as mine, so perhaps I do belong in their group. But who are they and why can't I remember?

Keegan returns a few minutes later, stating the rest of the house is clear. "You're lucky only one came after you," he says to me. "They normally travel in packs."

"What is it?" I ask, finally putting my gun back in its holster, only because my arm is getting tired. I still don't trust the newcomers, so my hand stays on the grip in case I need to use it quickly.

"It's a Mulgrim," the older man answers.

"A what?" I ask, not understanding the term.

"You really don't remember what a Mulgrim is?" the older man asks, puzzled. "It's a nocturnal wolf that can only be seen when a special light is cast on it."

"Like this," Keegan says. He removes another flashlight from his belt and shines it over towards the body, but nothing shows. Then he shines the light he used earlier and the beast is clear as day. "They move like smoke, which allows them to easily sneak up on their prey. The one you killed looks to have been rabid so it was probably abandoned by its pack, which is why it came alone."

"Where do they come from?"

"They're the result of decades of radiation exposure to the wolves that had called the Kai Mountains home," the older man says. "They roam the territory freely now since we took over the mountain."

As Keegan secures his flashlights to his belt Jules and Cody return, giving an all clear. Cody, the young one, is all set to leave, but the older man isn't budging.

"It'll be safer for us to stay here for the night," the older man says as he leans his back against the wall.

"You've got to be kidding," Jules says. "We'll be dead before the sun comes up."

Keegan takes off a pack from his back and removes a metal box, which when opened contains an injector and several cartridges of a blue liquid. "I came prepared, sissy boy," he says, displaying the contents for all to see.

"Give Sara an injection now," the older man says. "We can't take any chances with her."

Keegan gestures for me to sit on the couch, which I do after some hesitation. He places one of the cartridges into the injector and is about to press the metallic device against my exposed bicep, but I pull away at the last minute.

"This isn't going to hurt," Keegan says, mocking me.

"It's not that," I respond. "How can I be sure what you're giving me isn't going to kill me?"

"If we were going to kill you, we would've done so already," Jules says, shifting his rifle from one shoulder to the other.

Keegan rolls his eyes, places the device against his skin, and presses a button, which shoots the liquid into his body. He loads another cartridge and does the same thing to Cody, then Jules. I finally relent. The liquid is cold as it penetrates, and I can actually feel it coursing through my veins and then entering my muscles. The older man, who Keegan calls Wavern, is the last to be injected.

"Satisfied?" Keegan asks, packing up the kit.

I grin in response.

"Covering all entry points out here will be difficult so let's move into one of the bedrooms," Wavern says.

I pick up my bag of bottles and follow the group to the last bedroom at the end of the hall next to the kitchen. Once we're all inside, Jules and Cody move a fractured dresser in front of the door while Keegan and Wavern cover the lone window with the mattress from a twin-sized bed. They have to use the metal frame of the bed to keep the mattress propped in place. We take seats at various points in the room. Everyone except me has their weapon out. It's hard to see faces since the room is so dark, but Wavern doesn't want anyone turning on a flashlight. None of the others question why, which bothers me. The door and window are covered, so I don't see what the harm can be with having a little bit of light in the room. I'm about to ask when Jules speaks.

"Where'd you get the water bottles?" he asks me.

"From a gas station down the road."

"And you think they're safe to drink?" Cody asks, surprised.

"They taste fine and the bottles themselves aren't compromised."

"That doesn't mean anything," Jules says.

"Don't scare her," Keegan says, jumping in. "If the seals at the top are intact, then they're fine. You know that material is made to withstand anything and everything. We'll be long dead and that plastic shit will still be around."

"Did you take anything else from the gas station?" Wavern asks.

"Just a pair of sunglasses." I go to reach for them on the top of my head, but they must've fallen off when I was sleeping.

"Good. If you'd eaten any of the food we'd be burying you shortly," he responds.

Silence falls between us, but I don't let it last.

"What did you inject me with?" I ask Keegan, even though I can barely see where he's sitting.

"It's an antitoxin called Cymatilis. It's used to prevent radiation poisoning, but the downside is that it only lasts in the body for six hours before metabolizing. This is why I carry refills," he answers, directing the last sentence towards Jules.

"Then why isn't she sick?" Cody asks, his voice cracking. "The bomb went off over twelve hours ago. The blast obviously didn't kill her, so the radiation should have."

At the mention of the bomb, my mind goes back to the nightmare I had of my body turning to dust. It had to have just been a nightmare, but it seemed so real.

"There's a lot of things that need answering," Wavern responds. "She'll be examined when we get back to Rinku, but for now we need to get some rest."

I'm too wired to sleep, but I don't know if it's from the injection or because of the fact that I'm alive when I shouldn't be. I wish I knew what the hell is going on. Wavern thinks he has questions? Huh, I've got plenty of my own. For instance, how the hell did I survive that blast without a scratch and why can I only remember my name? I'm surprisingly calm about all of this, when I should be freaking out, which makes me question my sanity at this moment.

I rest the back of my head against the wall while someone moves around, probably changing positions. I'm knocked into and notice that Keegan is now sitting next to me, a little too close for comfort.

"How are you holding up?" he whispers to me once he's settled.

"Fine," I whisper back.

"I didn't think we were going to find you, but Wavern wouldn't let us quit. He was determined that we locate you no matter how long it took."

"Even if all you found was a body, or pieces of one? Why even bother looking for me if you all thought I was dead?"

"Not all of us thought that," Keegan replies, sounding hurt.

"How did you find me?"

"We waited for the heatwave to subside before we left Rinku. The satellites broadcast the blast to our control center. From his lookout in the mountains, Wavern saw you enter the abandoned city seconds before the detonation. He radioed for us to gear up and meet him by the compound's entrance. When we reached the city's outer edge, Wavern caught sight of you heading down the road. We followed, but then lost track of you when the sun set."

"That city was abandoned? Are you sure?"

"Lymont, like much of the Aslu Territory, has been desolate for decades. You were the only one there when the bomb went off," Keegan says.

"But I saw body parts strewn about. And whose blood is all over my boots?" I ask, getting agitated and raising my voice slightly.

"I don't know, Sara, but the area was completely devoid of people."

"Then why was I there?"

"We were hoping you could tell us," Jules says from across the room.

"I didn't say anything when I left Rinku?"

"You weren't in the control center when roll call was made," Wavern says. "It wasn't until the satellites picked you up that we even realized you were out of the compound, but by then it was too late. The bomb was only seconds away."

"Who dropped it?"

"We don't know," Keegan replies nervously.

"What?" I ask, shocked by the answer. "How do you not know?"

"Not everything is so easy, Sara," Jules answers. "We try to predict when they'll strike, which is why we have our lookouts. We haven't seen aircraft dropping the bombs, so we're pretty sure they're being launched. We've never been able to detect from where. The projectiles don't even show on the satellites until they're close to impact. It's almost like they're shielded from detection until the last possible moment."

"How long has this been going on?" I ask.

"Far too long," Wavern replies. "Now, get some sleep since we have a long day ahead of us."

I lean my head against the wall and close my eyes. I try to clear my mind of all thoughts, so I can at least relax but the nightmare keeps replaying. I'm finally about to drift off when a strange, high-pitched howl pierces the quiet. It sounds almost like fingernails on slate and it's hurting my ears. I'm about to say something when Keegan puts his hand over my mouth. The howling receives a response from several sources close by.

"A pack of Mulgrim," Keegan whispers to me. "They must sense the body of the one you killed."

"Are we safe here?" I whisper back, not liking the idea of being cornered in a room with monsters just outside.

"We should be. They won't come near the corpse because they can smell its sickness, but they probably also smell us. This could make for a long night," Wavern says.

"What do we do?"

"Nothing at the moment," Jules answers. "If we keep quiet, they should move on. The door and window are covered, which will make it difficult for them to breach the room."

"But not impossible," I say.

"Correct," Keegan replies.

I find myself holding my breath periodically, as if trying to prevent the Mulgrim from hearing me. No one else seems too bothered by the pack being so close, but I can't get myself into the same state. Instead, I clench my muscles every time they call out, which only adds to the stress running through my veins.

Two

A buzzing sound wakes me from my slumber. I turn over and notice Keegan turning off an alarm on his pack and then preparing the injector while Jules and Cody slide the dresser back from the door. We eat a quick breakfast of dried fruit and granola before we're each injected with another dose of Cymatilis. There are just enough bottles of water for all of us to wash down the food that's sticking to the back of our throats. The sun has barely risen when Wavern insists we start heading back to Rinku. He does a perimeter check to make sure the area is clear of Mulgrim. Keegan and Jules take the lead while I stay in the middle of the group. I make a request to stop in Lymont, which from my understanding, we need to pass in order to get to Rinku.

"Why would you want to stop there?" Jules asks over his shoulder.

"You all insist that I was alone when the bomb went off and I want to prove that I wasn't," I say defensively.

"It's a little further east than we need to go, but okay we'll stop… briefly," Keegan replies, causing Jules to give him a bewildered look.

I'm not sure why Keegan is so agreeable to stopping when the others clearly don't want to. I just hope when we get to Lymont those body fragments are still there, and that the Mulgrim haven't eaten them.

Everyone is quiet as we make our way to the city, and I can't decide if I'm happy about that or if I should be unsettled. Maybe if I remembered more about myself I could decide. Not having any inkling as to who I am is disturbing to say the least. I'm putting all my trust into these four men and I don't even know who they really are. They could be lying to me and I'd have no way of knowing. I have a lot of questions to ask and I'm almost tempted to start badgering these men with them, but I can't seem to open my mouth to get the words out. I search my mind for the proper phrasing I want to use, but Cody speaks before I can.

"So, you really don't remember anything?" he asks.

"No," I respond as I adjust the cap on my head.

Wavern took the sunglasses, which were lying on the floor beside the couch, from me before we left the house, so the only protection I have for my face is the hat. At least it's something, since the others have nothing blocking the harsh rays. The sun feels hotter this morning than yesterday, and the parched ground has more cracks in it. Or am I just hallucinating from the heat? No one else seems to be as affected by the temperature as I am. Either that or they're hiding it really well.

"Do you remember the bomb going off?" Jules asks.

"No. I only remember waking up buried under a pile of rubble and having to push my way out of it." I wait a few minutes before asking the first question that finally pops into my head. "What type of bomb was it?"

Keegan and Jules throw glances at each other, probably wanting the other one to answer.

"Atomic," Wavern finally responds.

"It wasn't a very powerful bomb," Keegan says. "It was one of the smallest we've seen so far."

"But it was enough," Wavern adds.

Then why am I still alive?

Maybe that wasn't a nightmare at all, but a memory surfacing. I wonder if I'll ever remember why I went to the city, but would I even want to know?

"We were lucky another one wasn't dropped in that neighborhood while we slept," Wavern says, adding to the stress I'm already feeling.

"Or when we left the compound," Jules adds.

"So, why was one launched when Sara left and not when we did?" Keegan asks.

"That's something we'll need to investigate when we get back to Rinku," Wavern says.

"When was the last time a bomb was dropped?" I ask.

"Eight years ago," Cody answers, his voice cracking in the process. "Hundreds died."

I decide not to ask any more questions for the time being, as I'm afraid I'll put myself into a panic attack if we keep talking about it.

It seems like the walk going to Lymont is taking longer than when I left it. We passed the gas station almost two hours ago, so we've got to be close. Another hour passes before the wreckage comes into view. More of the structures have collapsed, but other than that it all looks the same as it did yesterday. Keegan has me take the lead, so I can direct them to where I came across the remains. It takes me only a few minutes to locate the section I was trapped under. The larger body parts have been dragged off, but there are some still scattered about.

"Well," Jules begins, "I wonder who that was."

"Let's take some back to Rinku. Nex can run a DNA scan and search our database," Wavern says.

Cody is selected for the task, while the rest of us look under charred sheet metal, rusted cable rods, and melted glass. I don't know what everyone is expecting to find—maybe pieces of another body. Thankfully we only spend a few minutes doing the search, as I'm not comfortable being in the city. Cody selects a partially dismembered finger and a tooth, which he wraps in plastic and tucks into his backpack, then we leave Lymont and head towards the mountains. There isn't a direct road that goes into Rinku, so we have to go around mounds of dead cacti, debris that look to have once been part of a building, dried riverbeds, and discolored bone slivers. I can't tell if they're human, and I'm not interested in finding out.

We go around a bend in the mountain and a cave-like opening comes into view. The entryway is narrow at first, but widens and begins to slant slightly downward as we go deeper. Keegan tells me the actual entrance into Rinku is a mile in from the opening. When we reach what I'm assuming is halfway down the tunnel, we pass a large, thick steel door on our right. It appears to be another entrance; however, I don't see any door handles or even a way to open the heavy barrier. When we finally reach the end of the tunnel, a similar door blocks our path. Next to it is a panel, which Keegan places his palm over. A blue light scans his print and the door hisses open, revealing a small room with two additional points of entry. Wavern removes the sunglasses from his face and the hat from my head, then tosses them aside before we enter. As soon as we're all inside, the door closes and masks drop from the ceiling. Keegan instructs me to put it on quickly. I barely have it secured when a cloudy gas floods the room, obscuring everyone from my sight. I try not to panic when I feel a substance touch my skin and adhere to it. The gas stops as red lights flicker on overhead and out from the smooth metallic walls. The substance from the gas dissipates within a minute or so and the room clears.

"Decontamination complete," a mechanical voice says, echoing around us.

The others remove their masks, so I do the same. They retract into the ceiling disappearing behind small, round covers that slide into place. Jules takes our weapons then heads over to the door on our right, while Wavern proceeds to the door on our left.

"You all head to the showers while I take Sara to the medical ward," Wavern says.

Jules pushes on a lever that covers the front of the door and shoves it open. Cody hands the remains to Wavern before quickly following. Keegan, however, hesitates. Wavern has to order him to return to the barracks as commanded. As the door closes behind a sullen Keegan, Wavern opens the other door. That's when I notice the metal for these doors is much thinner than the main entrance, which seems odd to me.

"What's with the varying thickness of the doors?" I ask.

"The outer doors shield us from the harsh radiation that's outside, and since we don't need that kind of protection inside the base the internal doors don't need to be as heavily reinforced," Wavern replies.

As the door closes, soft lighting illuminates the edge of the floor and ceiling. From this I'm able to determine that the tunnel is carved out of solid stone. The air is surprisingly cool, which feels nice coming from an overheated environment. The journey to the medical ward is taking a lot longer than it did from the opening of the cave to the main entrance. Wavern explains to me that the medical ward is on the far side of the compound, which sits in the widest section of the Kai Mountain range.

"Normally a medical team would be waiting for us by the decontamination room, but since we didn't tell them we needed assistance we're stuck walking the whole damn thing," Wavern says, gesturing down the hall.

About every hundred feet or so along the sides of the tunnel are tall, thin plasma screens, vertically adhered to the wall. I stop to look at one, but Wavern insists that we continue.

"You don't have to concern yourself with those at the moment," he says as he quickens his pace.

"What is it?" I ask, trying to catch up.

"It's the Daily Slate. All passageways have them, as well as the mess hall, the rec room, the medical ward, the control center, and the barracks. It displays the daily schedule for each squad, the weather outside, and what's happening in the home city of Demos."

"Where's that?"

"In the Nove Mountains, approximately one hundred and seventy-five miles west of here."

"Are there any other cities close by?"

"Not anymore."

I can tell from Wavern's clipped answers that I should stop with the questions. I'm sure I'll learn about everything in time, but I get the uncomfortable feeling that time isn't on my side.

The tunnel gives way to an open expanse which is divided by a thick glass wall. Wavern has to clear his throat to get somebody's attention. Two women, whom I presume are nurses, turn around and their mouths drop open at the sight of us. One of them hits a panic button by the entrance which causes a heavy metal door to slide out from the walls behind us, cutting us off from the tunnel. The nurses rush toward me after throwing on white, plastic suits and masks, and then push me towards the first room on our left. Wavern starts to enter but he's ordered to wait outside. As the door closes I'm taken towards the back, stripped, and shoved into a shower stall. The water that pours down from the spout in the ceiling is hot to the point of scalding.

"I've already been through decontamination," I protest as the women lather up two sponges and begin to scrub me from head to toe.

"You've been out there way too long, Sara. We need to make sure you're free from all contaminants," one says.

"Besides, your return wasn't expected," the other one adds.

"So I heard," I mumble.

The water is shut off. I'm handed a towel, and a pair of white cotton pants with a matching top. I dress while the nurses prep the lone bed for me to lie down on. Once I'm settled, Wavern is allowed to enter, but he's not alone. A tall woman with long dark hair tucked into a braid joins the nurses by my side. The woman holds a tablet in her hands and judging by her flipping her finger across the screen, she seems to be going over some sort of information.

"Hi, Sara, I'm Nex, the physician for Rinku," the woman says, shaking my hand. "Wavern tells me that you don't have any memory of who you are, so I'd like to run some tests just to make sure there isn't any permanent brain damage from when you were in Lymont."

Nex hands the tablet to one of the nurses and instructs her to take the remains that Cody collected down to the lab to examine them. The other nurse pulls various vials and a syringe from the cabinet against the far wall. While the nurse prepares my right arm to draw blood, Nex examines my other limbs. She pulls up each pant leg and carefully looks at every inch of my skin, but I have no idea what she's looking for. I feel the pinch of the needle going in as Nex takes a look at my left arm. She picks up my hand and flips it over so it's palm side up, then halts when she notices something on my inner wrist.

"Where did this come from?" she asks.

I pull my hand from hers to examine what she found. Tattooed into my skin is a small, black, six-legged spider, something I didn't notice before because it was under the leather wristband I'd been wearing. From the way Nex reacted, I take it that I didn't have this marking before. She goes over to the wall on my right and pushes a button, which turns on a screen embedded into the wall. She taps the corner to pull up records and then scrolls through the files, finally stopping when she comes across the one with my name: Gentry, Sara. The screen fills with photos of me, along with my medical history, military background, and family relations. She taps on several of the photos, but the spider isn't on any of them.

"When were those last taken?" I ask, curious as to when this could've been etched into my flesh.

"This picture here," Nex says, pointing to one in the far upper corner, "was taken the night before you fled the compound."

"So I must have gotten it between that night and yesterday."

"That's not possible," Wavern says, stepping around Nex to get closer to me. "That mark hasn't been seen in over sixty years, and it's banned. The faction it belonged to has long since vanished, so there isn't any logical way that you could've been tattooed with it. Besides, you can only obtain tattoos in Demos, and you haven't been there in months. You would've needed to sign out one of the terrain vehicles and drive the two and a half hours to reach the city. Our squad was part of the watch team the other night, so when you left your post you would've gone straight to Lymont."

"Brea take those down to the lab and put them through a full panel spectrum," Nex says to the nurse as she's placing a bandage on my arm where the needle left its mark. "Sara, why don't you get comfortable while I talk to Wavern outside."

The three slip from the room. The glass isolation door slides into place and locks as a curtain swings in front of it, blocking my view of Wavern and Nex's conversation. I have no intention of getting comfortable, and instead get down from the bed and go over to the screen displaying my life. I first look at the pictures. I'm grinning and laughing in a few with Keegan, Jules, Cody, and another man who looks to be the same age as Keegan. All the photos look to have been taken here in Rinku because none show the sun or anything outside, only carved stone or metallic walls. The pictures only go back eight years, so there isn't anything of when I was younger. I tap on my medical files next. All show I've had routine physicals, immunizations, and I've never had any major illnesses or surgeries. Oh, and I have a small tattoo of a butterfly on the right side of my lower back.

Glad to know that I'm physically healthy… at least, I was.

My military background shows I've been in Wavern's squad for the eight years I've been in Rinku, which means he recruited me when I was fifteen and probably around the time of the last bombing. At least that's what the math says when I deduct my current age, which is listed in my medical file. I show high marks in tactical training, weapons handling, and physical endurance. I've never been reprimanded or punished, and my current ranking is just below Jules which places me third in line for command of our squad, Wavern being first.

I close that file and select the one for familial relations. What appears is simply a family tree with only a few names and even fewer pictures. My parents are listed, but there are no photos. I glance down at my picture and notice that there's a green square around it. I tap the image and the file swings to the left while another one shows on the right, and in between the two is a picture of myself and Keegan, linked together as husband and wife.

Well, that explains why he was reluctant to leave the decontamination chamber with the others.

The chart that appears for him is almost identical to mine, with his parents' names listed, but no corresponding photos. I close the file just as the door opens. I'm leaning against the bed when Nex and Wavern enter, both with puzzled expressions on their faces.

"I need to take some scans of your skeletal structure, Sara, before I can release you back into general population," Nex says, gesturing for me to get back into bed.

"What for?" I ask, annoyed.

"It's procedure," Wavern replies, a little too casually.

I begrudgingly get back onto the bed. Wavern says he'll return in a while, as he needs to check in with the rest of the squad, and then leaves. The door closes behind him, leaving just Nex and myself. She pulls a machine out of the wall behind my head and settles it a few inches above my body.

"This will only take a few minutes," she says, patting my shoulder.

She steps towards the shower stall, pulls a heavy curtain out from behind the opening in the wall, and begins to push a series of buttons. The Roentgen machine moves up and down as it takes images of my insides then displays them on the screen next to me, adding them to my medical file. The machine stops when Nex exits from the radiation guard and puts everything back in its place. Next, she steps over to the display and scrolls through the images. I'm not sure what exactly she's looking for and she's not saying anything.

"Hmm," she finally utters before the silence becomes too unbearable.

"What?"

"Everything appears normal. You don't have any broken bones, which is odd considering you were supposedly in a bomb blast. No scarring on your muscles, and your blood work came back clean."

"Then I was lucky," I respond, swinging my legs out over the side of the bed.

"No, Sara, you weren't." Nex turns to face me but keeps her distance. "The blood on your boots and those human remains that you found, and Cody collected, were consistent with those coming from a victim of the bombing, but I can't explain how it could be possible."

"Whose are they?"

"Yours."

"How the hell can that be?" I practically scream at her. "I'm right here. You said so yourself that there isn't anything wrong with me. How can I be missing pieces of my body if everything is here?" I gesture to my arms and legs. "You have to be mistaken in your identification."

"We ran the print from the finger collected and it's yours. I had a tissue sample extracted from the remains as well as pulp from the tooth and ran them through our DNA database, which also came back as a perfect match to you."

"But I'm not dead, obviously. Something has to be wrong with your database."

"I thought that, too, so the lab technician compared the blood we drew today to that in the database. It's also a match to the remains. Those are pieces of you out there, not anyone else's."

"Then how am I still here?"

Panic grips me and I choke on the sobs forming. I can't get air in and the room starts to spin. The nightmare slams back into my head as I realize it was a memory, and that I was mutilated and then incinerated in the blast. In my hysterics, I catch glimpses of Nex rushing over to the cabinet and removing an injector, which she places against my neck. A warm fluid enters my body, and I begin to relax before drifting off to sleep.

The stone steps are slippery, so I'm forced to place my hand against the wall for balance as I slowly descend. The surface is hot and dry, but down here it's damp and much cooler. No wonder he likes to hide down here while the rest of us suffer. I only have a few minutes to search his quarters and I have no idea what exactly I'm looking for. I just need something, anything that'll prove I'm right about his lies, especially before he sends me to the conversion room like he has everyone else he's turned into his slave. If I become his, I'll be lost forever.

The light is scarce, so my eyes have to adjust to the darkness. My feet hit an even plane and the wall gives way to open space. I stand still and wait for my eyes to adapt to my new surroundings. The chamber I'm in is small and contains two stalls on my right, both with chicken wire covered by wood planks being used as doorways. The first stall has a broken couch by the back wall, egg-sized pieces of green glass dangling from strings across the top of the doorway, and various cabinets haphazardly placed. The second stall has a bed covered in stained sheets, flat pillows, and a bedspread with small tufts of stuffing sticking out from holes that are probably years old. I don't know what I expected to find down here, but definitely not these few things.

I decide to go through the cabinet drawers, but there isn't anything of significance in them from what I can tell. As I move from one cabinet to another, the sound of scuffing feet catches my attention. I slink towards the back of the stall, hoping it's not him returning. I thought he'd be gone longer because he was in the process of turning someone and that can take time. The person must've given in quickly, which means I'm probably next.

But it's him and he isn't alone. I've not been able to see his face—not yet anyway, as his entire body is covered in a long black cloak with a heavy hood. Dust gets kicked up as he walks, clinging to the edges of the garment. His companion is the female he took to the conversion room. She's about my age, barefooted, wearing tattered rags, and her strawberry-blond hair is medium in length. She's laughing as they descend the stairs but I can't quite hear what he's saying, as he mumbles a lot when he talks.

The two pass me and enter the second stall, the woman discarding her clothes as they go. I assume he takes the cloak off when he's claiming his prize, but I have yet to actually experience this myself. I've only heard rumors. I need to find a way out before this happens to me, but I have no clue as to where I am or even how to get the hell out of here. I have no idea as to the exact length of time I've been down here as there's no way to tell as the sun will only rise in this dominion when new followers decide to join his collective, which hasn't happened in what feels like a few days. We're not permitted to wander too far off the trails that circle his lair, or we'll be eaten by his predators… or so we've been told. I've yet to see that happen.

The noises from the next stall hit a climatic pitch then fall silent. The cramping in my legs gets worse the longer I squat, but I don't dare move in case one or both of them is awake. The woman moans as they go at it again, only this time he prolongs her pleasure to the point where she's begging for him to stop… screaming, actually, as she sounds like she's in pain. He howls with delight and keeps going. Her cries pierce the stale air, followed by his laughter. I try to cover my ears, but I'm using my hands to keep my balance so I wind up falling over and knocking into one of the cabinets. All noises stop and the only thing I hear is the breath escaping my lips. I don't dare move, especially when I feel him close by. I can't see him, but I know he's there. I close my eyes and try to calm myself, but I sense him looming over me… watching me… wanting me… coming for me.

Three

"I don't care, Wavern. I'm not allowing you to keep her trapped in isolation like a rat," Keegan's voice penetrates the fog that I'm slowly coming out of.

"We need to get to the bottom of this," Wavern says, his face reddened in anger.

"I don't care what the database says, that wasn't Sara we scooped up in Lymont."

"I know you must have a lot of questions," Nex says, trying to diffuse the tense situation.

"The only question I have is when are you going to release my wife?"

"Not until at least tomorrow," Nex answers. "There are a few more tests I need to conduct just to make sure."

"To make sure of what? That she's Sara? You already did that. The only thing different about her is that insignificant mark on her left wrist, which could've come from anything she was touching when the bomb ignited."

"He has a point," one of the nurses from earlier says.

"You're not helping, Macom," Nex says, scolding the young woman. "We need to do this for the protection of the compound. I've sent everything over to Andra, and until she's satisfied Sara stays here."

"This is fucking bullshit!" Keegan shouts. "I want my wife!"

"She's not going anywhere without Andra's approval!" Wavern yells back. "Don't make me confine you to quarters. I need you in the control center later today since it's our shift again."

"I'm not done with this," Keegan says, pointing a finger in Wavern's face. "You're not going to keep me away from her."

Wavern gets close to Keegan, their noses almost touching. "You listen here, soldier. Sara's health and safety is top priority. She's here until Andra says otherwise. Disagree with it all you want, but that's the order I'm giving."

Keegan storms out, a vein bulging in his neck and his hands balled into fists. He's probably leaving before getting himself into real trouble, since his temper has always done him in no matter who it's aimed at.

Wait, am I starting to remember? God, I hope so.

"I'll return once the change in rotation has ended," Wavern says, then leaves.

Macom goes to one of the cabinets and removes a thin razor and glass dish. She comes over to the left side of the bed, adjusts my arm so the spider tattoo is showing, and gently scrapes a few cells from it. The whole process takes mere seconds, is painless, and doesn't alter any portion of the image.

"Is that for your other tests?" I ask Nex once the nurse has left.

"Yes, it is. I'd like to know what type of pigment was used, which might help us to narrow down where it came from."

"So, you don't buy Keegan's reasoning?"

Nex looks up from her tablet. "You heard that?"

I nod.

"Well, no, I don't agree with his statement, and I'll tell you why." Nex drops her arms to her side as she approaches my bed. "First, Lymont has been abandoned for so long that there wouldn't be anything with fresh paint on it to stain you. Second, the bomb would've burned it *off*, not *into* your skin. And third, I have pieces of you in a chill box down in the lab and yet here you are very much alive, well, and whole."

But without an intact memory. Was that a memory rising to the surface while I slept, or was it simply another nightmare? I wish there was an easy way to distinguish between the two.

"You sound almost resentful that I'm here," I say. "Did you not want me to return from Lymont?"

"You weren't supposed to be there, Sara, and now you're being ridiculous," she says sternly. "I'm just struggling with what could've happened to you. If only you could remember, it would solve everything." She steps back, takes a deep breath, and regains her composure. "I just want to make sure that you're you and not someone else, which at this point seems to be an impossibility. I have more tests running in the lab now, but won't have those results until tomorrow." She heads towards the door then stops. "I'll have a food tray brought to you within the hour." She exits, leaving the door open behind her.

I lie there, staring up at the ceiling and trying to recall anything about myself, but it's like it's all been wiped clean. Instead of wallowing in my despair, I get down from the bed and go over to the display. I spend the next several hours carefully reading my history and memorizing the faces in the photos, as well as watching several videos that were taken during my wedding to Keegan.

No matter how many times I read over the information, nothing is jogging my memory. That one snippet about Keegan managed to float its way back in, so I'm not sure why nothing else has. I move over to Keegan's file to find out as much about him as I can. He's an only child like me, and his parents are deceased as well. His military background practically mirrors my own, though my scores are much higher. We've been married for just a few months, but apparently have known each other since I was recruited by Wavern. Keegan is three years older than I am and came to Rinku at the age of eighteen. Both of our records start when we arrived in the compound. There isn't anything from before then, which seems odd.

I begin to wonder where we came from before being sent to Rinku. If the cities have been abandoned for a long time, it's obvious we didn't originate from them. Could we have come from Demos?

I'm just about done reading Keegan's medical file when food is brought to me. Macom tells me it's dinner and that I slept through lunch. I didn't think I was out that long from when Nex injected me. I remove the cover and am surprised to find fresh vegetables, bread, and chicken on my plate. I'm not sure what I was expecting, mashed-up food preserves perhaps, but nothing like this. I clean my plate, washing it all down with a tall glass of lemonade. Macom returns a few minutes later and removes the tray. I feel completely bored and utterly useless lying in bed doing nothing, but I'm not alone for long. A tall older woman with shoulder-length silver hair enters my room, slowly closing the door behind her.

"How are you feeling, Sara?" she asks as she cautiously approaches the foot of my bed.

"I'm all right."

Her cheeks crinkle as she smiles. "That's good to hear, especially since you've been through quite an ordeal."

I keep my mouth closed since I'm sure she's waiting for a specific reaction from me.

"My name is Andra and I'm the leader for this compound." She takes a few more steps then stops. "Nex has advised me of your condition and I've told those who found you not to speak about it to anyone. We don't need the whole compound up in arms over this. That would be dangerous… for you."

"So, what lie are we going with?" I ask, sarcasm dripping from my tongue.

"It appears your attitude towards me hasn't changed, which is saying something." She clears her throat, adjusts the starched collar around her thin neck, and grazes my blanket with the tips of her thin fingers. "As far as everyone else is aware, you were able to find shelter before the blast but received a severe concussion when debris fell on you. This will explain your lack of memory and why you aren't significantly injured."

"But it doesn't explain why I was in Lymont to begin with."

She smiles thinly. "True, but I'm sure you can come up with something plausible."

I detest this woman.

"When do I get out of here?" I ask as the air between us becomes increasingly hostile.

"Once the majority of the soldiers are back in their section of the barracks I'll have Wavern come and collect you. I *am* going to restrict you for the next few days as to what your duties will be. Normally, each squad is responsible for the daily functions of this compound, but until I can fully trust you, that right won't be afforded to you."

"So, I'm sort of under house arrest."

"You can think of it that way if you want, but I view it as a safety precaution." She steps back towards the door, then pauses. "Do you remember anything about why you fled from here and into Lymont?" she asks over her shoulder.

"No. I wish I did."

With that, she opens the door and leaves. I flop back down onto my pillow and stare at the ceiling once again. I feel like I'm being punished for something I had no control over. I still say the tests and database are wrong. Those remains aren't mine… they can't be.

But what if they are?

My head begins to pound the more I think about it, so I close my eyes and begin to drift off. I'm really not that tired, but I'm emotionally exhausted.

A woman's screams of pain fill the darkness around me. I try to go and help, but it's almost like I'm cemented in place. The space around me is dark and cold, and no matter what I do I can't move. Once my eyes have focused, I look up and notice I'm suspended by my arms by ropes. My legs dangle below me by chains that dig into my flesh, and are secured to a bolt in the floor. Every muscle aches more the longer I'm dangling, escalating to a point where I pray for my limbs to rip from my body. The cold air is slowly replaced by hot, moist breath that seems to be coming from all around me. I want to struggle, but I become weaker the longer I hang. I sense someone's eyes on me, measuring me. One touch of him against my skin and I burn, my body ignites into a candle, and I fall from the tethers and into his vault.

I'm jarred awake when I hit the bottom in my dream. I have no idea what time it is, or even if it's still the same day. I try to shake off the discomfort I feel from the images that plague my mind. I use the facilities, but when I exit the small room next to the shower Wavern is standing at the foot of my bed.

"Andra has approved your release, so I'm going to escort you to your room in the barracks," he says, then gestures for me to follow him.

"Where's Keegan?"

"He's in the one of the lookouts. You'll see him when his shift is over."

We leave the isolation room and head left. Our progress is stalled by a thick glass wall between us and another section of the medical ward. Wavern goes over to the wall and places his palm on an imager, just like the one used to enter the compound. The glass doors part, allowing us passage. This half of the ward is similar to the one we just exited, except the rooms here have curtains blocking their entrances instead of glass doors. The hallway between the ward and the barracks is a small one. We move from smooth, cool stone floors to skin-biting metal grating. The entire floor is covered in it, so it makes walking barefoot extremely difficult.

We round the corner and are greeted by an elongated section that houses sets of metal stairs in the middle of the floor, which go to the levels below. Showers, bathrooms, and locker rooms for men and a separate one for women take up the sides of the floor, and two individual tunnels lay at the far end. They look vaguely familiar, but I can't remember where each one goes. Wavern takes me down the length of the section, explaining that the tunnel on the right goes to the mess hall while the tunnel on the left heads towards the rec room. Andra has her personal quarters on this floor, right between the tunnel for the rec room and the women's locker room. We go back around then head down the stairs. The level below is identical to the one above, but the lighting here isn't as bright.

"Most of the other squads are in for the night, so we minimize the lighting to save on power," Wavern says. "There are ten decks in the barracks. This deck houses the quarters for Squads One through Eight. Currently there are only two hundred residents in the compound, but the barracks was built to hold approximately five thousand."

"How many people per squad?"

"Twenty at the moment. I had the rest of our squad stay behind when we went searching for you because they still had a job to perform. Our squad is back here." He gestures towards the far-right corner. I glance around the area and notice that each door is labeled with the squad number and the name of the leader. "However, you and Keegan are down here."

We descend to the next deck. The lighting is still minimal and the grate-style floor has followed us, but there are only six quarters on this level.

"Every third level has laundry facilities, which are over there," he says, pointing to the section of doors behind us. "Squads Nine and Ten, along with you and Keegan, are the only ones down here. We have family housing on this floor, which are located in the corners. You and Keegan are the only married couple in the compound, so you have one of the family quarters."

I take another look through the grating, but this time it's blocked off. The stairs are even cut off in the middle of their descent. I can't tell what type of substance is covering the deck below, but it looks to have been there for some time as a thin coating of dust covers the top.

"What's that?" I ask, pointing to it.

"We keep the empty decks closed off to preserve power and life support. If we ever needed to expand, the seal can be easily removed."

He taps my shoulder and guides me to a door in the back right corner. He turns the knob easily and I'm surprised that it's not locked. I ask him if any of the doors lock and he replies no, except for the isolation rooms in the medical ward, and Andra's apartment. The family quarters is by no means large, but it's adequate for a family of four. We enter the living room, which is furnished with several couches, a coffee table, and floor lamps that all sit on heavily scratched wood flooring. Against the wall by the door is a long plasma screen, similar to the one I saw in the tunnel on our way to the medical ward, only this one is in a horizontal position. The screen is divided the same way as the others but Wavern tells me that I can change the channel on this one, which you can't do with the others. On the left behind the living room is one of two bedrooms. In between them sits a small bathroom with a toilet, sink, and tub. There aren't any closets to be found, but there are a number of wall-mounted lockers.

I can tell from the items in the room on the left that it's the master bedroom. A queen-sized bed sits against the center of the far wall, flanked on either side by end tables topped with small lamps. A six-drawer dresser is opposite the lockers. There seem to be very few personal items, but the few there are in the room have been lovingly affixed to the wall or placed on top of the dresser. A lone picture sits on one of the end tables. I pick up the flimsy frame and study the image. It looks to have been taken when Keegan and I got married. A long banner hangs in the background, congratulating us on our nuptials.

"Keegan will be in the lookout until oh-six-hundred hours. You can visit the mess hall and the rec room, but for now that's as far as Andra wants you to go. Breakfast is served at oh-four-hundred hours. I would suggest getting to the mess hall early, otherwise you'll get stuck with the remnants, which are usually cold," Wavern says as we make our way back into the living room.

"What if I need to get a hold of someone? I don't see any communication devices."

"They're not in the quarters, but there is one per deck in the barracks as well as in the mess hall, rec room, control center, medical ward, and each lookout. You just need to pick up the receiver and hold down the white button to make an announcement over the universal paging system. There's a panel alongside the receiver that allows you to call a specific location if you want. That way it's not broadcast to the whole compound. Now, is there anything else you need?"

I shake my head.

"Then I'll see you later in the day."

He gently closes the door behind him, leaving me in partial darkness since we'd only turned on a couple of the lights. I return to the bedroom and rummage through the lockers, trying to determine which one is mine. When I find it, I change out of my white hospital garb and into khaki pants, gray cotton socks, and a black shirt. My boots, still with the blood spatter on them, sit at the bottom of my locker. I don't feel like venturing out at the moment, so I leave them there. I hop into the bathroom to quickly work out the knots in my hair before returning to the living room. I feel a little chilled as I try to get comfortable on the plush couch, so I pull the blanket off the back and wrap myself in it.

I glance at the screen, finally noticing the time, which is twenty-three-fourteen. The current temperature outside is sixty-five degrees, with heavy rains expected to begin in the next hour. Below that is the list of squadrons and their current posts. Two, Four, and Eight are the only ones scheduled at the moment for various tasks throughout the compound. The others are off duty. The bottom portion of the screen shows that it's eighty degrees in Demos, with no rain predicted. *No events scheduled for today* flashes beneath the temperature.

I reach for the remote, which almost blends in with the coffee table because of its clear design. It's thin, extremely lightweight, and I only need to roll my finger over one of the sides to change the channel. The other side operates the volume. I'm not sure how many channel selections I have, so I go through them all until I come back to the main screen. Luckily, there are only a handful. Most of them are showing children's shows such as cartoons or puppet programs. I finally settle on a talk show, but unfortunately I don't understand anything the two people are discussing. They seem more focused on throwing insults at each other than having a true discussion. I'm in the midst of dozing off when alert chimes bring me around.

"When was the last time you were at the Factory?" a young woman in orange gently says as she mugs for the camera. Her strawberry-blond hair hangs loosely around her bare shoulders as she works on selling her wares. "We have new items every day and can fill all your supply needs whether you live in Demos or one of the compounds."

The camera slowly backs away, elongating her figure. The outfit she has on is a sleeveless dress that flows around her ankles, with slits up both sides, exposing her thighs and almost her hips as well. Her arms are covered in gold bracelets, from her wrists to her elbows. She looks about my age, and has perfectly tanned skin—whereas I'm pale from lack of sunlight.

She also has an air of familiarity about her.

"Do you have everything you need for the upcoming memorial?" she continues, even though I've lost interest and am about to change the channel.

My eye catches something on her left wrist. The bracelets have slipped slightly since she's holding up a menu to select catering options for the memorial. I sit up and move closer to the screen to study the image since it's so small. From what I can see of the tattoo it's identical to mine.

"You only have a few days, so get over to the Factory before it's too late," the woman says with a smile.

I feel her comment is aimed at me.

She has to be the one I saw in that dream. There's too much of a coincidence to think otherwise. Who is she and why does she have the tattoo? I eagerly wait for the commercial to air again, but it doesn't. I want another look at the woman's face, so I can memorize it since the only thing my mind captured was the spider tattoo. I flip through the different channels, hoping to catch the commercial again, but I don't. I grow tired and anxious sitting on the couch doing nothing, so I go into the bedroom, put on my boots, slip on another set of leather wristbands, and head out. I don't want people asking about the tattoo as I'm not supposed to have it, and covering it up with the wristbands will prevent that. I know I'm restricted to visiting only two areas but staying in my quarters isn't making me feel any better.

Once I'm on the top deck, I take the tunnel leading to the rec room. It's about half the size of the medical ward with a large sectional couch, a pool table, bar, and three dartboards stationed at the back. Two plasma screens displaying the Daily Slate are hanging from opposite walls, so they can be seen no matter where in the room you're standing. The couch faces a portion of the wall that's covered with what looks like a white linen sheet, which is pulled tight along its edges and is currently showing an old-style movie that's being projected onto it from a device dangling from the ceiling a couple of feet away. Only a few people occupy the space and are mainly on the couch watching the movie. I stroll over to one of the dartboards, extract several darts, then go to the mark on the floor indicating where you need to stand when throwing.

I'm not sure why I choose to play, but it seems like something that'll keep both my mind and body occupied. It takes me a couple of rounds before my first dart actually makes contact with the board. My arm is sore an hour later, but I keep playing. I want the distraction even though my mind has started to wander. All I can think about is the spider tattoo and the remains in Lymont.

The two have to fit together somehow. I'm here, yet dead at the same time, which is an impossibility. Will I ever find the answers? Should I even go looking for them to begin with? The faster the questions pop into my head, the harder I throw the darts. I hurl one so fast and hard that it hits the bullseye dead on, but when I go to retrieve it I notice it's sunk into the board's wooden backing a good inch or two. I don't think I have the strength to do that, but somehow I managed it.

"Hey!" someone from behind me shouts.

I ignore him until he calls me by name.

"You all right, Sara?" the man asks as he cautiously approaches.

"I just… I'm… yes, I'm fine."

The man looks to be around Keegan's age, but a little taller and with bigger muscles. He resembles the person I saw in the one photo back in the medical ward. His clothing is the same as mine. I think that's all we have to wear down here—drab military fatigues. His dark hair is cut extremely close to the scalp and he has a massive scar running down the length of his right arm. He stops inches from me, but keeps his hands behind his back even though I sense he wants to reach out and touch me.

"You don't look fine," he says. "Let me get you a drink."

He goes over to the bar, pulls out a tall thin bottle, and pours its contents into two shot glasses. I join him and swallow the liquid before he has a chance to claim his drink. I refill the glass, but after the fourth drink I start to feel lightheaded.

"You've never been very good at holding your liquor," the man says, taking the glass away from me before I can fill it again.

"Then I need more practice," I respond, reaching for it.

"Yeah, I let you get drunk and Keegan will have my head." The man gently shoves me down onto one of the fabric-covered barstools, then proceeds to pour himself another drink.

"He's working, so he'll never find out."

"Wow, Sara, deceiving your husband? That's not like you," he says, chuckling.

"I'm not the same person," I snap back.

"So we've heard."

"What's that supposed to mean?" I ask, my temper rising.

"That you have no real memories because of the bomb blast. Or at least that's what they're telling us," he answers, setting his glass down and leaning against the bar.

"You don't believe it?" I ask.

"Now, I didn't say that—"

"But you implied it," I interrupt.

"It seems like your near-death experience has made you testy," he says with a smile and a wink. "I've missed that in you."

"Who the hell are you?" I ask, sliding down from the stool.

"Grimm Thomas. I'm the leader of Squad Two." He holds out his grease-stained hand for me to shake, but I only stare at it. He pulls it back when he realizes I'm not going to touch it, which causes him to shudder slightly. "Has Keegan realized how much you've changed?" he asks, his tone cold.

"How have I changed?"

"You used to be fun, easy to tease, and always had a smile on your face. We would harass each other to no end, but laugh about it. It's like your whole personality has been altered. You're coming off as rigid, which isn't like you."

"Maybe I'm still in shock from the blast," I say, feeling defensive.

He pours another drink and swallows it in one gulp. "Yeah, let's go with that. I'll see you later." He doesn't look at me when he leaves, but I follow his departure.

I wish there was a way I could recall what I was like before I came to in the rubble. Am I really that different? I need answers and quickly.

Screw Andra's rules.

I exit the rec room through the tunnel next to the dartboards, enter what looks to be the mess hall, and wind my way around the many tables until I reach another tunnel that empties into a vast room. The walls and floors are covered in metal grating, with four large consoles spread over the space, two long conference tables on either side of a large central station, a communication console in front of that, and seven exits along the back wall. Each station is occupied, but the only faces I recognize are Cody's and Wavern's. The latter looks startled when he notices me. He climbs down from the large center station and waves those staring at me back to work.

"Sara, you can't be in here," he says, putting his hand on my back and trying to turn me around.

"I need answers," I respond without moving. "I want to talk to Keegan."

"You can't right now. He's in one of the lookouts and can't come down until the next rotation."

"Please, Wavern, I can't stay cooped up in that apartment. Let me go outside. Maybe back to Lymont so I can take another look around. Maybe we missed something."

"You know very well that I can't let you do that. The Mulgrim will be hiding in our tunnel to avoid the acid rain that's falling, which will burn clear down to your bones if you stay in it too long." I simply continue to stand there, waiting. He can tell I'm not going to let up so he calls for Cody, who's sitting at one of the back consoles. "Cody, take Sara into the mess hall. She needs some company and you're the only one I can spare at the moment. Keep her in there until breakfast, then I'll send Keegan down."

"Sure, Wavern," Cody responds, shrugging his shoulders.

The two of us head into the mess hall and take seats in the far corner of the room. Cody is the last person I want to talk to because he's the youngest of everyone and I'm not sure how well he knows me. Keegan would be better as he's my husband, so I'm not sure why Wavern is suddenly concerned with him staying in the lookout. He had all those in the lookouts leave to go searching for me, so why the change? Maybe Andra reprimanded him for the action and now Wavern is being overly cautious.

"What do you want to talk about?" Cody asks, placing his hands in his lap after we've sat down. He seems a little nervous, but I can't figure out why.

"How long have you known me?"

"A few months, why?"

"What was I like before the other day?"

"Fun, sarcastic, always smiling. Quick-witted, dependable, scary smart."

"Have I been known to lose my temper or get frustrated easily?"

"No, not really. It would usually take a lot to get you pissed off. As for the frustration, I've never actually seen it. I only know that you won't give up on anything until you've learned it or fixed it. You're tenacious. Why, did someone say something?"

"Grimm. I ran into him in the rec room after I drilled a dart almost completely through the dartboard."

Cody's eyes widen, then he clears his throat to regain his composure. "Don't listen to Grimm. He's had his nose out of joint the moment he got here." Cody leans forward. "You say you almost put a dart completely through the board?"

I nod.

"Those things are super thick. I wonder how you did it," he responds, leaning back.

"I got frustrated and just started throwing them harder each time."

He looks puzzled by my response, which makes me think no one has ever done that before. Is that also how I've changed? Am I stronger and have a quicker temper? I knew talking to Cody wasn't going to get me far. I can't even think of the right questions to ask that he would possibly know the answers to, so I decide to change tactics. Cody mentioned he's known me for only a few months, so if he can tell me a little bit about his past perhaps it might trigger some memories of my own.

"How old were you when Wavern drafted you into Rinku?"

"Oh, I wasn't drafted by him. I was originally sent to the Virtus compound about eight years ago."

"Why did you decide to join at such a young age?"

He lets out a little laugh, but quickly regrets it. "I keep forgetting that you don't remember. None of us came voluntarily, Sara. Each of us was orphaned by the war that devastated the planet. Trust me, if I could be doing something else I would. Being a soldier isn't my first choice."

"When was the war?"

"Well over sixty years ago."

"Then how could we possibly be orphans from it? That doesn't make any sense."

He leans across the table and places his palms on the metallic surface. "Depending upon where you were when the nukes fell determined how much radiation your family line absorbed. My family was close to the fallout, so it took several generations before a completely healthy person was born, which is me. The leaders all felt that it would be best if those who can better deal with the poisonous air be placed in the compounds and turned into soldiers. We can tolerate the toxicity better than anyone in Demos, so we make great soldiers if war breaks out again."

"What happened to those who weren't affected by the radiation?"

"They were moved to Demos, which is protected by the Occlyn Ring. It's embedded in the rock that makes up the Nove Mountain range, and generates a force field around the city, preventing anything from entering its atmosphere. Demos was little more than a few houses and shops when the war began, but now the city fills the entire valley."

"How'd you wind up in Rinku if you weren't originally sent here?"

Cody's face darkens as he slips down into his seat. He rubs his arms, and that's when I notice he's wearing a long-sleeved shirt. I think back to the other night. He had the same type of shirt on then, too. Everyone else I've seen has either worn a short-sleeved or sleeveless shirt. I take a hold of one of his hands and pull it towards me. He doesn't fight me being so forward, nor does he stop me when I push up his sleeve. Just like his face, his arm is covered with scars, only they're deep gouges with chunks of flesh missing. I study the markings and remember that Wavern and Grimm have similar scars on their bodies.

"What happened?" I ask, rolling his arm over until it's palm up.

"I was down in the kitchen in Virtus preparing lunch when an explosion ripped through the compound," he answers, his voice sounding distant. "It took almost two days for me to be rescued—and I was one of the lucky ones."

"How many were lost?"

"One-hundred-and-ninety-seven died. There were only thirty survivors, split between the two remaining compounds."

"Grimm is one of them, isn't he?"

"Yes," Cody answers, tears slowly trickling down his face.

"Was Wavern there?"

Cody finally looks up. "His vehicle had just entered the garage for Virtus when it happened, so he was able to escape almost unscathed."

"Does anyone know how it happened? What caused the explosion?"

Cody pulls his arm from my hand and rolls down the sleeve to cover his wounds. "The preliminary investigation suggested that it came from the hydroponics bay, across from the kitchen that's one level below the mess hall. That was the area with the most damage… so they say."

"You sound skeptical. Why is that?" I ask.

"Because I was in the kitchen when the blast occurred and the kitchen feeds right into the hydroponics bay so I would've known. It came from the control center, or at least one of its levels. I want to say it was Level Three, which houses the life support systems, but I can't be sure."

"Was Virtus set up the same way as Rinku?"

"Yes. All the compounds have the same layout, with one exception. Rinku is the only one buried in a mountain range, with dual exits onto the surface from the garage. The other two have an above-ground entrance, which leads to a tightly winding stairwell providing access to the decon chamber."

"Why do you think they're not telling the truth about where the blast possibly originated?"

"Because they don't want us to know that it wasn't an accident," Cody answers, his voice heavy with excitement as he practically jumps up and down in his seat. "Someone deliberately destroyed the compound."

"Do you know why someone would do that? What would be their motive?" I ask in a calming manner, hoping to get him to settle down.

"I don't know. Maybe to take out the compounds, so they can gain access to Demos?"

"You can only enter the city through the compounds?" I ask, puzzled by his statement.

"Yes. Each has a connecting transport tunnel from the garage to a parking pad just outside the entrance to the city. You have to get inside one of the compounds in order to gain access to these tunnels."

"But in order to get into the compound, you have to be programmed into the biometrics for the imagers at the entrances," I counter.

I think I'm starting to remember mow. That answer came out too easily and quickly. Or maybe I just picked up on it because of how we entered Rinku.

Cody stares at me for a few seconds before answering. "Yes, you do."

"Well, we're all stationed in here to protect the city and its citizens. If we wanted to harm them, we wouldn't need to destroy a compound to do it. We could just go right into the city."

"I suppose," he replies, sounding as if his balloon has been popped.

I let silence settle between us as I try to gather my thoughts as to what to talk about next. I'm happy that Cody is very forthcoming with his information, but I still feel like I'm not asking the right questions. I recall the commercial from earlier, so that's the new tack I take.

"Cody," I begin, shaking his arm since he's drifted off. His head lolls for a moment before his eyes flutter open. "What's the Factory?"

"Huh? Oh, the Factory? It's where everyone gets their supplies such as clothing, housewares, linens, and foodstuffs. Basically anything you could ask for, they'll have it or make it. The complex takes up about seventy percent of Zone C in Demos. Why?"

"I saw an ad for it earlier. The woman in the commercial was trying to sell decorations for an upcoming memorial."

"Oh, yeah. That." Cody seems to drift off again, but it only lasts a split second. "You'd think after a while they'd want to stop remembering the war that almost ended everything and move on. I know I do."

"The one that scarred the planet?"

He scowls at me. "Is there any other?"

Well, that was a stupid question to ask on my part. Of course it would be that one. God, Sara, get your head out of your ass.

"Look, I need to get back to my post. I'll catch up with you later."

As Cody stands to leave I'm about to throw out another question, when footsteps to our right catch my attention. Several people emerge from a staircase across the room. They're wearing aprons over their regulation clothing. A few move over to a dumbwaiter behind a long counter. Hot food is slowly removed from the small lift and transferred to the counter, filling the dishware with food for the diners. A couple of others check a cart which houses plates, cups, and utensils.

"Breakfast is now being served," a young woman says over the paging system.

Lines quickly form into the mess hall from the rec room and barracks. I know I should get up and grab something, but I'm too mesmerized by the craziness around me. The workers can't seem to dish out the food fast enough for those in line. Voices rise over the clanking of dishes, and the tables around me quickly fill up, so I'm forced to get up and join the parade. I try not to notice when eyes follow me through the whole process. Once my dish is full I go back to my section of table, only this time I sit with my back against the wall. I don't want anyone being able to sneak up behind me and I want to see who all is staring at me because I know it's quite a few of them. The room fills to capacity, but no one dares to sit anywhere close to me. If there isn't another spot available, they retreat into the rec room or say they're going to eat in the barracks.

They know something is off with me. No one believes the shit lie Andra told, so I wonder if they'll ever look at me or treat me the same ever again. This is going to make life down here unbearable.

I can't take the staring any longer so I throw my half-eaten food into the trash, place my dishes on a conveyor in the wall by the utensil cart, and go back to my quarters. I can't stand being in the compound any longer. My insides are screaming for me to get out, to run outside. I don't know how I tolerated living in such a confined space for so long before I lost my memory. I know I've only been back here a little over a day, but I feel like I'm going mad. It's probably more from the not knowing than the actual isolation. I need to get myself to calm down.

"*Sara.*"

My name is hissed across the living room as I stand there with my hands on my hips, but when I turn, no one is there.

"*Sara.*"

This time the voice is louder, deeper, and echoes in my head.

"Sara, find the others."

I close my eyes and will the disjointed voice to silence, but it roars back with ferocity.

"You will never be rid of me, Sara. I'm part of you and you're part of me. We are intertwined for eternity."

"Where are you?" I practically shout as I open my eyes.

"Close as I've always been."

"What do you want from me?"

"You already have that answer. Find the others before you're discovered."

"I don't understand."

A piercing scream fills my mind, forcing me to grip my head in an attempt to get it to stop. I buckle to my knees from the pain the sound is inflicting on me.

"Stop, please!" I beg. It feels like my head is about to explode.

Silence ensues, but the pain is still intense. I slowly lower my hands, but I stay on my knees. "Who are you?"

"I'm your master, your creator, and your destroyer. I am the Arliss."

With that, all light extinguishes behind my eyes as I collapse to the floor and slip from reality.

Four

I sense I'm in a tunnel, but can't see anything around me. Flashes of light spark in the corners of my eyes, which only gives me snippets of Keegan's face intermingled with something much darker. I don't know why I'm seeing him, since he's back in Rinku and not anywhere near the hell I'm currently in. The images merge into the man in the black cloak from my dream, but his true face and form are still hidden. Cold creeps into my veins when I remember the tattoo on the wrist of the woman from the Factory commercial.

Find the others.

Is that what he's referencing? If so, how many others are there, and what was meant by his comment 'before you're discovered'? Cody's story about the destruction of Virtus plays out in front of me like a movie, but how? I wasn't even there, yet I feel like I'm living it through someone's eyes. I just don't know whose. I feel myself being pulled from the dream as a pair of dark-skinned hands grip a metal pipe, bending it with ease. As the person's left wrist turns with the motion, I catch a glimpse of a spider tattoo. I try to call out, but the air in my lungs is violently pushed out as I'm ripped into pieces.

The tunnel opens into a small cavern with a low ceiling. Wet stones make up the walls around me as hard, cold metal bites into my bare back. My limbs ache from strain being applied by ropes as they try to stretch my body to its maximum. The only light is being cast down from a chiseled hole above me, creating a makeshift skylight. The ropes burn into my flesh as I try to move. Tiny pinpricks appear and then disappear on my fully exposed body, as if being blown across by an invisible wind. The pain is excruciating and unrelenting. Every time I open my mouth to scream from the agony, I lose all ability to breathe.

"Give in," a voice whispers into my ear.

"No," I squeak out.

My answer is met with sharp pain, which causes my voice to catch in my throat.

"Submit, Sara," the voice whispers.

"Never," I try to reply.

The pinpricks blow across me once again, only this time they draw blood. Small streams flow down my sides. Again, when I go to scream, no air.

"You will eventually. Everyone else who has come here does," the voice says, only this time it's coming from the foot end of the metal slab I'm strapped to.

"Everyone else is weak," I croak and then prepare for the pain, though it doesn't come.

"Interesting," the voice replies, getting closer. "What makes you think that?"

"They became your slaves, willing to do anything to prevent their deaths."

"And you wouldn't do the same for immortality?"

"I'm already dead. There's no going back to who I was."

A burst of hot, moist air envelops my shoulders. The rustling of a rough material next to me causes my body to go rigid. He's so close that I can taste his salty breath. Warm fingers gently run the length of my arm for several minutes, causing my heart to quicken and my pulse to race with both excitement and fear.

"What if I told you I could return you to the exact place where you died, but you'd awaken completely unharmed?"

"Impossible."

"Nothing is impossible for me, Sara," he says with a wide smile, exposing his sharp teeth.

I pause and let his words sink in. I'd be able to see Keegan again and explain my actions to him and the others, but it would be at a cost. There's no way this thing can return me to the living world if my body was obliterated. The question rolling around in my mind now is: why is he willing to send me back, and what does he get out it?

I shouldn't be contemplating his offer, but I am.

"You lie," I blurt out with all the force I can muster. "Just let me die."

"Sorry, Sara, but that's not an option. You were pulled away from the ether where all dead souls first travel to by me, and for a purpose. The world you came from was once mine. I want it back, and you're going to help me get it."

"Why would I do that?"

"Because it's why you were sent here, Sara." His voice travels slowly around the slab as he moves, but he never comes into view. I only catch glimpses of his cloak when it swings into the sunlight, which lets me know he's right next to me.

"You're a special person who I needed to find, and you proved to be the most challenging. If you hadn't escaped from the compound and run into Lymont, I may never have located you. How fortuitous."

"I'm not going to help you," I say forcefully. "You're the reason our world is in its current condition."

"Oh, what lies your leaders tell you," he hisses. "They wanted the world to change, to evolve into something only madmen would want, and they succeeded. Look closer at your world, Sara—it's not what you think. I know you've discovered some of the haunting things kept under lock and key. Otherwise, you wouldn't have fled, only to die soon after. You knew the bomb would be launched the moment you stepped outside that door, yet you ran anyway, right into my arms. It's almost like you were begging me to come for you… to save you, which I have."

"You're crazy. I don't want to go back. Please just let me die," I say, pleading, yet I don't remember why I don't want to return.

Why is that? Did the blast erase that from my mind or am I in too much pain and anguish to think straight?

"Not even to see your loving husband again? You're his whole world, Sara. What will he do if you're not in it? Keegan is searching for you right now, desperate to find you alive."

"That's not possible. I've been here for weeks. There's no way he's still looking for me."

"Time is irrelevant here. A day in my nest is a minute for your world. The dust from the blast has just finally settled down, allowing your friends to go looking for you. What should we let them find: pieces of your remains, or you alive and perfectly fine?"

"What do you want from me?" I cry as the thought of Keegan only finding bits and pieces of me horrific.

"You do whatever I ask when I request it. Everyone else in your position has been so willing, some practically begging for what I'm offering you. Your resistance makes me want you even more. Submit, Sara, and we'll live in happiness for all eternity."

I thrash around, trying to free myself from the restraints, but I only manage to dig them deeper into my skin. He laughs at my efforts, a vicious chortle that doesn't seem to stop. My arms become slick from blood seeping from my fresh wounds, but if I'm dead how can I be bleeding?

Oh, God, is this real?

"What did you do to me?" I yell.

"The same thing I do to all I bring here," he answers, his cloak fully coming into my view. His hood remains up, preventing me from seeing his face as he steps closer, leaning over me. "You're whole again, Sara. You became mine the moment you accepted Haron's hand at the lake."

"I didn't know," I whisper as tears form.

He bends down until his face is practically touching mine. "Of course you did. They all know when they approach the surface of the water. Everyone's decision to survive is made just before they willingly move from the ether and into the lake."

"I thought you said you pulled me from the ether, but now you're saying I made that decision?"

"Yes," he hisses into my ear. "Everyone is given the option to either stay in the ether until it ends and you're sucked into oblivion, or you follow the stream that leads to the lake. Your natural instinct was to choose the stream, and now here you are." He raises his head slightly. "Your death has brought you home, but your resurrection will bring you everlasting life and the admiration of millions for generations to come."

I close my eyes as the tears that had been pooling in the corners finally fall onto the table. The ropes are loosened slightly, which eases the tension in my limbs. I feel powerless, weak, and vulnerable. I doubt I made this decision for myself as I wanted to die, which is why I ran into Lymont. He claims there are others like me, that we're all destined for the same thing. I wonder what he has in store for my world if he does make a return.

This can't be happening, but it is. I want to keep struggling, but my heart has already succumbed... it did the moment I got here.

"Submit, Sara. Allow me inside and you can return to your world," he says to me, his lips brushing the edge of my ear.

"As your slave?"

"No," he whispers.

I open my eyes as he climbs on top of me, finally removing his cloak. His skin is pale, his eyes a bright blue, his lips full, and his dark shoulder-length hair tickles my cheeks. I've been wanting to see him in the flesh since the moment I arrived, but not this way. I know what he wants and what I have to say to give my permission. If I don't, this game of his will continue forever until he ultimately wins. He claims I have a choice, but in the same *breath he says I don't. I have no options. I'm his, I just won't admit it. He lowers himself the rest of the way, our bodies pressed solidly against each other. I want to turn my head, but he places a hand gently around my throat to prevent movement.*

"Say it, Sara, and all will be well," he says, brushing my lips with his.

I close my eyes and will myself to escape, if not physically then mentally.

"Yes, Arliss," escapes from my mouth. "I'm yours."

His lips take mine as he enters my body. Warmth spreads between us and I moan from the motions. I don't want to show my pleasure or the fact that I'm desiring him more than I should, but I sense he already knows this. My muscles begin to ache and my blood boils, but he keeps going. I feel as if I'm about to explode from both pain and pleasure, and I love every second of it. I don't want it to stop or I'll die.

This must have been how that woman felt the other night.

My body can't take the sensuality he's giving me anymore, and I begin to scream, which only intensifies his arousal. Pain explodes behind my eyes as he pushes me to the breaking point, my throat becoming raw with my cries.

Five

"No!" I shout, bolting up, my head nearly colliding with Keegan's.

My gaze swings around the room as I try to catch my breath and get my bearings. I'm on my bed in the apartment, my clothes are soaked. Trickles of sweat race down my cheeks, dripping into my lap.

"You're okay," Keegan says, though my heart is pounding so hard in my ears I struggle to understand him. "I got you," he continues, rubbing my arms.

"What happened?" I ask, panting since air won't stay in my lungs.

"I found you unconscious on the floor. You've been fighting something in a deep sleep for several hours."

I lean against the headboard and take in a trembling breath. "I feel like I'm going to be sick."

"I'll get you something from the mess hall. You probably just need to eat."

Keegan rushes out of the room. When I know the front door is closed, I slip out of bed and head straight for the bathroom. My stomach is still churning, but the desire to become sick is passing. The drying sweat makes me feel chilled, so I strip down, but before stepping into the shower I check both my arms and legs for ligature marks because the dream felt so real. My skin is free from any blemishes, with the exception of the spider and butterfly tattoos, yet I can still sense the ropes' presence. I feel sore, angry, and violated from that nightmare, but something in the back of my mind keeps telling me that it was all real.

Every disgusting bit of it.

I turn the shower on hot, close the glass door after stepping inside, and slide to the bottom of the tub. I pull my knees up to my chest, wrap my arms around them, and shudder as I recall the Arliss' touch, his breath on my body, and the passion I experienced like never before. The water is almost scalding but I sit through it, punishing myself for what I did, or believe I did. I turn the temperature down just as my skin begins to turn red. Steam has completely filled the tiny space, so much so that I can barely see my hand in front of my face.

The phrase *I shouldn't be alive,* keeps echoing in my mind. *What did I agree to?* I slam my head hard against the tile, hoping to knock myself out, but I only wind up giving myself a headache. I need to get out of here and find the others, but how and where? What does he want me to do once I locate them? Why am I even contemplating any of this?

The door to the bathroom squeaks open, which pulls some of the steam out into the hall. Keegan kneels down next to the tub, opens the partition, and turns off the water. He leans in slightly but keeps his distance probably out of fear of what his wife might have been turned into. I'm sure he's heard that the remains located in Lymont are mine and he doesn't know what to make of it. He was so adamant about having his wife return to him, but now he's avoiding touching me. I must have blurted out something while I was unconscious for him to be acting this way.

"I brought you some eggs and toast," he says calmly. "Do you think you could eat them?"

I move my head so I'm facing him, and just stare.

"Maybe Nex should have another look at you."

"No," I respond hastily. "I just need a few minutes."

He smiles, pats my leg, and leaves.

I stand and reach for a towel to wrap myself in before I get cold. I'm drawn to the mirror covered in steam over the vanity. I reach for it, then draw back. I'm afraid to look at my reflection, terrified of what might look back. I know I'm me now. The real me, reborn by the Arliss. Perhaps I'm afraid I'll notice pieces of him in my image if I look at the mirror the wrong way.

As I reach for the door handle, a voice hisses in my head.

"You're mine now, Sara, and don't you forget it."

I shake my head and enter the small hallway between the master bedroom and the living room. Keegan is sitting on the couch, my food on the coffee table. I sit next to him, pick up my plate, and try to eat. The food isn't as fresh as it was hours ago, and Wavern did say it doesn't get better the longer you wait to eat. I glance at the display and notice the Daily Slate has been updated. Squad Eight is off the rest of today and most of tomorrow. However, they need to report to a launch site, along with Squad Two, at nineteen-hundred hours tomorrow. My eyes move down the screen and that's when I see that the memorial is scheduled to begin at seven tomorrow night. This is the first time I notice that the time for the two sections of the Daily Slate are posted in different formats, when all other information is transcribed the same.

"Ah, yes," the Arliss whispers in my ear, *"the celebration of my demise. How thoughtful of them."*

I almost choke on my food at his remark.

"Yes, Sara, I can see and hear everything you can. Thank you for letting me inside."

I want to shout at him to go away, but Keegan is watching me. He'd really think I'd lost my mind if I just started talking to an invisible person.

Keegan pats me on the back as I try to swallow the bits of egg that are refusing to go down. He fetches a glass of water when his efforts fail, and it takes several big gulps before the food finally budges. I put my plate back on the coffee table and lean into the couch, trying to bury myself in its cushions.

"Do you want to talk about it?" Keegan asks after several awkward moments of silence.

"Talk about what?"

"Why you're still alive?"

"I thought you didn't believe I was dead when you went looking for me. Now you're questioning it?" I ask, getting defensive.

"I'm just trying to understand what happened!" he exclaims. "You have to admit that what we found in Lymont is pretty strange."

"You think I'm someone else, don't you?"

"No, babe, of course not," he says, pulling me into his arms. "I'm sorry if that's how this is coming across. I'm just trying to make heads or tails out of all of this. You're sure you can't remember anything before the blast?"

Before, no, but shortly thereafter, yes, I think to myself.

"No, nothing," I respond. "Look, can we just forget it ever happened and move on? It's not something I'm comfortable talking about."

"We can't simply forget about it, Sara," Keegan responds, also becoming defensive. "We need to figure out what happened out there. Better yet, why you weren't at your station that morning and in Lymont instead?"

"What post was I supposed to be at that day?"

"Lookout number four, only you didn't show when Wavern conducted rollcall. It wasn't until I climbed into lookout number two that we knew you were heading towards Lymont," he says.

"Doesn't the compound have internal security cameras? Surely those would've picked up my movements before I got out."

"They did, but they don't explain why you went out in the first place."

"I keep telling you, I don't know and I'm probably never going to remember, so why can't everyone just drop it?" I comment as I push away from him and back into the corner of the couch.

Keegan gives me a puzzled look. "Who else said something to you?"

"No one. Well, not in those exact words."

"Who?" he asks forcefully.

I pull my legs up under me, as if trying to create a cocoon for myself. "Grimm. According to him, my whole personality has changed. He doesn't believe the shit Andra is spreading, and neither does anyone else from what I've seen."

"All the more reason *not* to drop this," Keegan practically shouts. "Be realistic; it was a miracle you survived, let alone without a scratch. People are going to talk and question what happened, and *you* should be one of them."

"Right now, I just want to move on from the last few days and go to bed."

I get up and head towards the bedroom, Keegan following closely behind. I drop my towel and slide under the covers. I'm too exhausted to care about going to bed naked. Besides, he's my husband so it's not like he's never seen me naked before. He sits on the other side of the bed, wringing his hands.

"Look," he begins without turning to face me, "I think it's best if I just stay with the rest of the squad for the time being."

"What? Why? You were practically fighting Wavern to get me out of the medical ward, and now you want to leave me alone?" I ask, becoming enraged.

"You need recovery time, and I'm not helping by bombarding you with insinuations and questions. Besides, we need to rebuild what we had so you feel comfortable around me again."

"You're making it sound like we've broken up or something. Our relationship is fine and I do feel comfortable around you. You're my damn husband, Keegan. What more do you want from me? Stay."

He turns, leans over to me, and kisses me hard. Heat radiates up my spine as I slide closer to him, wanting more, but he pulls away.

"In time, Sara, but for now you need rest."

"This is bullshit!" I shout. "What the hell is wrong with you?"

"Nothing!" he yells in return. "Fine, do you want the truth? I need time to adjust. Grimm is right, you have changed. I want my wife back and she's not here."

"What makes you say that? I haven't changed."

He grabs my left wrist and points to the tattoo. "Where the hell did this come from, Sara?"

"I told you, I don't know!"

"You're a fucking liar! Grimm gave you this tattoo, didn't he? Just like he gave you the butterfly on your lower back. I could never persuade you to get a tattoo, but the minute he suggests it you're all for it. Is this a way you two can secretly fuck each other without actually physically touching?"

"What the hell are you talking about?" I ask, astounded by the accusation.

"He has this exact image branded on his left wrist, he's the only person I've ever seen with it, and he's had it since I can remember. He's always wanted you, but I got you first. Is this a way for the two of you to go behind my back, a way to fulfill the desires you've kept hidden from everyone?"

Keegan pushes me into the mattress, gripping my arm so tightly my hand begins to turn purple from the lack of blood. "If this turns out to be his handiwork, I'll kill him… and you." He shoves me away, turns off the lights, and slams the front door as he leaves.

I'm puzzled and stunned by his allegations. I remember Keegan being jealous at times of how close Grimm and I used to be, but that was ages ago. It all changed when I married Keegan, or at least I thought it had. Does Grimm really have this mark on his left wrist? If so, how come no one else has made the connection?

I need to find out why I ran into Lymont, now more than ever. The Arliss made it sound like I'd stumbled upon some horrendous piece of information, but what would be so bad that I'd kill myself over in order to keep it quiet? I close my eyes and try to get some sleep, but it's hours before my mind finally grows tired.

I can tell I'm not alone in my bedroom before I even open my eyes. What I'm not expecting is the person sitting next to me on the bed. Grimm glares down at me, his mouth open in a wide smile. I'm about to sit up, when I remember I don't have any clothes on, so I quickly pull the covers up tighter against my neck.

"Don't you look happy to see me," he says, winking.

"Go away," I respond, trying to bury myself under the blankets.

He grabs them just before I'm able to cover my head. "Not so fast. Andra has temporarily reassigned you to my unit and I need you to get your ass in gear, pronto."

"Lucky me," I say, my voice dripping with sarcasm. "Why am I being reassigned?"

"For your safety… and ours."

"What does that mean?"

"Let's just say many in the compound are leery of you and your miraculous return. Andra feels that if you're to remain with Wavern, his judgement might get compromised if he needs to take quick action against you. He views you like a daughter, which could get him and the rest of the squad into some serious trouble. But you see, I have no problem if I need to beat the shit out of you," Grimm answers, smiling wider.

I roll my eyes as I'm not in the mood to debate the change. "Could you leave so I can get dressed?" I ask, pushing him off the bed with my feet.

He winks again, stands, and goes out the bedroom door, neglecting to close it behind himself. I quickly dart over and slam the door shut, grab the last set of clean clothes from my locker, lace up my boots, and search all over for my wristbands, only to remember I left them on the bathroom counter. I slip into the hall then into the bathroom where I brush my hair, pull it up into a ponytail, and secure the leather bracelets. Grimm is leaning against the wall by the door, impatiently waiting when I enter the living room. He hurries me out of my quarters, up the stairs, through the rec room, and into what he calls the weapons and ammunition bunker.

The room is small and resembles a hollowed-out-shell, with a staircase leading down to our immediate right, and another tunnel just to the left of that. Metal lockers fill the space, almost making me feel claustrophobic. Grimm opens an upper locker and removes two holsters, and straps one to each of his thighs. I notice there are names on all the lockers, so I go looking for mine, which is one row over and down along the floor. Jules probably would've returned my weapons and equipment here, but when I open the door the locker is empty.

"You didn't really think I'd let you go armed, now, did you?" Grimm asks, poking his head around the corner. "Besides, the weapons aren't kept in here, just their rigging."

"Then why is this called the weapons and ammunition bunker?" I ask, getting mad.

He points to the floor with one finger while gesturing for me to be silent with another. That's when I hear muffled sounds of rounds being fired.

"The shooting range is below us. The level below that houses all the firearms, bullets, parts, maintenance, and storage for this bunker. No one except Squad Five has access to that level. We wouldn't just want anyone getting a hold of our weapons, now, would we?"

I know that last comment is aimed at me, but I act like I don't hear it. He nudges my shoulder and directs me to the other tunnel, which is slightly longer than most others in the compound. Lights pop on as we enter, illuminating the room from underneath the wire-mesh cages that line the walls, and from two cylindrical conveyors that sit in the center of the room. Grimm stops me and gestures towards the cages.

"Since you obviously don't remember, let me explain this room to you," he says with extreme sarcasm. "The cages on the left house our survival packs. This is where you would store your medical gear, food packets, any additional ammunition, your cameras, radios, and surveillance equipment. The doors to the right of those cages lead out of the compound. It's a soft seal door, but when you're about twenty feet from the main tunnel you reach the hard seal door, which requires a scan of your palm in order to open." He pauses, probably waiting for my reaction in regard to the requirements to escape the enclosure, but I'm already well aware that I left on purpose. "The door next to that comes from the decon chamber. Over on our right are all our radios, cameras, and surveillance equipment. The opening to the left of those cages will take you straight into the control center."

"What about those?" I ask, pointing to silver suits hanging from hooks.

"That's our hazmat gear, in case anyone was thinking of exposing us to a lethal amount of radiation." Again he pauses and stares at me, but I don't respond.

This kind of treatment is going to get old real fast.

We step to the control panel near some conveyors at the center of the room. Grimm enters a sequence of numbers for the left conveyor and a few moments later it rises, carrying two guns and several clips of ammunition. He takes one of the survival packs, slipping the clips inside before placing it on his back.

"What's this other conveyor for?"

Grimm glances back at me. "Medical supplies, but we won't be needing any since we won't be going outside. Or, should I say, *I'm* not going to go outside. If you bolt again, you're on your own. I'm not crazy like Wavern."

I want to snap back at him but my brain is coming up empty, so instead I roll my eyes.

We enter the tunnel that'll take us to the control center, then once we're inside we make a quick left and head down another long, dank hallway. This one is void of the plasma screens that display the Daily Slate, which makes the passageway even darker and more ominous. We come to an intersection with another tunnel that links the decon chamber to the medical ward. I'm surprised I didn't notice the intersection the other day when Wavern was taking me back, but I guess I was too focused on the plasma screens to really notice. The floor has a sharp upward slant, forcing us to climb, thankfully not at a steep angle. After twenty minutes, we finally emerge into a vast hangar-like structure filled with vehicle parts, a few mechanics, and the smell of oil. The ceiling goes up at least five stories, with heavy iron doors blocking each end from the harsh climate outside. There are four large transports and two four-seater ATVs sitting on individual pads scattered about the concrete floor. As I glance around, I notice that two pads are empty. The place is dirty, poorly lit, and smells like popcorn.

"What's with the odor?" I ask when Grimm stops in the center of the floor.

"Because all our natural resources were obliterated in the war, we've had to get creative. We use plant byproducts from the hydroponics bay to create the fuel needed to run these things. It's a sweet-smelling substance that works, but can give you an awful headache if you're around it all day."

I follow him over to one of the four-seater ATVs along the back wall. He goes to a key rack, removes a set, and then gestures for me to get into the passenger side. Since there aren't any doors, I just simply climb in. Once we're in motion, we head for the massive iron door on our left, but just before we hit it Grimm veers to the right and we plunge down a steep tunnel for several minutes before finally leveling off on a two-lane road cut into the tunnel below the surface. Lights are secured in the rock walls and ceiling. There are heavily encased fans every few feet over our heads, probably to vent the exhaust from the vehicles.

"Where are we going?" I finally ask after ten minutes of silence.

"Demos—or the Factory, to be more specific," Grimm answers without taking his eyes off the road.

"How long will it take us to get there?"

"Almost two and a half hours," he replies.

"How far away is it?"

"About one-hundred-and-seventy-five miles west of here. Why, did you think it was closer? Rinku is the outermost compound. We were designed to protect the Aslu Territory, for all the good that did."

"And the other two compounds? Where are they?"

"Other side of the Nove Mountain range in the Ulun Territory. They're a ten-minute and thirty-minute trek to Demos, respectively."

"But Virtus was destroyed, wasn't it? Leaving just the one compound?"

"Just Quarn, yes. It's the only one that's still inhabited."

"Cody told me what happened in Virtus."

Grimm's manner grows dark as he furrows his brow. "Did he now? And what exactly did he say?"

I quickly debate what to admit to Grimm. "He said there was an explosion in the hydroponics bay. Many were killed and only thirty survivors. He told me you were one of them."

Grimm doesn't respond.

"Where in the compound were you when everything happened?"

"Why?" he asks, becoming guarded.

"I'm just curious."

He slams on the brakes. Thankfully I'd strapped myself into the seat, because at the speed we're going I would've gone through the windshield otherwise. "What exactly did Cody tell you?"

"Only that he was in the kitchen when it happened."

"He didn't mention anything about his crackpot idea that the explosion initiated from one of the levels below the control center?"

"No," I say, lying. "Why? Do *you* believe it happened under the control center?"

Grimm presses the accelerator, shooting us down the pavement. "I wouldn't know. I was heading back from Demos when it happened. I was only a few miles away when the explosion ripped everything to hell. Luckily the tunnel didn't collapse, otherwise I wouldn't be here."

"Then how'd you get the scar on your arm?"

He glares at me for a few moments, then turns his attention back to the road. "From pulling Cody out of what was left of the kitchen."

"He's lying," a voice whispers in my head, but I can't tell if it's the Arliss' or my own. *"He doesn't believe it happened in the hydroponics bay either. You should push him on the topic."*

I ignore the voice and try to get a look at Grimm's left wrist, since he doesn't have it covered. I can't see the image clearly, but there's definitely something there.

"Keegan told me you have an interesting mark on your left wrist," I say.

"Yeah, so? You knew that. It's no secret."

"What is it?"

"Why?"

"Does it look anything like this?" I ask, pulling off the wristband and showing him the tattoo.

Again, he slams on the brakes, this time to seize my hand and examine the spider. He sets his left arm next to mine to compare the two. The images are almost identical, except mine is black whereas his has no coloring at all. His looks more like a branding than a tattoo.

"Where'd you get it?" he asks, his eyes transfixed on the mark.

"I don't know," I respond as I pull my arm away and slip the wristband back on. "I came back from Lymont with it. Where'd you get yours?"

"It was branded on me when I was a kid. Some asshole thought it'd be funny to scar me with the Nathair mark."

"What an interesting development. I must know more," the Arliss hisses in my head.

"Who are the Nathair?"

"They were a group of men and women who thought bringing an ancient creature back to life would save the world as it was on the verge of dying. Instead, they brought nothing but death and destruction to millions. Anyone caught with the Nathair symbol was subject to execution while the war raged on. When it was over the mark was banned, but by then all the Nathair were dead as was the creature they brought to life. The fucker who branded me with the mark thought it would be hilarious to scar me as a traitor for life."

"Who was it?"

Grimm hesitates in responding, so I have to keep prodding him for the answer.

"It was Keegan," he finally blurts out.

"Seriously?" I ask, stunned.

"Yes, seriously," Grimm says heatedly. "I told you the guy is an asshole."

"Did he get into trouble for it?"

"Of course not," Grimm answers with resentment.

"How come?"

"His family was held in high regard before the war, so it translated over even after it had ended. I think the notoriety has gone to his head. He thinks he can get away with anything," Grimm says angrily. "And I bet your husband blames me for your tattoo."

"What makes you think that?"

"Because he's a jealous fucker," Grimm says, jerking the vehicle forward. "He won't care how this mark wound up on your body. He'll attribute it to me anyway because he's under the delusion that I'm trying to steal you away from him. He'll look at it as an act of revenge for when he branded me. I swear that guy is going to wind up with my fist down his throat one day. I still can't understand what you see in him."

I now remember why I married Keegan, but decide to keep my mouth shut. I don't need to be in another argument if I can avoid it—especially with someone I care about. My relationship with Grimm is starting to rise to the surface, which is making me both anxious and uncomfortable, so we ride the remainder of the way in silence. I fill the time by trying to determine how to locate the others for the Arliss, which is going to be difficult because I don't even know how many people I'm looking for.

I wonder if Grimm is one of them, but I doubt it since Keegan marked him and not the Arliss. The tattoo must be a way for us to identify each other. I'm not sure what he wants with them, or even me exactly, yet I feel if I don't do this I'll get pulled back into his nest for more torment and pain. I know the woman from the Factory commercial is one, and it's fortunate that we're heading there now, but….

"Why are we going to the Factory?" I ask.

"To get provisions for tomorrow's memorial," Grimm responds, his voice much calmer now.

"How come it's just the two of us?"

"I sent the rest of the squad ahead right before I came and got you. They're in two large transports, so they can move everything around. As I'm just carting you, I don't need such a big vehicle."

We finally begin to ascend, albeit gradually, when a low rumble catches my attention. The closer we move towards the sound, the louder it gets and changes in pitch.

"What is that?" I ask.

"That, my dear, is the Occlyn Ring. It's housed inside the mountain and spins continuously to provide the force field Demos requires. All tunnels were dug underneath it since you can't actually penetrate the ring itself."

Surprisingly, the ring isn't shaking the tunnel even though it's almost deafening when we drive right under it. The road rises again about twenty feet later and leads us into another hangar, which has an assortment of parking pads with only a few vehicles on them. Grimm stops along the wall closest to a pair of tall sliding glass doors that appear to lead to a city full of color, light, and smiling faces. I follow him through the doors and into the warm, welcoming atmosphere.

The air in Demos smells clean and fresh, a pleasant change from Rinku's. The walkway is made up of tightly-packed stone pavers and is at least the same width as the road in the tunnel. On either side of us are lofty structures constructed of glass, stone, and steel, rising nearly to the top of the force field, which shimmers in blue against the reddish sky. Some of the buildings have balconies, while others have wide terraces, each ornately decorated. Grimm tells me as we make our way down the road that they're the apartments for the citizens of Demos. As we pass them I notice pebbled paths weaving around the buildings, linking them together in a sort of labyrinth, which extends deeply on either side of the road.

It takes several minutes for us to reach the city's center, which consists of an open-air plaza around a massive pool with a very elaborate fountain in the middle. I pause to take in the sights as Grimm continues walking.

There are five roads extending out from the center, making the layout of the city resemble that of a tire, with the roads being the spokes. To the left of the pool is an area dedicated to what look to be educational buildings, hospitals, government offices, and maintenance bays. To the right of that are groups of shops in various styles and colors, all leading towards a tall wooden structure that looks out of place in the city. To the right of the pool is an entire area filled with parks and reflecting ponds. I can't help but stare as families gather on the grass and children play nearby.

"Oh, what paradise," the Arliss whispers. *"Such beautiful creatures. Alas, their fate has already been determined, and not by me I might add."*

"Hurry up," Grimm says, coming back to retrieve me.

He grabs my arm and drags me away from the splendor. We round the pool and continue straight ahead, down the road with the shops. Grimm stops at the entrance to the odd-looking building. The structure looks to be haphazardly constructed, almost like segments have been added on to it over the years. The exterior is covered in dark wood shingles, and as we make our way through the double doors I notice the interior wall coverings are made up of the same material. The furnishings, however, are constructed of polished wood and wrought iron, giving the place a rustic atmosphere.

We stop at a counter which blocks us from getting further inside, as wrought iron rails obstruct the lone aisle in. An older man in a white suit smiles when we approach. His teeth are perfectly straight, his salt and pepper hair is cut short along the temples, and his posture is impeccable. I feel like a hunchback compared to him.

"How may I assist you, Grimm?" the man asks, placing his hands on the counter, palms down.

"I was checking where we are with the provisions for tomorrow. My squad should've arrived a bit ago to collect them," Grimm replies, sounding very authoritative.

"The items are almost finished being assembled below. Your squad is by the back exit, waiting. It shouldn't be too much longer."

Grimm smiles, but he seems tense. "If you don't mind, I'd like to have a look around to see if there's anything additional we may need for the compounds and the plaza."

"Of course," the man says as he reaches for a latch, which unhinges a gate to our right. "Just let our employees know if you find anything else you may need."

Grimm pushes me gently through the gate, as I'm too entranced by the odd smile the man is providing. He looks stoned, yet appears to have all his faculties. I find him somewhat unpleasant and the whole encounter disturbing, but I don't know why. Grimm guides me a little deeper into the shop before finally letting me go.

"Don't touch anything," he says, waving a finger in my face. "I need to go check in with my squad, but I'll be back momentarily. You can look around, but don't wander from the main floor. I don't want to spend the rest of my day hunting for you in this maze." He disappears into the racks of food stuffs.

I feel as if I'm being treated like a child and bullied into obeying orders. I shake my head and decide to take a look around while I have the chance.

The place is crammed with shelves of varying sizes and heights, all housing something different. The entire main floor is dedicated to food stuffs, so there isn't much to see. In the center are two elevators, along with two spiral staircases leading upward. I look up, noticing the center of the building has no ceiling, and I can see a vast second level. The stairs and elevators are made of the same polished wood as the shelving units, but the elevators have wrought-iron gates for their entrances. I know Grimm said to stay on the main floor, but I want to see what the rest of the establishment looks like, so I head up one of the staircases.

The second floor is cluttered with just about anything you could want. Colorful trinkets dangle from wires hooked into the vaulted ceiling. Glass ornaments hang precariously over the opening to the main floor. I have to constantly watch where I'm putting my feet since the floor is severely uneven. I catch glimpses of other people milling about the area, all with their hands behind their backs as if not to tempt themselves into touching something. A young man in white quickly approaches me when I reach the furniture section of the floor.

"Looking for anything in particular, Sara?" he asks in a very jovial tone, giving off the same creepy vibe as the greeter downstairs.

"No, thank you," I respond, startled by the fact this man knows my name. "I'm just waiting for a friend."

"Ah, I see. Well, may I suggest that while you're waiting you might perhaps be interested in the party decorations and supplies we carry for the memorial. They're located in the back-right corner on the main floor," he says, smiling.

"Um, sure, I'll go take a look."

He stays in his spot, staring at me while I hurry over to one of the staircases in order to get away from him and his disturbing manner. Once I'm back on the main floor, I turn left and enter the party section. Only I wouldn't say the items here are suitable for a party. Black and dark blue streamers dangle down from the shelving units, which are stocked with plates, cups, wreaths and garlands, memorial plaques that you can write on, hand-painted wooden tombstones, dolls with crosses as eyes, and paper lanterns that have a mushroom cloud etched on their sides. The whole display is morbid and unsettling.

I turn my back to it and begin to go towards the front of the store, when a tall, dark-skinned man blocks my path. His features are hidden by a thick, heavy hood, but when he looks down at me I catch a glimpse of his face, which seems somehow familiar. My mind races to place a name with the face as he abruptly turns and walks quickly to the rear of the store.

It can't be him, I think to myself. *That can't be Tennison. He died when Virtus was destroyed.*

I start to follow the man, when a woman with strawberry-blond hair and wearing an orange dress catches my eye. She's heading deeper into the party supplies section. I hesitate to follow her, but something tells me I need to. She changes direction when she notices me and begins moving towards the front of the store. I continue to follow her, but at a greater distance. The bracelets on her arms chime with every step, as if calling to me. We're almost to the counter when she doubles back to the stairs. When I get closer she stops, turns, and smiles at me.

"Hello, Sara," she says, then grabs my arm and pulls me into the gap between the staircase and the elevator wall.

"How do you know who I am?"

"You're one of his," she states. "And so am I." She pulls up the bracelets on her left arm, revealing the tattoo that I already know is there. She then taps on my left wristband, indicating mine. "This allows us to identify each other."

"How do you know I have one?"

"Because he told me so," she says, hissing slightly and sounding like the Arliss. "They're imprinted on us just before we return." She rubs her chin before continuing. "We've met before, you know. Quite recently, but I'm sure that memory has been blocked like all your other ones."

"Why do you say that?"

"It's what happens when you decide to bind yourself to him. Upon your return to the living world, your memories are temporarily blocked. It's how he's able to stay inside you, watch you, and control you. Your memories will return when your body has had time to adjust to his presence. Some memories should've already surfaced by now."

"You're the woman I saw the Arliss take into that room, the one with the mattress."

"Yes," she replies, smiling.

"How many of us are there? I'm supposed to find them."

She caresses my cheek with the back of her hand, which sends chills down my spine. "All in good time, Sara. As for now, enjoy the memorial… as it will be the last one." She kisses me gently on the lips and leaves.

"Such a sweet girl Casey is, don't you think?" the Arliss hisses in my ear. *"I have such big plans for her… too bad they all involve her dying."*

Six

"Sara." My name echoes through the aisles as I emerge from the gap. "God damn it, where are you?"

"Right here," I respond, trying to sound as annoyed as possible. "I stayed on the main floor, just like you directed." I make sure my comment is filled with sarcasm as I gesture widely with my arms and pretend to take a bow.

"Don't be such a bitch," Grimm says, rolling his eyes. "Let's go, everything is ready."

We head to the back of the main floor where a pickup counter is located, along with the exit for the Factory. Half of Grimm's squad is pushing large carts loaded with fireworks out the door and down the path to the hangar, while the others carry the nightmarish items from the party supply section. We turn left at the plaza, but only those with the carts continue. The rest make their way into the parks and begin to set up the decorations as citizens carry tables and chairs from one of the other shops, setting them down on the grassy areas.

"Is that for tomorrow?" I ask as we continue down the path.

"Yes. The compounds are in charge of all arrangements for the memorial. Tomorrow the citizens of Demos will gather in Zone D to celebrate surviving the war while the rest of us have somber ceremonies in the compounds. At night, the fireworks will be set off from two old missile silos in the southern part of the Nove Mountain range. Squads Two and Eight are in charge of those this year."

"Is Zone D where the parks are?"

I can sense his agitation at my question, but the more questions I ask the more memories begin to surface.

"Yes. Demos is divided into five zones. Zone A and E are where the residential buildings sit. Zone B contains all the government buildings, such as schools, hospitals, and maintenance sheds. Zone C has the Factory and all retail shops. Zone D has the parks and reflecting ponds. As you can see, each zone is separated by the stone roads." He gestures widely, over-exaggerating his movements.

"I get it," I snap. "God, you're irritating as always."

He stops so abruptly that I almost ram into him. "Are you starting to remember things?" he asks as he turns around and speaks in a tone filled with both joy and concern.

"What do you think?" I ask with such sarcasm that I even feel it's over the top.

He pulls me into his arms and hugs me so hard I can barely breathe. "Yes! I'm getting my buddy back!"

"Let me go. You stink."

He laughs as he releases me. "You always thought my pungent aroma was sexy."

"Maybe in your dreams," I say.

"That's my girl," he says, leaning over and squeezing me one last time.

"Don't get too excited, it's coming back very slowly," I add as he starts to walk again, this time with a slight hop in his step. "I'm probably going to keep bugging you with questions until I fully recover."

"Keegan can help you with those."

I snort. "He's avoiding me and is now staying with the rest of the squad for the moment."

"Lovers' quarrel?"

"Hardly. It's like you said to me yesterday—I've changed, and he says he needs time to adjust."

"That's bullshit, Sara, and you know it. Keegan has always been there for you, and annoyingly so for most of the time. Sometimes to the point of ridiculousness."

"How would you know? You've only been in Rinku for a few months."

"I've known you since we were little. We were both raised in the abandonment home, in the southern section of the Kai Mountains. That was until Tennison, who was the leader for Virtus, came and recruited me. Once I was all trained up, I made sure to come and see you as much as possible. Then Wavern took you to Rinku unexpectedly, where you met

Keegan, so I only saw you periodically when our paths crossed here in Demos."

"Who lives in the home now?"

"No one. It was where those who survived the war and its fallout were placed. The new leaders didn't want the survivors polluting the pure air of Demos, which is why we're the only ones permitted outside in the toxic environment. Over time, our families developed a tolerance for the horrid conditions. Depending on where someone's ancestors were when the war happened, determined the amount of exposure received and the length of time it would take to cycle through till someone was born healthy in that person's blood line. Andra is a first-generation survivor as her parents were helping with the completion of the Occyln Ring when the bombs started to fall. They'd just gotten it to complete one full rotation when all hell broke loose. Wavern is the next oldest, but from then on it's pretty much people in their early forties or younger. Thousands of people never saw the sky again." Grimm lets silence fall between us, but not for long. "It was a good thing Wavern took you out when he did, otherwise you wouldn't be here."

"What are you talking about?"

"The abandonment home was destroyed a few days after you left. Everyone, with the exception of a handful of kids, was killed. Those who survived were found huddled in a partially collapsed dorm room."

I wonder if Cody was one of them. He's too young to be a part of the compound, so I'll have to ask him.

"How was it destroyed?"

"By a bomb, much like the one that fell on Lymont the other day."

"Does anyone know where it came from?"

"There have been speculations over the years as to who could be responsible, but no one has ever been able to prove it."

"Who do they think it was?"

He stops, pulls me aside from the group, and answers in a hushed tone. "The one who was supposed to have been defeated by the war. The being responsible for the way our world looks today. The monster who annihilated millions of people. They call him the Arliss."

Uncontrollable laughter rings in my head. *"Oh my, such lies you've all been fed. If only he and everyone else knew the truth. And that day is fast approaching."*

My head begins to pound from the noise, so I'm forced to rub my temples to ease the pain. I think Grimm notices my sudden change, but doesn't ask about it. We rejoin the group just as they're exiting Demos, into the hangar. The fireworks are loaded into the large transports while Grimm and I jump into the four-seater. We follow the vehicles out of the hangar and back onto the road to Rinku, but just past the Occlyn Ring one of the transports veers down a road on the right.

"Where are they going?" I ask.

"They're going to launch site number two. That road leads you to Quarn as well, and that opening there," he begins as we pass a similar road on our left, "will lead you to what's left of Virtus."

We haven't gone far when the second transport turns right and heads down another road, which Grimm says goes to launch site number one. The squad will spend the remainder of the day organizing and setting up the displays for tomorrow. Once they're finished, they'll go back to the city and pick up the rest of the team before heading back to Rinku.

"What was our childhood like in the abandonment home?" I ask when we're about halfway to the compound.

"Tolerable. There wasn't much to do, so we pretty much had to come up with ways to entertain ourselves when they weren't badgering us with military drills, technical training, and survival skills. They started us at an extremely young age, to prepare us for our lives in the compounds. You and I accelerated quickly through the program, even though we're three years apart. We would turn our lessons into a competition, which is why we get along so well."

"How old were you when you were recruited by Tennison?"

"Eighteen—the standard age."

"So you'd been in Virtus only a short time when Wavern came and collected me."

"Yes."

"Do you know why he took me at fifteen?"

"No, and it's always been bothering me. I've just never been in a position to ask him."

I decide to stop the questions for the remainder of the ride since my mind is feeling overloaded, so I lean back and close my eyes. They aren't closed for long when I feel us ascend. It didn't feel like I'd dozed off, but as I open my eyes we pull into the garage for Rinku. Grimm swings the vehicle around in order to park it back on its pad. As he shuts off the engine, I start to unbuckle myself, but stop when I see Keegan standing in the center of the room with his arms folded over his chest. His cheeks are red and I swear I see steam coming out of his ears.

"Hey man," Grimm says when he spots Keegan. "Everything is just about all set for tomorrow."

Keegan stomps over to us, and as Grimm turns his back to remove the keys from the ignition Keegan throws him to the cement floor.

"What the hell, Keegan? What's your problem?" Grimm asks, trying to get back to his feet.

Keegan bends down, grabs Grimm by the collar, and punches him hard. I finally manage to unbuckle myself just as two men working on a couple of the transports rush over and pull Keegan off Grimm. The men struggle to keep Keegan back.

"Where'd you take her?" Keegan demands, spit flying.

"Who? Sara?" Grimm asks, clearly puzzled by the question. "We went to Demos, you know that."

"Why is she with you?" Keegan yells as he continues to try to free himself.

"Andra reassigned her to my squad this morning. Didn't Wavern tell you?" Grimm asks as he wipes blood from his lip.

"He told me, I just didn't believe it. I bet that made your day though, didn't it, Grimm? You've always had a thing for my wife, and now that she's lost her memory you can swoop right in and take her as your own. But you've already done that, haven't you? Giving her that tattoo… marking your territory."

Grimm gets to his feet. "You've lost it, man," he says, jabbing a finger in Keegan's face. "Being cooped up in here has made you crazy. Sara loves *you*, stupid, but with the way you're acting right now she may not for long."

This only antagonizes Keegan even more. He breaks free and slams Grimm onto the cement again. The two throw punches, roll around on the floor, and kick each other until Wavern comes running up from the tunnel.

"Enough, both of you," Wavern says, pulling them apart. "Grimm, go see Brea in the medical ward to get patched up. Keegan, you're confined to quarters until further notice." Wavern pauses, still trying to catch his breath. "I thought this was all settled years ago. Knock this shit off, or I'll move you both to Quarn, where Demmer can deal with your crap."

Wavern lets Keegan go. He and Grimm leave, but Wavern has one of the mechanics go with them. I'm too stunned to move, so Wavern has to nudge me and gestures for me to follow him back into the tunnel. I'm confused as to what just happened, since I actually don't remember Keegan ever acting like that before. I begin to have flashes of Keegan and Grimm arguing in the past. Although I can't recall what they were fighting about, I remember it never got violent. Any torment Keegan directed at Grimm was when we were kids—nothing this bad since we moved to the compounds.

"I didn't think he was going to take it that badly," Wavern finally says after we pass the tunnel to the medical ward. He sounds both remorseful and puzzled. "I had my doubts about bringing Grimm into the compound when Virtus was destroyed, but everything had cooled off by then. Keegan and Grimm were actually trying to get along. I just don't understand what could've changed and so quickly."

This time I think Wavern is talking more to himself than to me, so I keep my mouth shut. I don't think he heard Keegan's outburst about Grimm marking his territory, so I'm not going to rehash it for him. Wavern looks like he's already under enough stress; I don't want to add to it. He taps my shoulder, having stopped a few paces behind me.

"I'm going to check on Grimm. Dinner is just about ready, so go eat. I'll be down to your quarters later to check on you."

Wavern turns around and heads back the way we came before I can respond. I continue to make my way through a very crowded control center as workers change shifts, and head into the mess hall. After grabbing my tray, I find Cody and Jules sitting in the back corner. They gesture for me to join them, and ask how I'm feeling, if I'm starting to remember anything, and what did I do today. I keep the fight between Keegan and Grimm to myself, but divulge most of everything else.

"That was a dark day," Jules says after I mention the bombing of the abandonment home. "Hundreds of people wiped out in the blink of an eye."

Cody stays silent, his skin turning pale as Jules continues to talk.

"Whole family lines made extinct. Everyone was shocked when survivors were found," Jules says before shoveling more food into his mouth. "Cody, weren't you one of the lucky ones?"

"Yeah," Cody squeaks out.

"How old were you when it happened?" I ask.

"Nine. I lost my siblings in the attack. Our parents had already been dead for several years from radiation poisoning."

"Does anyone know why it was bombed?" I ask.

"There has been speculation," Jules replies. "There are some of those, me included, who think it was done intentionally by the governing body to keep the people in the home from straining the world's dwindling resources. Others speculate it was the work of the Arliss."

"I thought he was dead, killed when the rest of humanity was. People still think he exists?" I ask.

"Not anymore," Cody mumbles.

"Who was the Arliss?" I ask after a few minutes of silence.

"No one really knows," Cody replies.

Jules snorts. "He was a monster who rose up from a dying world to turn those who'd summoned him into his slaves," Jules says curtly. "They didn't exactly get what they bargained for. The Arliss was manipulative, overpowering, cunning, and able to turn whole communities into his captives without lifting a finger. Our leaders just aren't telling us the full story, because they fear his return. You can't kill that kind of monster without repercussions," Jules adds.

Cody grows increasingly pale, shoves his tray aside, and gets up to leave without saying another word. Jules and I stare after him as he disappears into the rec room.

"Poor kid," Jules says after a few minutes of silence. "He was so young when it happened, and then to have everyone he knew die in Virtus…"

"What do you mean?" I ask.

"Tennison was the only leader who offered to take in the handful of kids who survived the bombing of the abandonment home."

"Why didn't the other compounds take any of the survivors?"

"Quarn was suffering from a flu epidemic, so Demmer didn't want anyone else to get infected. I'm not sure why Andra didn't want anyone. I do know she was pretty adamant about it, even going against the governing body. She absolutely refused to let any of them into Rinku. However, after the incident in Virtus she didn't have much of a choice. The leaders said they would replace her with Wavern if she didn't take half of the survivors."

My memory of that day slowly returns.

The compound leaders, along with the squad leaders and their highest ranked members, were called to a special session in the meeting hall in Zone B. The governing body, which rules over our entire society, forced Andra to take people from Virtus, under threat of losing her position. I can't recall why she was so defiant, or even if she actually stated why she refused to take anyone. To this day I believe she holds Wavern responsible for her hand being forced. Maybe that's why she didn't put up much of a fight when Wavern bolted out to Lymont to get me. I bet she was hoping none of us would return, which would've made her life easier.

"She didn't speak to any of us for weeks," I add.

Jules gives me a quizzical look.

"My memories are slowly returning, but there are still major gaps that need filling."

He smiles, finishes his meal, and tells me he'll see me later. I take care of my tray and dishes when I'm done a few minutes later. As I pass through the rec room I try to find Cody among the others filing in to play games or watch a movie, but he's nowhere to be seen. I go back to my suite, exhausted from the day. To my surprise, Keegan is sitting on the couch when I enter. I wasn't expecting him to be here. I assumed he'd go to the squad's quarters when Wavern ordered him to leave the garage.

"Have you eaten?" I ask, closing the door behind me.

"I'm not hungry," he replies, his eyes glued to the plasma screen that's showing some sort of news program from Demos.

"What the hell is the matter with you?" I ask, standing in front of him with my arms folded across my chest. "You haven't been violent towards Grimm since we were kids, or anyone else for that matter. Why now?"

His gaze drifts up towards my face, anger clearly pulsating from his irises. "So, we remember things now, do we? Good for you," he says sarcastically.

"What the fuck is your problem?"

"Everything... nothing!" he yells, then leans forward and runs his fingers through his hair. "I don't know," he says, sounding concerned. "Ever since that bomb dropped on Lymont, I just can't stop thinking about how I almost lost you. I don't want to go through that again." He reaches for me, wraps his arms around my waist and pulls me into him, resting his head against my abdomen. "Seeing you with Grimm makes me feel as if I'm losing you, and I just can't let that happen."

"You're being ridiculous. I married you, not him. I love you, not him."

"Then why did you go out there?" Keegan asks, looking into my eyes. "You knew it was forbidden to go outside into that harsh environment, so why would you disobey a direct order?"

I put my hand on the top of his head. "I wish I could remember."

"I know why," the Arliss hisses in my ear. *"Come back and perhaps I'll tell you."*

I ignore him, or at least try to. I want to respond, but I know I can't without Keegan asking all kinds of questions. I stroke his hair while I wonder why the Arliss would want me to return, since he sent me back here to begin with.

As if he hears my thoughts, he responds.

"I need you to bring me a replacement," he says. *"One of my loyalists has deceived me and needs to be punished for the betrayal. You need to bring me their replacement so my plan can be placed into motion. Preferably Grimm… he seems like a capable fellow, and he's already wearing my mark."*

I feel sickened by his words. I wouldn't want the Arliss to come into contact with anyone I know, but inside I feel compelled to follow… to obey. I try to pull myself away from Keegan, his touch feeling toxic. His grip on my waist tightens and he begins to pull me down on top of him, reclining against the couch.

"Please don't go," he whispers just before our lips meet.

I'm very confused by his behavior and clinginess. He's always been a take-charge type of person, not someone who falls apart easily. What could've caused this rapid change? My mind swirls with emotions as we cling to each other. Heat builds to the point of ignition. Our clothes are strewn around the room as we make our way into the bedroom. I try to focus on the moment, to love my husband for who he was, and not the stranger I feel he has become. After several moments, I finally lose myself and try not to look back.

Seven

Keegan falls asleep quickly, but I'm wired and restless. I toss on my clothes and sit on the couch. According to the time on the Daily Slate it's a few minutes after twenty-hundred hours. I'm in the process of changing the channel when there's a knock on the door. It's Wavern.

"I came to see if Keegan is here," he says, hovering in the doorway.

"He's sleeping."

"Can I come in?"

I step out of the way then close the door behind him. "How's Grimm?" I ask as he takes a seat on the couch.

"He'll survive. Andra saw the fight on the security feed in her apartment. Keegan has been placed on a five-day suspension and is confined to quarters," Wavern tells me.

"He's not going to take that well."

"Nope, but then again he shouldn't have gone after Grimm like he did. He's lucky the punishment isn't harsher for attacking a superior officer. If I had my way, he'd be spending the next week working in the farms for the Factory. Those people are barred from leaving, so they never see sunlight."

"Why do you think Keegan attacked Grimm?" I ask.

"Keegan's had something stuck up his ass since Grimm came to live in Rinku, especially once Grimm was promoted to lead Squad Two. Technically, Keegan should've been placed in charge, but because of his arguments with some of the other leaders he was passed over."

"He doesn't get along with the other squad leaders?"

"Not so much them, but certainly the compound leaders. He and Andra are constantly butting heads, and he and Demmer have gotten into it a couple of times." Wavern pats the cushion next to him for me to sit. "We were all surprised when you married Keegan," he says quietly. "It felt rushed. You two had only been dating for a few weeks, at least from what we could tell.

The minute Grimm came onboard after Virtus was destroyed, you and Keegan got married. I think it was more his idea than yours."

"It was, and then again it wasn't," I comment.

"What do you mean?"

"I loved the attention Keegan gave me. I'd missed being close to someone for so long that over the years we became intimate," I say. "We hadn't been dating for only a few weeks; we'd been sleeping together for several years. When Grimm moved into the compound I was afraid I'd made a mistake with Keegan, so we decided to get married to keep our relationship together. At least, that was my reasoning for the union. Keegan wanted to make sure Grimm had no chance with me."

"Had you known Grimm before coming to the compound?"

"Yes. He and I grew up together in the abandonment home. We were close… really close up until the day Tennison recruited him," I say as I rub the butterfly tattoo before abruptly standing. "I resented Grimm for leaving me there," I blurt out. "Especially when the home was destroyed a short time later." Tears begin pouring down my face. "He left me there to die… tossed me aside like garbage, when I'd given him everything."

"You were only fifteen, Sara. Surely by now you know none of that was true. He had no control over leaving the home… none of you did."

"I wanted to punish Grimm," I say, balling my hands into fists as the tears stop. "I thought marrying Keegan would do that… that he'd feel discarded like I did."

"That's toxic, Sara. If Keegan is aware of any of this, I can see why he reacted the way he did today. I'm sure if Andra had known about how far back you and Grimm go, she never would've moved you into his squad."

"But she did know!" I shout. "Keegan told her right before Grimm moved in."

"Why would she put you on Grimm's team if she knew the type of reaction Keegan would display?"

"Because that's exactly what she wanted Keegan to do. Probably hoping that he'd kill Grimm in the process. And me as well," I say, sinking back into the couch.

"Why would she want either of you dead?"

"I don't know... I'm just rambling. Why did you recruit me at fifteen?" I ask.

"The abandonment home's head mistress called me up and told me about you. It wasn't an unusual request of hers, as she would often tell me about kids that were showing exceptional talent. That's how I learned about Grimm, but Tennison got to him before I could."

"But I was three years below the minimum age."

"And one of the smartest people in that awful place. Haron felt horrible when Grimm left. She thought you'd do well with me, seeing as you'd already mastered every class and were becoming difficult for her to handle. I think she wanted to make sure you were placed correctly and quickly, before you got out of hand and wound up in the farms at the Factory."

Haron. Where have I heard that name before?

"You know where, Sara. Give it some time, it'll click."

I glance up and notice Keegan standing in the doorway to the bedroom. He's put on pants, but nothing else. He has his arms crossed over his chest and his eyes are focused on Wavern.

"I didn't hear you get up," I say, stumbling as I get to my feet.

"I didn't want to interrupt the conversation," he says heatedly. "Why are you here, Wavern?"

"To tell you that you're on notice," he says, standing. "Per Andra, you're on suspension and confined to quarters for the next five days."

"What the hell for?"

"Attacking Grimm," Wavern says authoritatively. "You know damn well you can't just hit a superior officer."

"He's no officer," Keegan mumbles.

"Your opinion about his ability aside, those are the orders. I'll have someone in the squad bring you your meals when Sara can't." Wavern heads towards the door. "Try to listen, Keegan. You're overreacting to Sara being placed into Grimm's squad. Once the memorial is over, I'll put in a request to have her returned to Squad Eight. In the meantime, keep your fucking temper in check or I'll have you arrested for dereliction of duty."

Wavern opens the door and slams it as he leaves, which causes the plasma screen on the wall to shake slightly. I turn to face Keegan and scowl at him.

"You're unbelievable," I say as I cross the room.

He grabs my arm. "Are you going someplace?"

"Yeah, to bed," I say, jerking my arm away.

"We're not done talking," he says, following me.

I dig in my locker for something to sleep in, but I only find a shirt. I need to do laundry desperately or I'll be walking around naked.

"There's nothing more to say," I comment as I change.

When I pull the shirt over my head, Keegan is now standing in front of me. I didn't even hear him move from the doorway. He takes my wrists and shoves my arms down to my sides with such force they feel as if they might snap. A darkness falls over him, turning his eyes red.

"Who are you?" I moan as pain shoots up my arms.

"I'm your husband, Sara. Who else would I be?"

"Why are your eyes red?"

"They're not," he says calmly as they change back to blue. "You must be hallucinating."

"I know what I saw."

He shoves me onto the bed. "I'm sure you think you saw something," he says, crawling on top of me. "But with the trauma you've been through lately, it's obvious your mind is playing tricks on you."

"It's not," I say hesitantly.

"Are you sure?"

I think back to the encounter earlier in the Factory. Maybe I imagined seeing Tennison standing before me. He's been gone for months now, or at least that's what we've been led to believe. I guess it could've been someone else. Maybe Keegan's right and I did imagine his eyes changing colors. The lighting in the bedroom isn't the greatest, so I could've been mistaken. It's been a long couple of days, I haven't been sleeping well, and I survived a nuclear blast.

My mind is definitely playing tricks on me.

"I'm just so tired," I say, relaxing as he strokes my arms.

"I hope not too tired," he says with a slight laugh.

His lips touch my body and I light up. He hasn't even started yet and I'm already moaning with pleasure, which my mind tries to tell me is odd but my body won't allow the message to be heard. Painful pinpricks cover my skin with each motion, just like it did with the Arliss, but this feels gratifying. I don't want him to stop even as the pain intensifies. I'm not sure why he's hurting me, but I don't want it to end. Everything about this is wrong, but right at the same time.

He's gone when I wake, which means he's going to be reprimanded or worse when Wavern finds out. I take a shower and put on the clothes from yesterday as that's all I have. I make sure my wrists are covered with the leather bands before heading out. I've missed breakfast, but since it's the memorial today the mess hall will serve food all day long. Many people usually spend this time hanging out in the rec room, trying to keep their minds occupied on other things. I decide to go to the firing range to get some practice in when a thought occurs to me. We have a lot of weapons and ammunition stored, but we only use them for practice down on the range, so why do we have so much?.

Am I missing something? Could Jules be right about our leaders fearing the Arliss' return? Is that why we have a large arsenal?

I shake my head to clear it since I can't afford such distractions when I'm about to shoot my gun. Mishaps happen that way. When I enter the weapons bunker I go right to my locker, completely forgetting that it's empty until after I've opened it. And besides, the guns aren't kept here, so why did I go to it?

"Looking for this?" A hand pops around my face, holding one of my weapons from the other day.

"Thanks," I say, taking it from Grimm's hand.

I turn to look at him. He has a bruise on one of his cheeks, a cut just above his eye, and scraped knuckles.

"You don't look too bad," I say with a casual smile.

"Huh, you should see the other guy." His joke falls flat, which causes an awkward pause between us. "Do you want company down at the range? I'm free for another couple of hours."

"I kind of need to be by myself at the moment, but come and get me when it's time to leave for Demos."

He forces a smile and leaves.

I head towards the stairs and go down. I and a few members of Squad Five are the only ones in the range. I get quizzical looks from them when I step up to one of the counters and request several clips of ammunition and a couple of targets. I'm sure Andra would have a fit if she knew Grimm gave me my gun, but I really couldn't care less at the moment. I load the clip, slide the target down the line, put on a pair of hard earmuffs that dangle from a nail along the back wall, and fire off a few rounds. With each pull of the trigger, I can feel the tension in my shoulders ease. I change out the targets and fire off another round, all while picturing the Arliss as my target.

His words echo in my head. Which loyalist betrayed him, and how? Why do I have to bring him another victim? What is his true purpose with me and the others? From there my mind wanders to the abandonment home and its destruction, then on to Cody, Keegan, and then Grimm. While all of this is running around in my head, I've automatically changed clips and targets several times over without even thinking. I don't snap out of it until one of my shots hits the back wall and ricochets towards the other side of the targeting aisle. I set my gun down and remove the earmuffs. As I turn to leave Wavern is standing in the doorway, blocking the stairs. I go over to the counter, and hand in my weapon and empty clips before joining him.

"Andra wants to see you," he says, then abruptly turns and heads up.

His severe tone catches me off guard, but I begrudgingly follow.

From Wavern's attitude I can tell he's not in a talking mood, so I refrain from asking the questions that are circling in my head. I wonder if Andra found out that Grimm gave me one of my guns back, or perhaps that I'm finally starting to remember things, or that Keegan left our apartment against her orders. My nervousness increases the closer we get to the barracks. Once we enter the area, Wavern takes a hard right and stops when we're halfway towards the women's locker room. He knocks gently on the door marked with Andra's name. We wait for several seconds before the door finally swings open, exposing a very luxurious apartment on the other side. I practically sink into the carpeting the moment I enter.

The living room walls are covered in white wainscoting with watercolor paintings sporadically placed on them. Two U-shaped couches sit just beyond the door, around a glass coffee table. To the left of the couches is a square metallic table with eleven chairs surrounding it. Next to that is a half wall supported by a thin column separating a kitchen and dining room from the rest of the area. Across from the front door is another door, but it's closed, so I have no idea what lies beyond. Along that same wall are three plasma screens: two showing rotations for Rinku and Quarn while the other one is off.

The third must've been for Virtus.

"I'll call you when we're done," Andra says to Wavern, then slowly closes the door on his stern face. "Have a seat, Sara," she says.

I sit on the couch by the long table, scooting myself so far back that my feet almost come off the floor. Andra takes the seat across from me and straightens her red silk shirt as she does so. She's formally dressed in a red pencil skirt, her hair neatly set into a bun at the nape of her neck. Her attire strikes me as odd considering where we live, but it could be because of what day it is.

"I'll make this conversation brief since you'll be leaving for Demos in a little while," Andra says very casually.

She clears her throat and offers me a glass of water from a tray resting in the center of the coffee table. I decline the drink, but thank her for the offer. I know she's stalling, but I can't figure out why.

"I've heard that your memories are starting to return," she says, pouring herself a glass.

"Yes, but slowly," I respond, emphasizing the word *slowly*.

"That's wonderful news." Andra looks like she's trying to smile, but it's forced and awkward. "What have you been able to recall?"

I have a feeling she's fishing for something in particular, so I try to be as vague as possible. "Just snippets of daily life here in Rinku. My normal routines such as weapons practice, observing through the lookouts, working in the kitchen, that sort of thing."

Her face fills with disappointment. "I was hoping you would remember why you went into Lymont. You know the rules about leaving the compound unauthorized."

"Yes, I remember the rules," I respond with a slight tone.

She frowns before taking another sip of her water.

"Why was I removed from Wavern's squad?" I ask.

She sets her glass down, crosses her legs, and leans forward. "Wavern acted recklessly when he ordered the others to follow him outside to look for you. I feel his attachment to you has clouded his judgement, so to remedy that you were moved."

"But why to Squad Two? Especially if you knew it would cause issues with Keegan."

"I knew nothing of the kind," she says quickly with a hint of anger. "Grimm and Keegan have had troubles, but that was in the past. I assumed they'd been resolved, especially after you married Keegan. The two of them have been warned of what the punishment will be the next time they're caught fighting."

"I thought Keegan was confined to quarters for the next several days."

"He was, but I've since changed my mind."

That would explain why Wavern is in a mood this morning and why Keegan wasn't in our quarters when I woke up.

"Wavern has requested that you return to Squad Eight after today. The request has been denied, so I would say the subject about your transfer among the squads is now closed," she says as her eyes narrow almost to the point of daggers. "Now, let me set a few new boundaries for you." She clears her throat, picks up her glass, and finishes her water before continuing. "You'll be placed into normal rotation, but under Squad Two, which means you'll be helping with the memorial and celebration in the city the rest of the day and tonight. You'll only be permitted to handle your weapons at the target range until you've recalled enough of your memories for me to know you aren't a threat to anyone, including yourself."

"You think I'm a threat to myself?" I blurt out, heat rising in my chest.

"Well, you did try to kill yourself, Sara. Why else would you have gone running like a lunatic from the compound into a toxic environment? You know full well someone or something launches nuclear bombs whenever they detect us outside. Our satellites aren't able to pick them up until a few seconds before impact. You've known this your whole life, which is why all our passageways are underground."

"Then why wasn't a bomb launched when everyone came looking for me? Or when we left that neighborhood?" I ask.

"I wish I could answer that. Wavern asked me the exact same question when you all returned, but I have no explanation."

I'm not buying any of it. "You seriously believe I was trying to kill myself?" I ask.

She's right, I was, but I'll never openly admit it.

"Yes, Sara, that's the only explanation for you leaving." She stands and settles back down next to me, patting my knee. "The minute you remember why you ran, I need to know immediately. It's essential to the safety of everyone, including yourself. I don't want anyone repeating your mistake."

She's failing at trying to sound sincere, so I fake a smile to show I understand.

Andra quickly stands and goes over to a receiver on the wall, where she calls Wavern to come and collect me.

"If I'm assigned to Grimm's squad, why isn't he being summoned?" I ask a little too harshly.

"He's already in Demos, my dear. Wavern will take you to him since he needs to meet Squad Eight at one of the launch sites anyway."

Wavern arrives a few minutes later with the same stern look on his face as when he left. He doesn't say anything to me as we exit the barracks and make our way to the garage, and remains silent until we're fastened into one of the four-seater ATVs and have maneuvered out of the garage, heading down the road towards Demos.

"Sometimes I don't understand that woman," he grumbles. "What did she want with you?"

"She was probing to see how much of my memory has come back."

"And what did you tell her?"

"The truth. Not much of it has, but she wants to know the minute I remember why I went into Lymont. She's convinced I tried to kill myself."

My body jerks violently forward when he slams on the brakes. "What?"

"She says that, because we've always been told and have always seen a bomb go off whenever someone is out on the surface, I must've known it would happen to me when I ran from Rinku."

"So her conclusion is that you wanted to get blown up?"

I nod.

His face contorts and I can't tell if he's about to burst out laughing or start yelling. "That's the stupidest thing I've ever heard," he finally says after composing himself. "There's no way in hell you would've done something so ridiculous. You're the toughest person I know, besides me of course. Andra must be losing her mind in her old age."

Wavern steps on the gas and we shoot forward. He doesn't stop again until we're halfway into the parking pad at Demos. Grimm is standing by the entrance to the city, with his arms folded across his chest and the hint of a smile on his face. He approaches us and goes over to Wavern's side.

"That didn't take as long as I thought," Grimm says, leaning against the doorframe.

"I don't think Andra got the answers she was looking for," Wavern replies with a glance towards me. "Has Jules come through yet?"

"Yes. He and Keegan took half the squad to the second launch site," Grimm says, but then his face darkens a little. "Cody isn't with your squad."

Wavern's eyes narrow and it looks like he's about to go off, but he manages to keep his composure. "Damn that kid. He told me this morning that he was going to be able to handle working in the launch site today. What excuse is he giving this time?"

"He claims the bombing at Lymont brought back too many memories from when the abandonment home was destroyed," Grimm replies as he hands Wavern two guns still in their holsters. "He's afraid to get anywhere near anything similar, such as fireworks. I thought it best if I took his weapons away."

Wavern rubs his face, obviously trying to determine what to do. "Well, he can't go back to the compound until this is over. Andra will have him demoted if he does," he says as he takes the holsters. "Does your squad need any help?"

"I can take him for today but he'll need to be watched, and I don't know how I'll manage to do that since everyone is already busy."

"I can watch him," I blurt out, as I feel they've forgotten I was there.

They stare at me for a few seconds, probably thinking it's not wise to have a flight risk watching over a basket case.

"Are you sure?" Grimm asks, sounding skeptical. "He's not acting right today."

"I'll keep him distracted, so it shouldn't be a problem."

"All right then," Wavern says with a small sigh. "He's your problem for the rest of today. Tomorrow I'll have Nex run some tests on his mental fitness." He hands me the guns, which I strap around each thigh.

I climb out of the ATV just before Wavern turns around and heads back down the tunnel. I follow Grimm into Demos, where the noise of celebration can be heard before the doors even open. Black and dark blue streamers hang from the balconies and terraces in Zones A and E. Small children run up and down the road, playing tag or blowing bubbles. Lively music wafts over our heads as we make our way to the center of the city. A casual observer would think this was a celebration, not a memorial.

Cody is leaning against one of the trees in Zone D, his eyes narrowed as he watches the citizens of Demos celebrate on the soft grass. He looks lost and almost infantile in his posturing. Grimm steps close, but doesn't touch him.

"Sara is going to keep you company," Grimm tells Cody quietly. "Why don't you two work on setting up the podium for Myr to give her speech from?"

Cody reluctantly pushes himself off the tree and meanders over to the large pool in the center. I follow at a slight distance while Grimm goes off into the parks. The two of us begin to assemble a platform where the governing body will sit as Myr, the leader of Demos, gives her speech.

We're halfway done when Cody starts to look anxious and uncomfortable before bolting towards the Factory. I have to race to catch up to him.

"Where are you going?" I ask, grabbing his arm and pulling him to a stop.

"Did you see him?" Cody asks, his voice high-pitched and shaky.

"Who?"

"Tennison."

"Cody, he died months ago in Virtus; you know that."

"He's not dead. I just saw him going towards the Factory."

I stare in the direction Cody is now pointing, but the road is empty. Whatever he saw seems to have moved on. That's if he actually saw anything at all. The stress of the day must be making him delusional.

"Let's get back to work," I say.

He's hesitant, but comes with me after a few more tugs. Because he's so distracted, it takes us a good part of the day to get the platform and podium ready. Grimm stops by to check on our progress, and isn't thrilled with Cody's lack of effort. He's in the process of reprimanding him when I pull Grimm off to the side.

"I think Cody needs to go back to the compound now," I say to him when we're out of earshot of Cody. "He's losing his mind. He thinks he saw Tennison."

I thought I saw him, too, yesterday, but I'm not about to admit it.

"Fuck, I knew the kid was unstable," Grimm grumbles. "The governing body just doesn't understand what kind of torment this so-called memorial causes people. If I take Cody back now, Andra will have him arrested for dereliction of duty, which would be worse than him staying here."

"Well, he *can't* stay here," I say. "He'll just get worse as the day progresses."

"There isn't anywhere else he can go," Grimm says, becoming hostile. "Look, just keep him calm and away from the crowds as best you can. The sun will be setting in a couple of hours, and the fireworks will launch a few minutes after that. He can return to the compound during that time."

"Fine," I say.

Grimm heads down the road between Zones A and E while I pull Cody over to a bench by an ice cream parlor that sits at the entrance to Zone C. I hold his hand and squeeze it, which seems to calm him down a little. I wish I knew why he's so shaken. Cody has always been a little unstable, but never outright deranged like he's acting now. He has me gravely concerned.

As the crowds starts to congregate around the plaza, Cody becomes more agitated, so I have him take a walk with me around Zone B, where there aren't any crowds. We wander up and down the paths that wind around the various buildings, then take a break in front of the library as a thought crosses my mind.

"Do you mind if we step inside for a little bit?" I ask.

"No, that's fine."

As we step through the rotating doors, I think about how I'm going to look up the history on the Arliss. Hopefully it's in the databases housed on the second floor. If not, I might have to get creative.

Eight

The library is practically deserted, with only a handful of people milling about the racks of books that cover the first floor. We head up a staircase in the center of the building to the second floor, which is filled with interactive workstations. I select one in the far corner. Cody has to pull a chair over so he can sit by me, since there's only one seat per station. I tap on the monitor and begin running through the various files, hoping I can easily find one on the Arliss. After ten minutes when I don't locate anything, I do a search on his name but again nothing.

"Try the word 'war'," Cody suggests.

I enter that as my search word, but what appears isn't exactly what I'm looking for. It's an editorial on the war between the Comhar of the Ulun Territory and the Levo of the Aslu Territory. I decide to give it a read anyway. What could it hurt?

The Rodinea Expanse, the last freshwater lake known to exist, has been a battleground between the Ulun and Aslu Territories for years. The border for these two powerful factions lies in the center of the expanse, so both sides technically have equal claim. However, with the world around us dying, life becoming almost impossible to sustain, and our resources running out, the Rodinea Expanse is the last hope for both the Comhar and Levo. Tensions between the two factions has risen to the point that each group has started construction of their own bunkers, and a city inside the Kai and Nove Mountain ranges protected by force fields to house their citizens if war does break out—which, at this point, is inevitable and could lead to further disintegration of our already fragile planet.

A map is provided in the upper right-hand corner of the editorial, so I select it to have a better look. The Rodinea Expanse is a massive lake that lies in a valley between both mountain ranges. I didn't even know this body of water existed since I've never seen it from the lookouts or Demos, so it probably didn't survive the war. The map goes on to mark the future sites for the three compounds, the city of Demos, and the abandonment home. I'm kind of surprised that the Levo in the Aslu Territory have only one compound marked, while the Comhar in Ulun have two strategically placed at either end of the Nove Mountains but on the other side, away from the lake and Demos.

Maybe they felt if the compounds were constructed on the same side as the expanse, then war would definitely break out. So, then, why not build them in the mountains like the Levo did? Perhaps it would've been too much of an undertaking since Demos was going there. The abandonment home rests in the mountains, but if my memory is correct it's cut into the edge of the mountainside, so there would've been more blasting than actual construction like there was for Demos.

"What's that?" Cody asks, pointing to a linked word at the bottom of the article.

"Let's see," I say, tapping on the word *Nathair*, which brings me to an article written by Myr for the fiftieth anniversary of the memorial.

Many have held the belief that our ancestors knew the key to protecting our world, ensuring our everlasting survival. However, that idea fell out of favor as society evolved and separated, isolating the two territories from each other for centuries. It wasn't until the impending war between the Levo and Comhar that this belief was resurrected. Hidden deep within the Nove Mountains, a worker who was clearing away a section of stone for the Occlyn Ring to be constructed came across a small, shallow cavity containing several stone texts, which were covered in an antiquated language of symbols. Intrigued by the find, the texts were brought to a historian in the Ulun Territory. She spent months studying the symbols and trying to locate as much information on our ancestors and their wild beliefs as possible. When she felt she had translated the symbols properly, she published a finding that our ancestors' idea about a being called the Arliss was the only creature capable of undoing the damage that had been done to our world, thereby saving it from extinction.

Few believed the misguided woman, while others called for her banishment to the Aslu Territory to live out her days with the Levo as a prisoner of war. Because she was a well-regarded young woman the leader of the Comhar permitted her to stay, but restricted her activities. She refused to be belittled or demeaned, and one night she managed to slip across the barrier that divides the territories. Little is known as to what occurred when she entered the depraved territory of Aslu, only that she was located two days later with a young man in the southern section of the Aslu Territory, several hundred miles east of the Kai Mountains.

Many Levo began to fall under the spell of this wicked man, the Arliss as he was determined to be called. They began turning on their own neighbors and murdering them as they slept if they refused to join him. The Comhar were no less susceptible to the lies and promises the Arliss made to gain followers. It became apparent to the leaders of both territories that the young man was quickly taking control of the weak-minded and making them into his disciples. These followers who called themselves the Nathair kept their existence hidden for several months, disguising themselves from the rest of society. The only way to determine who was a Nathair was by the small black spider tattoo on the inner part of their left wrist.

A new strategy had to be implemented before the Arliss overpowered both communities. The leaders for the Levo and Comhar put aside their differences, focused on completing their respective safe havens and compounds, and then declared war on the Arliss together. Many lives were lost during the conflict, but the greatest number was when the Arliss forced the leaders to launch a nuclear attack against those they had once sheltered, leaving the world blistered and the expanse dead. Those who survived annihilation and were free of the Nathair's mark were ushered to the abandonment home, as a way to contain the radiation that pulsed through their bodies from seeping into a healthy population that currently called Demos home. The Arliss and the Nathair were destroyed, but in their wake our world was left in worse condition than when the conflict between the two territories began.

All historical records or artifacts that had once been preserved were immediately destroyed as a way to cleanse the new society from the curse of the old. The Levo and Comhar no longer exist because they joined together for a common purpose, thus ending all clashes between the two groups. A new world has been created, but one that needs tender loving care. If we endure another attempted eradication, our world and its people will be lost forever.

The Arliss is trying to return, but if he's successful, life as we know it will end as that was almost the outcome during his last visit. The woman was wrong in believing the Arliss would save us… he's meant to destroy us, but how do you stop a creature that's immortal? There has to be a way. He didn't just come out of nowhere; he has to have an origin. But how do I figure it out without asking him?

"I need some air," Cody says, then stumbles away.

I leave the workstation and follow him outside the library. He looks pale and is having a hard time catching his breath. He has to sit on the curb and put his head between his knees to calm himself down.

"What's wrong?" I ask, rubbing his back.

"Didn't you just read the same shit I did?" he practically shouts. "Our own government dropped those bombs… it wasn't the Arliss like they've always forced into our heads."

"They didn't have a choice, Cody. The Arliss was destroying the world and they had to stop him, so, technically, the world was destroyed by the Arliss."

Who hasn't said a word to me in a while, which should cause me some concern, but I'm grateful for the peace and quiet at the moment.

"But that's exactly what they did… made this world unlivable. Myr claims that the two factions came together but my family originated in Aslu, making me a Levo; and we were treated like shit, even when I was a kid. The majority of those who live in Demos are Comhar descendants. The Levo were led to the abandonment home to die out, not to be protected."

"If that were true, the governing body would've just let the Levo stay in the toxic environment instead of placing them in the abandonment home. Neither of us would be here if they hadn't."

He glares at me. "I guess that part of your memory hasn't returned," he grumbles.

"What?"

"You're a fucking Comhar, Sara, just like Keegan and Wavern."

"How the hell do you know that?"

"Because even though we all grew up in the same place, we were treated differently because of who our families were. Grimm knows all too well what they'll let a Comhar get away with."

"Grimm's family was Levo?"

"Yes, which is why Keegan wasn't punished for what he did to him, or any child of a Levo descendant for that matter."

Maybe that's another reason Keegan got so upset with Grimm yesterday. He sees Grimm as beneath him because of who his ancestors were and since I have the same heritage he doesn't approve of me being friends with Grimm. Keegan needs to get a fucking grip and move on.

Why did I marry that asshole? I could've found a less degrading way to get back at Grimm for a wrong he really never committed.

And why did Keegan's eyes turn red? I know I didn't imagine that, no matter how much he tried to convince me. I wonder if Nex would know if it's a medical condition.

Oh, the lies I tell myself.

Cody is finally settling down when trumpets blast over speakers that hang from the streetlights which are slowly turning on as the sun sets. We head back to the plaza, but remain by the outskirts of Zone B as the crowds are much smaller there. Myr, a small woman with horn-rimmed glasses, a severely curved spine, and choppy silver hair stands up to the podium and adjusts the microphone.

"Good evening, citizens of Demos and soldiers of Rinku and Quarn," she begins, her voice steady. "Tonight marks the passing of another year of mourning after the war that destroyed our world and our lives. As we gather here to commemorate the millions who suffered at the hands of the Arliss, be mindful of the need we have for each other in order to heal the blistered soil and dried lakes. Only together, as one community, can we accomplish this feat. As of yesterday, a new beginning has begun. The Rodinea Expanse, once barren, is now filled with clean water, made safe by an Occlyn Ring of its own."

"How is that possible?" I ask no one in particular. "They would've had to go outside to accomplish that, which means bombs would've dropped. How'd they avoid them?"

"That's a good question," Cody says.

"This couldn't have been done without the efforts of everyone here, and in the compounds today," Myr continues. "And this is only the start for us reclaiming our world. Without an incident in eight years, our people are finally able to traverse the surface without fear."

My mouth falls open at that remark. I wait for someone from Rinku to correct her, especially Andra, who is sitting in the row of chairs behind Myr, but no one says a word.

"I told you that your leaders lie," the Arliss laughs. *"Look closer, Sara, and you'll see the truth, as did all those who died before you."*

"After years of scouting, tracking, and countless numbers of radar images from our satellites, I can say with confidence that there are no more bombs anywhere on our world. We have finally freed ourselves from the fear of annihilation. The question remains as to who was responsible for the bombings after the Arliss was defeated, but it's time now for us to put that all behind us and look to our future. With the assistance of our compound leaders, the former Ulun Territory will be the first to build a hydroponics bay above ground, which will be constructed one mile west of the Nove Mountains," Myr says with enthusiasm. "This great undertaking is years in the making, and construction will begin tomorrow. I'm looking forward to one day leaving the city of Demos behind and inhabiting the plains as our ancestors did." Applause erupts from every inch of the plaza and she has to wait for it to die down before completing her speech. "As we gather here tonight, let's not forget those we've lost this past year. When you look up at the fireworks, always remember that those who've died are being sent up to the heavens to look down upon us and smile."

"What's she talking about?" I ask as I lean over to Cody, so he can hear me through the thunderous claps and cheers.

"The ashes of those who've died since the last memorial are mixed in with the gun powder for the fireworks. It's a way of ridding the surface of corpses," he says grimly.

The lights lining the roads dim as rockets shoot into the sky outside the city, exploding into dazzling colors. I've never been a fan of how the citizens of Demos celebrate their survival when millions perished in the war and its aftermath. I'm not even sure why the compounds are involved in the event, since those killed were our ancestors. I'm sure the people here are more than capable of handling this day without any assistance from us, but I doubt that'll ever change… even when they do escape this electrified prison.

I look over the crowd as they gasp with delight from the spectacle, each person's eyes glued to the fireworks as they explode just beyond the dome. I glance over at Cody to see how he's fairing, but he's gone. I scan the crowds for him, finally spotting him making his way down a path between two residential buildings in Zone A. I call after him, but he ignores me and rushes towards a group of onlookers, nearly knocking a few of them over as he passes.

"Cody, wait!" I holler as I try to catch up.

He darts around the various groups, making his way to the road between Zones A and E. I finally reach him when we hit the outer edge of the festivities.

"Let me go!" he yells as I grab onto him.

"Where are you going?"

"It's him."

"Who Cody?"

"Tennison… I have to see what he's up to."

"Why?"

He turns to me with such terror in his eyes it chills me to the bone. "He murdered my friends and I need to know why."

Cody rips his arm out of my hand and bolts towards the parking pad. Once he's through the doors, he heads down the tunnel. I continue to follow him even when he veers left into the tunnel leading to what remains of Virtus. We run nonstop, but I don't see anything in front of him. The tunnel is empty.

"Cody, stop!" I shout as he picks up speed.

The collapsed entrance into the Virtus garage comes into view and he disappears through the damaged beams and cracked floor. I slow my approach and gingerly pick my way through the rubble until I'm in the garage itself. Transports and four-seater ATVs lie on their sides, surrounded by singed concrete and warped metal that make up what remains of the walls. Unlike the garage in Rinku this one only has a single access point for vehicles, so I assume the opening I find across the way must lead into the actual compound. I stand in the doorway and listen as Cody's footsteps echo into silence. I chase after him, but at a much slower rate since the tunnel isn't level or complete. I'm forced to crawl over chunks of concrete and metal rods as I venture further in.

I eventually come to a fork in the tunnel, and without any sounds or movement, I have no idea which direction he could've gone. If I keep going straight I should hit the control center, so I decide to continue following that tunnel. When I reach the location where the control center should be, all I find is a crater descending into darkness. My foot kicks a small piece of debris, sending it down into the gloom before I hear it hit water—that must've flooded the lower levels after the explosion.

"Cody!" I call out, my voice reverberating eerily.

Footsteps rapidly approach, but from the entrance to the mess hall. I think I see a lone figure standing in the doorway, but in the darkness it might just be my imagination. A flashlight flickers on from the tunnel to my right and someone aims it at the figure. The light illuminates a tall dark-skinned man, breathing heavily, leaning against the wall as if it's holding him upright. One of his eyes is pure white where his iris has been obliterated, his right arm is missing below the elbow, and the cloak he has secured around his bulky frame is dripping wet.

"You shouldn't have come," he says, his voice deep and unfaltering.

"Tennison? You're alive?" I ask. "How?"

"Go back the way you came," he says. "You'll only find death here."

"Wait a minute," Cody says as he steps out from his tunnel, the flashlight tightly held in his hand. "Why did you do it? Why'd you blow up the compound?"

Tennison simply stares at the two of us.

"I kept trying to tell them it was your fault, but no one believed me," Cody says, his voice rising. "You'd been acting odd for days, but everyone pretended not to notice. They put me in isolation until I recanted my story. You destroyed everything!"

"Leave, Cody!" Tennison shouts, which causes the room to shake. "And take that thing with you," he says, pointing to me.

Cody looks at me, puzzled. "But that's Sara."

"No, it's not. Sara's dead. She was killed in the bomb blast in Lymont that everyone is covering up. Just like I was killed years ago and no one talked about it. They all called it a miracle that I survived, but then it was never spoken about again. They can't admit there's a force at work here they don't understand, and it terrifies them," Tennison says.

"You're not making any sense," Cody responds, sliding his foot along the side where the flooring still remains.

Tennison raises a gun, aiming it at Cody. "Don't think I don't see you trying to move closer. Stay where you are."

Cody stops, a look of shock on his face as he's now close enough to see Tennison's wreck of a face and body. "What happened to you?" he asks, his body trembling.

Tennison remains silent.

"Tell me!" Cody shouts.

"Go back to Rinku and never mention me again," Tennison responds.

Cody lunges for him. The gun goes off. The bullet hits Cody in the torso and sends him into the crater.

"He should've left well enough alone," Tennison says, pointing the gun at me. "They all should have."

"What's the matter with you? Cody just wants answers, as we all do," I say heatedly.

"Then ask the Arliss," Tennison says, seething as he pulls the trigger.

I jump in after Cody and the bullet flies past my head. I dive below the water and search for his body with my hands, since I can't see anything even with the little illumination from the flashlight as it spins towards the bottom of the crater. I find his shirt, grab it, and pull him to the surface. He moans as I try to find someplace to move him to when another bullet rips past my ear. I grapple with Cody's weight while I get a hold of one of the holsters, then I remove the gun and fire it blindly in Tennison's direction. A large splash hits me, pulling me away from Cody and causing me to drop the gun. I force myself to the surface just as Tennison wraps his arm around my throat.

"You're not taking me back there," he pants in my ear.

"Let me go," I growl as I try to remove the other gun.

"Only when you're truly dead."

I reach for a steel rod I see protruding from the cement, grab it and swing it around, nailing Tennison in the temple, causing him to loosen his grip. He brings his left arm up, his gun still held in his hand, though he's a bit wobbly from the blow to his head. I'm able to push the weapon to the side as it discharges, but the bullet ricochets and pierces my right arm, and I drop the rod. I holler from the impact, but keep my focus on Tennison. As I reach for the grip of his gun my hand slides down his cloak, pulling it away from his wrist, and in the dull light I see it… the spider tattoo.

"It's you," I gasp. "You're the one the Arliss wants to replace."

"Which is why you have to die," he says, shooting me in my shoulder.

I cry out, but don't let go. I finally manage to free the other gun strapped to my leg, then place the barrel against Tennison's forehead and pull the trigger. The recoil sends me backwards, causing me to hit my head on a shelf of concrete, dazing me enough that I begin to sink, and the water envelops me.

Nine

I see it now… the fragment of memory restoring itself to a complete picture, only it's not my memory—I'm seeing it all through Tennison's mind. He's tired of being forced to murder those he calls his friends just so the Arliss can find the perfect host. How many has it been over the last several years? Two? Four? Just enough not to cause anyone to become suspicious. He made sure their deaths looked like accidents, but none of them came back. They all refused the Arliss' offer, putting Tennison into a corner he could no longer tolerate. He's hoping the explosion will kill him, send him back to the Arliss so he can finally die, as that's the only way he can now. He knows his actions will lead to countless deaths, but then maybe the Arliss will finally get what he wants and leave him alone if he manages to survive.

He sabotaged the pipes for the oxygen tanks in the life support systems two levels below the control center. Cracks formed in the metal, causing the gas to leak. When it reached an ignition source, in this case the stoves in the kitchen one level up and over, the compound exploded and fire ate everything and almost everyone. He should've been incinerated, but he wound up only maimed.

Now, the Arliss wants Tennison replaced, so the bullet I just sent into the man's head will remain, therefore ending his life for good. But, how did Tennison come across the Arliss? He mentioned that he had died years ago, which would've been well before the compound was destroyed. How and where did that happen?

And why does my chest burn and my head hurt?

The weight crushing my body is immense, but when I open my eyes I see sunlight dancing above water covering my body. I break the surface and draw in a deep breath so I can cough and get air back into my lungs. I stand in what looks to be a lake, but I only see the near shore directly in front of me. A lone individual occupies it—a dark-skinned woman with long, braided red hair, and wearing a flowing dress with cutouts in the shoulders. She's leaning forward, her hand extended to assist me out of the water.

"Welcome home, Sara," she says with a genuine smile.

"Where am I?"

"The Fomorian Plateau," she says. "The space between life and death, and the home of the Arliss."

"I'm dead? I can't be!"

"No, you're quite alive, I assure you. You're just unconscious, but since you've been to the plateau before you can easily pass between the two worlds. You don't have to be dead to come here… not anymore, anyway."

"You're Haron," I say. "The headmistress for the abandonment home."

She nods.

"How did you wind up here?"

"The Arliss saved me from extinction, just as he saved you. I greet those who are new to his realm, especially because I know most of them already."

"How many have traveled here since the bombing of the home?"

She lowers her head. "Too many, I'm afraid. The Arliss is very particular as to who he sends back. Many don't last through the day in the conversion room," she says, gesturing to a mound of boulders to her right.

"Where's Cody?" I ask, panicking.

"He's settling down in his room, but he's quite all right," she says calmly.

"I need to see him."

"Of course, but let's get you into some dry clothes first," she says, gesturing to two cylindrical towers in the distance. "Your room is all prepared for you."

Before following her, I glance back at the lake, its dark waters obscuring everything underneath, which gives me chills. How do I get back to my world from here? I don't remember how I did it the last time, but I'm sure I'll find out.

The landscape for the plateau consists of compacted sand covered in pebbles and small cacti. I spot a rock wall behind the towers and am shocked to see how dark it is behind the wall. The sun is high above our heads, but no amount of light seems to be able to touch whatever lies beyond it. Haron directs me to the tower on the left, which is constructed out of adobe. We climb the stairs just on the other side of the entrance until we reach the fourth floor, which is the top level. There's only one door on the entire floor, and when she opens it I freeze in my spot. The Arliss is sitting casually on a large bed that rests in the center of the room. Heavy curtains cover the windows, blocking all sunlight, so the only illumination is from a couple of floor lamps. The Arliss is no longer wearing his cloak, his skin has darkened, and his frame is bulkier.

"Thank you, Haron, I'll take it from here," he says.

She bows and heads down the stairs.

"Don't hover, Sara, it's rude," he says.

A force pulls me into the room and slams the door closed behind me, locking me in.

"I want out of here!" I shout.

"In time," he says, licking his lips.

"Why aren't you in a cloak, and why does your body look different?" I ask hurriedly due to unease.

"I only use the cloak for those who are new to the fold… at least until they accept me into their lives. As for my body, well, let's just say it's preparing for a much-needed change," he says, smiling as he stands and saunters over to me. "I want to thank you for following orders. I would've preferred Grimm, but Cody will make an excellent host."

"You leave him alone!"

"Ah, but it's too late. He's already accepted me," the Arliss says, leaning close. "He allowed me in rather quickly, too, I might add… almost like he's been waiting for me to collect him."

"How's that possible? He just got here."

"Once again, you forget time doesn't really exist in the plateau. Cody has been here for over a day, but I'll be returning him to your world along with you in a little while. He needs more time to adjust to the idea of becoming… a new person," the Arliss says with a sly smile.

"What do you want with us?"

The Arliss places a hand on my shoulder, causing me to wince. I'd forgotten about being shot, but with his touch the pain from my wound radiates down my arm. He lifts up my sleeve revealing the bullet hole, which surprisingly isn't bleeding, though it isn't healed either. He examines my other arm to discover a second bullet wound; this one also is neither bleeding nor healed.

"Lover, you're hurt," he says as he caresses the wound.

"Why aren't I bleeding?" I ask, unnerved. "I bled when you tortured me the last time I was here."

"Wounds sustained in the natural world will never bleed here because of the alteration in time. Your injury is technically frozen in place, but when you do go back it will start to bleed again like all wounds. Now, if you're hurt here then, yes, you will bleed, but your wounds won't travel back with you when you return home," he says.

"Then, how was I brought back if there wasn't anything left of me after the blast in Lymont?"

"You'd already been marked for me, so it was easy to guide your soul from the ether. I simply reconstructed your form," he replies. "Once the mark has been placed, it's only a matter of time before you find yourself in the Fomorian Plateau."

"Marked? How and by whom?"

"I'm entitled to keep some secrets, Sara," he says, reaching out with his other hand to brush my cheek.

"Don't touch me," I utter.

"I can do whatever I want to you. You gave yourself to me, remember? I own you."

"You tricked me," I say angrily.

"I would never do such a thing," he says, pretending to be offended. "Besides, I'm not the one you should be upset with. It wasn't my idea to bring you here in the first place, but I'm ever so grateful to the person who chose you." He wraps his hands around my neck and tilts my head. "And now for the final act of making you mine," he says before biting me.

I should feel pain, but all I feel is lust and desire. He practically shoves his tongue down my throat as I try to fight him off while I work on regaining control over my senses, but it only causes him to squeeze my throat harder. I close my eyes as his hands begin to wander over my body before finally removing my clothes. He tosses me onto the bed, strips, and penetrates me with such force I feel like I'll split in two. I finally give in and howl with pleasure as he caresses every inch of my body. My mind fills with thoughts of death and destruction, which urges me to beg for more. I can't stop myself from succumbing to the Arliss over and over again. He fills me up, making whole what was once empty… a desolation I didn't know existed. My fingernails sink into his back, drawing blood, which causes him to scream in delight. I finally hit a peak so mind-blowing I shriek before collapsing into exhaustion.

"There, now, that's better," the Arliss says.

I sense my personality changing, becoming warped, destructive, and lustful. I try to push those feelings aside, but it only makes them surge. I'm no longer Sara but an Arliss slave, programmed to be whatever he asks me to be.

"What do you want with us?" I ask again as I try to catch my breath.

"You'll know when the time is right," he replies. "But for now, relax; just don't go past the wall. That's beyond my boundaries." He kisses me, puts his clothes back on, and heads towards the door.

"I want to see Cody," I say before he leaves.

"He'll be up in a little while, but you need some rest. You have a big day ahead of you."

I want to protest, but my eyelids are too heavy to keep open.

The screaming is what wakes me, and thankfully it's not mine. I wrap the sheet around my body as I get out of bed and go to the open window, pushing the curtains aside in order to see out. Night has set in; thousands of stars sparkle overhead. The water in the lake laps gently against the quiet shore as another scream rises from a group of boulders on the right, a pale light shining from a vast opening between the boulders. I slip away from the window, dress, and head down the stairs. No one else is around as I exit the building and head towards the boulders. Cries of pain float along the cool air as I slowly climb up the rocks. When I reach the top, I have to quickly drop my head so the Arliss doesn't see me through the opening. The light below is being generated by hundreds of candles. I glimpse Tennison strapped to a metal table in the conversion room as the Arliss paces around him, slashing his body with a sharp blade every few moments.

"You disappoint me," the Arliss says as he continues his trek around the room. "I had such hopes for you, but now I've had to resort to other means."

"Leave the kid alone," Tennison moans as blood trickles down his arms, legs, and torso.

"Why? He obviously wants to be here and, besides, you shouldn't have lured him away from Demos. He'd still be alive if you'd stayed in Virtus like you were supposed to," the Arliss hisses.

"I didn't know Cody was following me."

"It's a good thing he did, otherwise Sara would've wound up back here empty-handed, and I wouldn't have liked that."

"Why did you turn her?" Tennison asks as his muscles spasm.

"I was asked to," the Arliss responds with a slight laugh.

"By whom?"

"You don't need to know that," the Arliss says. "But I will tell you this: without this particular person, I wouldn't have gotten as far as I did. They've been masterful at bringing me my subjects. There's only been a handful who have refused me, but no one will miss them."

"What did you do to those who refused your horrendous proposition?"

"The same thing I'm going to do to you shortly… that is, if you live." The Arliss leans over Tennison, blocking his face from my view. "Feed you to the wolves."

"Go ahead; at least I'll finally be free from you," Tennison says sternly, a blood-curdling scream following.

As the Arliss moves out of the way I notice that Tennison's left wrist has a deep gash across it, and blood is pouring from the wound.

"Now if you'll excuse me, I have some planning to do," the Arliss says before exiting through a doorway.

I wait until he's out of sight before climbing down and entering the conversion room. Tennison's whimpers fill the air, but as soon as he notices me he becomes quiet.

"What do you want?" he asks as his body shakes and beads of sweat dot his face.

"Was Cody right? Did you blow up Virtus?"

"What does it matter if I did?"

"It matters to Cody."

"Yes, all right? I did it," Tennison says through gritted teeth. "Satisfied?"

"Why'd you do it?"

"To stop him."

"The Arliss?"

"No, Keegan."

My voice catches in my throat and it takes me a few moments before I can squeak it out. "As in my husband Keegan?"

"The very same," Tennison says weakly as he struggles to stay conscious. The wound is so deep and he's lost so much blood there's nothing I can do for him now.

"Why? What was he going to do?"

"He already did it."

"Did what?" I ask, my voice rising with irritation.

Tennison rolls his head to the side as his eyes fill with tears. "Turn you."

"Keegan didn't turn me—the Arliss did," I say angrily.

"I know you were listening… when the Arliss said… your change was requested. Who… do you think… requested it?" Tennison asks, his voice starting to fail. "It was supposed to be Keegan… who came to the compound that day… not Wavern. I thought… that if I destroyed… everything, Keegan… would be lost among the rubble… buried forever. No one was… supposed to… survive."

"But that means he knows the Arliss and that's not possible. He'd have to have died at some point in his life for that to happen, and as far as I know he never has."

"Look closer, Sara. Keegan isn't who you think he is."

"His red eyes," I mutter.

"What?" Tennison asks, fighting to stay alive.

"Keegan's eyes turned red the other night. He tried to convince me I was imagining it, but I know what I saw."

"Are you sure… they were red?"

I nod.

"The followers of the Arliss… don't have red eyes," Tennison says, panicking. "Nothing about their physical features changes… only their senses." Tennison's breathing becomes labored. "Get out of there, Sara," Tennison says as his eyes widen. "Don't trust anyone. Get as far away from Demos and the compounds… as you can." His lungs rattle as he takes his last breath.

"It's a shame Tennison had to die," Haron says behind me. I hadn't even heard her enter.

"Which time?" I ask sarcastically.

"Both," she answers softly.

"How'd he die the first time?"

Haron approaches the table and places a hand on Tennison's arm. "The same way you did, only in the Ulun Territory. He slipped out of the compound undetected during a rotation change. No one knew he was gone until he entered the hatch into the decon chamber the following morning."

"And someone dropped a nuke on him?" I ask.

She nods.

"Didn't they see the bomb fall like they did when I died? Didn't anyone question his miraculous return?"

"Yes and, from my understanding, when those who died in the Virtus explosion arrived on the plateau they explained that Demmer and Andra had the entire compound cover up the incident. Tennison was thoroughly examined when he returned and nothing inconsistent was found, so the matter was dropped."

"Did he ever say why he left?"

"He told me upon his arrival that he'd been forced to leave… to flee the compound for his own safety. But it was utter nonsense. Tennison was the compound leader, so he was in charge of everyone in Virtus. There couldn't have been a single person dumb enough to make that man leave the safety of that compound. It had to be another reason."

"If he hated the Arliss so much, why'd he agree to help him?" I ask.

"I don't know. I guess that piece of information died with him."

"The Arliss said I was marked before I died. Was Tennison?"

"Yes, but I don't know by whom or how, so don't ask me."

"Tennison believes it was Keegan. Do you think that's possible?"

"Anything is possible if Keegan is involved. I've never cared for that man, even when he was a child. I don't care who his grandfather was, they should've allowed me to punish him for the hell he imposed on the other children."

"Who was his grandfather?"

"Some big war hero. He got trapped in the Aslu Territory when the bombs fell, but managed to save hundreds of lives by forcing them to climb the Kai Mountains to safety on the other side. He wound up dying of radiation poisoning like all the others, but this was well after his daughter was born—Keegan's mother."

"I thought the bombs were dropped in both territories and the valley between the mountains. How could anything have been safer on the other side?"

"Bombs were dropped on both sides, but far fewer were launched into the Ulun Territory than into Aslu. Right after the war, there were a few rumors floating around that the Comhar used the Arliss as an excuse to eradicate the world of the Levo. That quickly died down when Myr took over the governing body, considering she's of Levo heritage."

"How'd you wind up here?" I ask, wanting to change the topic.

"I followed the stream from the ether. I didn't want to die… I wasn't ready for it, but who is? I'd seen others floating in that direction, so I followed, hoping it would lead to salvation. And it did," she says, pointing to the opening over our head. "Now, I'll need to take care of the body. This is something you won't want to see."

I leave the conversion room, horrified by the idea that Keegan could be involved with what happened to me. Is that why I ran into Lymont? Because I found out what, or who, he really is? If only I could remember. But that still doesn't explain who launched the nuke. It had to have been Andra, but again I have to wonder why and, more importantly, how. Myr said the satellites no longer detected the existence of bombs anywhere in the world, so how was one launched at me the other day? Or even Tennison several years ago, for that matter? I'm making myself sick the more I think about it, so when I'm back in the room I remove my clothes as they're still damp from the lake, get under the sheet, and try to put it all behind me.

Ear-splitting howls bring me around and I realize it's the same sound a Mulgrim makes. Could that be what lies on the other side of the wall? But they're originally from the Kai Mountains, so how are they moving between our world and the plateau? Is there another way in?

Another howl shatters the quiet, this one causing my eyes to fly open. When they focus I spot Cody sitting beside me on the edge of my bed looking distraught. The sheet I had wrapped myself in when I went to sleep has slipped off, exposing me. I should be embarrassed since Cody is sitting right there, but for some reason I'm not. Being in the Fomorian Plateau has made me bolder, as did the Arliss turning me into whatever I am now.

Fucking Keegan! I'll need to repay him for this when I get back.

"What's wrong?" I ask casually.

"Is this where you went after the bomb fell on Lymont? Were you actually killed in the blast? Were those your body parts we found?" Cody asks quickly, eyes averted.

I slide over to him, sit up, and lean against his back with one of my arms draped over his shoulder. "What makes you ask?"

He raises his left hand and shows me the spider tattoo that is now imprinted into his skin. "He gave this to you, didn't he?"

"Yes… to all your questions," I reply, pressing my face into his shoulder.

"Did you promise him anything to secure your return?"

"Yes. I gave him my devotion, loyalty, and apparently my body," I say seductively. Normally I wouldn't be acting like this, especially towards Cody. But in any case this is now who I am, so I'm going to have to figure out a way to control this new lusty nature of mine, especially when I get home. "What did you promise?"

"I'd rather not say."

"You can tell me, Cody. I won't tell anyone," I say, wrapping my legs tightly around his waist.

If I'm like this in the Fomorian Plateau, what will I be like when I return to my world? I have a hard time believing this is what Keegan wanted for me. He's jealous of Grimm, and I haven't even slept with the guy. How's Keegan going to react when he realizes this is what he asked the Arliss to do to me? I need to find a way to get my life back, and quickly before I make too many mistakes… especially if they're irreversible.

But how?

Cody grows increasingly uncomfortable with my forwardness, but I don't back down. He reluctantly places a hand on my thigh and begins to caress it almost absentmindedly.

"Tell me," I whisper in his ear, which causes him to shiver.

"I promised him my soul," Cody finally blurts out.

"Well, that's not so bad," I say, relaxing my hold around his waist. "At least you'll be alive."

"No, Sara, I won't be!" he shouts as tears fill his eyes. "The Arliss is going to take possession of my body, making it his. I'll cease to exist."

"And that scares you," I say rather coolly.

What the fuck is wrong with me? Why am I acting so heartless about his situation? Is that another trait of being an Arliss slave?

"Yes, of course," he says, jumping to his feet. "Sara, of all people I thought you would be just as upset about this as I am, but you're acting like it's no big deal. This is my life we're talking about. How can you be so cold?"

"If it's so terrible, why did you make such a promise?" I snap.

"So I could survive… for at least the time being."

"Then don't blame me for your mistake," I say angrily. "At least you had a choice in this. I didn't."

"Excuse me? How exactly is this a choice?"

"You didn't have to take the stream into the lake when you died. You could've continued on in the ether until your existence ended. No one dragged you here," I say as I wrap the sheet around myself as I'm now the one uncomfortable, wishing he would leave.

"But you came here of your own accord," Cody says, puzzled. "It was your decision to run out of the compound. You knew a bomb would fall… one always does."

"I wish everyone would stop reminding me about that," I grumble.

"Well, we wouldn't have to keep bringing it up if you'd admit the truth about it," he says heatedly.

"Fine!" I shout, jumping off the bed, still wrapped in the sheet. "I wanted to die… to get away from everything and everyone. Death was the only option for me. I couldn't continue living in a world like that anymore."

"Why?"

His question forces me to look inward once more. I try to pull the memory that's lurking in the back of my mind. When it finally hits, I sink to the floor. My mouth hangs open and tears stream down my face.

"Oh, my God," I mumble. "I remember now. Andra caught me in her office, the one she has in her apartment. Something had been bothering me about why she'd refused to take in survivors from Virtus. Her reasoning didn't make any sense, so I went digging around in her files while she was in the control center early that morning, just before I was supposed to go on duty."

"What did she say was the reason?" Cody asks, kneeling in front of me and placing his hands on my arms.

"She didn't want to deal with any more fallout victims, especially those who weren't from a pure bloodline."

"So, she didn't want to take in any more Levo refugees basically."

"I wasn't sure, so that's why I went through her files. I didn't find anything at first, but then I came across a roster of the residents still living in the abandonment home. It was logical for her to have it since that's how they recruit, but something was off about it. A line had been scratched through the names of those who'd already been moved into the compounds as well as the dates of their transfer. I had to read through the list twice just to make sure I was seeing it accurately," I say, my gaze wandering. "I'd been the last of the Comhar line to be removed from the home. Once I was gone, only Levo children were left, so I dug further into the file. Only, there wasn't anything left to find."

"It still doesn't explain why you left the compound," Cody says as he puts his hands down.

"I was about to leave when a beeping sound filled the room. I searched all over for it, only to find it was coming from behind a panel in the wall in front of her desk. When I opened it, I discovered monitors displaying areas in the Aslu Territory; some of the sections I'd never seen before, except one. The remnants of the abandonment home were clear as day on the display, but from the outside. I could see into the top level, or what's left of it, from what seemed like a mile or so away from the structure itself. As my eyes scanned the other screens I noticed one of them flashing red, with a message that said movement had been detected in Telus Mesa, but the only thing I saw was some strange animal scurrying across the cracked soil. I tapped the image to clear the alert like we do for the screens in the control center, but instead of disappearing it gave me an option."

I pause because my mind is starting to work faster than my mouth, and I'm afraid I'll stumble over the words as they come out.

"What was it asking?" Cody asks after too much silence has lapsed.

"It wanted to know if a bomb should be launched or not."

Cody leans back as if I've become too toxic to be near. "What are you saying, Sara?"

"Andra has been the one launching the bombs. She's the one who destroyed the abandonment home," I reply, choking on my sobs.

"Are you sure?"

"Yes."

"But where would she be housing the nukes? Myr said the surface is clear of them."

"It is clear of them because they're in the satellites," I reply. "Andra came in the moment that request began flashing. She was mad when she saw me, and seized my arm before I could touch anything else. She then flashed a wicked smile and asked if I wanted a demonstration. I shook my head, but she commanded the satellite to launch a bomb anyway. It hit just a half-mile away from the mesa, incinerating vegetation that was trying to grow. I knew right then that I couldn't be in a world with people like her. I needed out, so I left the compound—knowing full well she'd send a nuke after me. In fact, I was counting on it."

Ten

"Maybe that's why a bomb wasn't launched when we went looking for you," Cody says, his voice trembling. "It would be too suspicious for Andra to send another one, when almost the entire compound had been notified of our search. She couldn't risk the exposure."

"We need to get out of here," I say, reaching for my still-damp clothes.

"How? If you haven't noticed, we're kind of dead."

"There's a way out, I just need to remember where it is," I say, slipping into my shirt.

"Going somewhere?" the Arliss hisses, standing in the doorway with Haron behind him.

"Yeah, Cody and I are leaving," I reply heatedly as I finish dressing.

"Oh, I don't think so," the Arliss says before snapping his fingers, which causes Cody to collapse to the floor, unconscious. "Not without me, that is."

"You don't need him," I say, protesting. "I'll get you someone else, just leave Cody alone."

The Arliss ambles up to me while Haron remains in the hallway. "I wish I could, but he's already made his choice," the Arliss says, caressing my cheek. "Besides, I've just discovered that an old enemy of mine is up in your world, roaming around freely, trying to take control over your people for himself, and I can't allow that to happen, now, can I?"

"Old enemy? I thought we were your only adversaries."

"No, my dear. Once again, your leaders lied to you," he says, turning his back to me as he steps away. "My true foe is a demon known as the Pheles. He's cruel, possessive, manipulative, deceitful, and destructive. He's also the fucking bastard who sealed me down here centuries ago. But, oh, how I relished the moment when the Levo entombed him in the Kai Mountains."

"How do you know he's returned?"

"I've seen him… through you, actually," the Arliss says, spinning back around.

My head begins to pound, so I close my eyes and try to push away the truth of what I already know. "He has red eyes, doesn't he?" I finally ask when I reopen my eyes.

"Yes, Sara, he does."

"Does he need to take possession of a body like you do in order to traverse my world?"

"Yes."

"When was he imprisoned in the mountains?"

"A few years after he placed me here."

"Then how did he live this long? The body he had would've needed nourishment and then eventually die. There's no way it can be the same one."

"He's immortal like I am, and there's only one Pheles that I know of in existence. It's your husband," the Arliss says.

"But that's not possible!" I yell. "When could the Pheles have taken him over? There isn't any place in the compound that thing could've been hiding. Plus, Rinku was around long before Keegan was alive, so you have to be wrong. Something else has Keegan under a spell." I sit on the bed and try to think of other ways the Arliss could be mistaken or lying, but nothing comes to mind. "You said the Pheles is possessive. How?"

"He latches himself onto one person for eternity. He becomes jealous over the littlest things easily, to the point of almost being abusive. If that person is mortal, he'll make them immortal by any means necessary."

"Like mark them? So when they die they wind up down here?"

"Exactly," the Arliss responds with deep concern.

"From your tone of voice, I take it Keegan isn't the one who marked me to come to the plateau."

"Correct. He didn't send you to me, but someone else close to you did."

"Who?"

"Does it matter?"

"Hell yes, it matters!" I shout as I bolt up from the bed. "I want that fucker's name!"

"I'll give it to you once I'm in Cody's body," the Arliss says sternly. "And for that I'll need your assistance."

"You want me to help you kill Cody?"

"He's already dead, Sara. We're just moving him to the next world."

"If his body is too badly injured to keep him alive, how is it going to support you?"

"It will, trust me," he says, smiling wide. "Now, shall we get going?"

I don't respond or move, as I'm trying to determine which is more important to me: finding out who sent me here, freeing Keegan from the Pheles, or trying to save Cody's life. Guilt tears at my heart when I choose the first. Cody is a sweet kid, and he deserves better, but I have to know who wanted me reborn as an Arliss slave.

I need to know so I can kill them.

"Let's go," I mutter.

Haron finally steps into the room, picks up Cody, and cradles him in her arms as we head downstairs and out into the darkness. When we enter the conversion room, I notice the metal table is empty and clean. Haron did a thorough job of disposing of any sign that Tennison existed. She sets Cody down on the table and secures him to it, when a scream hangs in the air, radiating down through the skylight.

"I thought Cody and I were the only ones here," I say as I turn to look at Haron.

"You are," the Arliss responds, heading for the exit.

The three of us run towards the beach as the sun abruptly rises, signaling a new arrival. An older man in white is crawling out of the water with one arm held tightly to his stomach. He collapses into a heap, as his breathing becomes labored. Haron is the first to reach him and when she rolls him onto his back I immediately recognize him as the greeter from the Factory.

"Please help me," the man moans, reaching to touch Haron's face with a blood-soaked hand.

I glance at his wound and become immediately sick, seeing that his hand is the only thing holding his guts in. I step away and vomit while the Arliss begins bombarding the man with questions.

"You're one of Casey's, aren't you?" the Arliss asks heatedly.

"Yes," the man responds weakly.

"That would explain how he got here," Haron says.

"Who did this to you?" the Arliss asks a little more calmly.

"Wavern, the leader for Squad Eight in Rinku," the man moans.

I spin around and sprint back towards them. "That's a lie!" I shout. "Wavern would never do anything like that. Besides, he's at one of the launch sites tending to the fireworks display that should still be going on, since only a minute or so has passed in my world. It takes over an hour to get through them all."

"I'm telling you the truth," the man whimpers, and he puts his hand back over his wound. "He caught me screwing his girlfriend, so he eviscerated me."

"Wavern doesn't have a girlfriend," I state.

The man's eyes bore into mine. "He does, Sara. He just hides it really well," the man says.

"Should we help him?" Haron asks when the man passes out, barely breathing.

"No," the Arliss responds. "Drag him to the wall and feed him to the wolves."

She nods, puts her arms under the man's shoulders, and begins hauling him away.

"What did you mean that he's one of Casey's?" I ask as the two of us return to the conversion room.

"Casey bit him, just like I did to you, making him hers for eternity. She's got several men under her control, some of which I question her choices about."

"And that automatically sent him here when he was killed?" I ask.

"Yes. You either have to be marked or bitten to follow the stream from the ether."

"But Cody wasn't marked or bitten, so how'd he wind up here?"

"He followed you."

"But he got here before I did," I say, protesting.

"He was more desperate to get to the plateau than you were, so he arrived faster."

"How do you get marked?" I ask once we're back under the skylight.

"It's a trick the Nathair learned from me when I was resurrected."

He turns and places a hand on the back of my head just behind my ear. His fingers gently rub over a tiny spot by my earlobe and that's when I feel it, a rise in the skin. I reach up to touch it with my finger. When I realize what the impression is, I bring up my left wrist and stare at the spider tattoo.

"How…how did this get on me?" I ask, my voice shaking.

"I told you, it's a trick I taught the Nathair. How else was I going to know who to convert?" he comments and winks.

"The Nathair are dead, made extinct by the war, so how did this make it onto my skin?"

"One Nathair made it to the safety of the abandonment home," he says slyly. "Thanks to Keegan's grandfather who, by the way, only led those from Comhar over the mountains. He let the Levo perish. It was a miracle that many of them found their way to the abandonment home without his guidance."

"So the person is a Comhar descendant?"

He nods. "And a very influential one at that."

Andra… it has to be Andra.

"He's been disposed of," Haron says, joining us as the sky showing above the room goes dark.

"Good," the Arliss says happily. "Now, let's get this over with."

He steps over to the far wall and presses on a rock that juts out oddly from the rest. A piece of the rock slides away, revealing a niche containing a green-colored stone covered in antiquated symbols. I immediately recognize one of them as the tattoo on my wrist, but there are at least a dozen others all spread out evenly along the smooth surface.

"What is that?" I ask as the Arliss brings the rock, which is the size of a fist, over to the table.

"It's called a Degrem Stone," he replies, setting it beside Cody's body. "All the symbols represent the different creatures that have called this world home at one time or another. This is my symbol," he says, pointing to the spider. "It's what I instructed the Nathair to use when I was reborn. This one over here is the Pheles symbol." He turns the stone over and points to a grouping of stars in a pentagram formation. "The other creatures have long been extinct, so there's no need to explain any of those to you."

"What do you do with the stone?"

"It merges souls into other bodies, but I need a follower to assist me with it since I can't do it on my own," he says.

"Why can't you have Haron help you?"

"Because I want you to learn how to work the stone," he says curtly. "Once I leave this plateau, Haron will cease to exist and I'll be in need of a new assistant if something were to happen."

"But you can't die, so why would you need me?" I ask crossly.

"I can't, but the body I possess still can. And in order for me to move into a new host I need an assistant, which *will* be you," he says, narrowing his eyes. "Now, enough with the questions and stalling." He places the stone in my hands and instructs me to set it on Cody's chest. "All you need to do is press and hold the spider image until I've entered the body. The symbol is burned into my soul, so the stone knows it's me it should transfer. Your mark is simply superficial."

He disrobes and grows impatient when I don't push on the symbol right away, so Haron has to step over and force my finger down. The stone glows a bright green, followed by an energy surge that grabs the Arliss, pulling him into Cody's body. The stone grows hot, becoming almost unbearable to handle, but Haron keeps her grip on me to make sure I don't let go. I cry out in pain as the stone goes from green to red, and my flesh begins to blister. I try to push Haron away but she's pressed herself against me, forcing me into the side of the table.

"Let me go!" I holler.

"Not yet. It's almost complete," Haron says calmly.

A shockwave escapes the stone, releasing my hand, and the glowing ceases. Haron takes possession of the stone as Cody's eyes begin to flicker. He takes a deep breath and then slowly exhales.

"Ah, it feels so good to be human again," the Arliss says, using Cody's voice.

"How could you do that to him?" I yell as I raise my hand, which I've balled into a fist. I swing to hit him, but his hand comes up surprisingly fast and stops me.

"I wouldn't do that if I were you," he says as he squeezes my fist, breaking my fingers in the process.

I scream and back away, cradling my disfigured hand.

"Put that back for me, Haron," the Arliss says as he slides off the table. He grabs my arm with such force that my shoulder pops. He pulls me out of the conversion room, practically dragging me to the shore of the lake. He shoves me into the water and holds my head under for several seconds. "Now, are you going to give me any trouble?" he asks as he lifts my head up and pushes me aside.

"No," I say, trembling.

"Good, because if you do I'll kill you in your world, and without me in the plateau, there isn't a stream to get you back in here, so you'll be dead for real." He starts to retreat to his dwelling, then stops. "Don't move until I get back. I need to finalize a few things before we leave."

I sit on the sand and try to calm myself down as he disappears below the set of boulders on the opposite side. I wasn't expecting him to be so strong in a human body. If he's like that in his world, what will he be like in mine? There's no way to prevent him from getting into my world now. I'm on the verge of tears, when Haron sits beside me.

"How could you let him do that?" I sob.

"He's my master, Sara, just like he's yours."

"But now you'll die when he leaves. Is that really something you want?"

"Of course not," she snaps. "However, it's what he wants. He's tired of being trapped down here and, frankly, so am I."

"He told me that if I now die up in my world, I can never come back here. Is that true?" I ask, trying to gain control over my emotions.

"Yes. The Fomorian Plateau is his realm and he controls everything that happens within it. According to the Arliss, he's the only being who can return to the plateau before another deceased creature can set foot here," she says, then leans very close to me. "But there's another way in that he purposefully neglects to mention. One mortals can use while still alive."

I look at her, surprised, but I keep my mouth shut and just let her talk.

"When you get back to your world, follow the wolves. They'll lead you to the portal that's been kept open for the past sixty years."

"The one the historian unlocked?" I ask.

She nods. "Because a Nathair descendent survived the war, that portal has remained open, which is how the wolves have been able to traverse between the two realms. When the Arliss returns to your world, the portal will stay open no matter what. It won't close until the Arliss, in his human form, and his followers, are dead. He'll be sent back to the plateau while the others flow into the ether, until the very end."

"What would happen if the Nathair is killed?"

"As long as the Arliss is out of the plateau, that portal will remain open even if the Nathair dies."

"What about the Pheles? Is he connected to the plateau?"

"That, I don't know," she says, sounding perplexed at the question. "Possibly, since his marking is on the Degrem Stone. That's what binds everything together down here."

"So, without the stone, the Fomorian Plateau would cease to exist and the Arliss wouldn't have a way to return. He'd die," I say, becoming excited by the thought.

"That sounds plausible," Haron says with a slight smile.

A plan starts to formulate in my head, which takes my mind away from the throbbing pain in my shoulder and fingers.

"Do you want to know the real reason Cody agreed to help the Arliss?" Haron asks after some silence. "He wanted revenge, particularly on anyone descended from a Comhar, which included you by the way."

"He was planning on killing me?"

She nods. "He was going to do to Rinku what Tennison did to Virtus, but Demos was his first target. As soon as the city fell, the compound was next. I heard him and the Arliss discussing it while Cody was determining if he wanted to agree to the Arliss' terms or not."

"I can't believe it," I mutter, stunned. "I thought Cody and I were friends. Has he always harbored these feelings towards me?"

"From what it sounded like to me, yes. He was just waiting for the appropriate time to unleash his wrath."

"No wonder the Arliss was happy when Cody followed me. He'd finally found the perfect person to manipulate into relinquishing their soul," I say.

Not another word is said between us. When the Arliss returns he's dressed in Cody's clothes, with the guns strapped to each thigh.

"Where'd you get those?" I ask as I stand.

"I took them from your clothes before you went to sleep," he says.

"Give them to me. Cody can't be wearing them when we return. He had them taken away by Grimm because he was acting unstable."

The Arliss doesn't argue and hands me the weapons, which I slip around my legs.

"Some ground rules we need to go over before leaving," the Arliss says. "First and foremost, you *have* to refer to me as Cody since I'm in the kid's body. Second, I won't be able to communicate with you telepathically like I have been. That power is only permitted in the plateau, but I will be staying as close to you as possible, so you don't fuck this up. And third, you tell Keegan or anyone else about me and your whole world perishes, understand? Being up there is a luxury for me, not a necessity."

"What about my fingers and shoulder?" I ask.

"They'll restore themselves once we're back in your world. But your bullet wounds will be bleeding, so you'd better hope whoever finds us can give you quick medical attention."

"Are you forgetting the wound Cody has in his torso? You'll also be bleeding when we get back, and a hell of a lot more than I will be."

"True, but the injury to Cody's body isn't fatal as long as I'm inside him, so I'm not too worried."

"What about his memories? Did you retain those?"

"Yes… all of them," he says with a devilish smile. "You're going to have so much fun when you get home. You'll wish for me to have intervened in your life sooner. Poor Keegan doesn't know what he's in for."

"Speaking of which, who made the request for you to turn me?"

"Someone who loves you very much," he says, taking my good hand and pulling me into the lake with him.

"Who?" I ask as I struggle to free myself.

The Arliss pulls me along as the floor of the lake slips away, and we're forced to swim to an island that rises before us. When we get closer, I notice the small landmass is made up of black lava rocks that resemble shards of glass. I get slightly cut up when the Arliss pulls me out of the water and directs me to a hole in the center of the island. Nothing but darkness fills the void and it's now that I remember this is the way back. A pit with no bottom and no air, so I'll be unconscious when my body makes the transition between the two worlds. The Arliss pushes me in front of him, places his hands on my back, and before he sends me off the edge he whispers the name of my betrayer.

"Wavern."

Eleven

Wavern? No! It can't be! The Arliss has to be lying, but what would be the point in doing that now? He's already gotten what he wants, so withholding or falsifying information now would be meaningless. Wavern is the one who saved me from the abandonment home, he's guided my life for the past eight years, and he treats me like a daughter, so how could he do this to me? And why? My thoughts cease as the air from my lungs is fully expelled and I lose all perception of time and surroundings.

I regain my senses when my head hits the water that sits below the control center in Virtus. How much time has passed? A minute? Maybe longer? I remember everything that transpired in the plateau, so time feels odd to me. My brain is having difficulty realizing that in my world I just hit my head on the concrete shelf perhaps only a few minutes ago, while my body knows I've been away for more than a day.

"Grab her!" someone above me shouts.

A pair of strong hands pulls me from the water and up onto the ledge above. I wince from my wounds.

"What the hell?" Grimm utters when he notices I'm bleeding from my right shoulder and arm. "Jules, toss me another med kit."

"Okay," Jules calls down from his perch in the control center. He disappears for a few moments and tosses a pack down to Grimm when he returns.

Grimm rips my shirt at the shoulder and begins applying pressure to stem the bleeding. I involuntarily cry out in pain and begin to shiver from the cold, so Jules drops a blanket down and I try to wrap it around myself as best I can.

"Where's Cody?" I ask as Grimm switches out bandages.

"He's on his way back to Rinku," Grimm says. "He's lost a lot of blood, but we were able to stabilize him enough to be moved. Did you shoot him?"

"Are you fucking serious?" I yell as a spasm of pain radiates down my arm. "Of course not."

"Then who did, Sara?" Grimm asks as he tapes gauze over the wound and moves onto the one in my arm. "You're the only one who had weapons."

My eyes look down to search the water, praying for Tennison's body to surface. It's now I realize that the compound is a lot brighter than when I left it. Lanterns sit at various corners of the control center, giving off so much light it looks like the sun is shining.

"Answer me, Sara!" Grimm shouts.

"Him," I say, pointing to Tennison's arm sticking out of the water between two metal rods. "He shot me as well, in case you care."

Grimm reaches for the arm, pulls it free, then drags the body towards us. "I don't believe it," Grimm says, his mouth hanging open as Tennison's one good eye stares blindly back at us. "Jules, get more people; we've got a body."

"You've got to be fucking kidding me," Jules grumbles. "I'll be right back." He disappears from sight.

"Why did you come in here?" Grimm asks, wrapping up my arm.

"I was chasing Cody, who was following Tennison, and we wound up here," I say, pulling the blanket tighter.

"We all thought Tennison died in the explosion. The last anyone saw of him, he was heading down to the life support level," Grimm says, cleaning up his mess then helping me to my feet.

"Are you still going to tell me you believe the detonation originated from the hydroponics bay?" I ask sarcastically as he slips the med kit into his pack.

"No," he replies. "Can you climb?"

"I can try," I say as Grimm slips the pack onto his back and reaches for a rope that's dangling against the splintered walls.

I wrap it around my left wrist and use my feet to navigate the ruins while pulling myself up. Grimm helps me when he can, and when we reach the control center I'm exhausted. He has me sit down so I can catch my breath before we continue.

"How did you find us?" I ask, my lungs screaming for air.

"Someone from my squad spotted you heading down the tunnel when they knew you were supposed to be on the city's plaza, so they came and got me. I was just entering the city when Wavern was leaving it. I wanted to double check before I sent a search party out for the two of you. He confirmed to me that you'd left, so we hopped into a couple of four-seater ATVs, grabbed Jules, and came down here."

"Why just Jules?"

"I didn't want to draw any unnecessary attention and if I took more people there would be questions."

"How did you know to come to the control center?"

"We heard the gunshots, so Jules and Wavern grabbed some lanterns while I ran ahead. I couldn't see anything until they got to me and that's when I saw Cody floating face down in the water and you struggling to surface underneath him. When I reached Cody, you went under. I was about to jump in after you when you came back up."

"Where's Wavern now?" I ask, getting back to my feet.

"He's driving Cody back to Rinku. He looked pretty upset, but he refused to let anyone else drive the kid to the compound."

He knows. Wavern knows the Arliss is now in Cody.

Jules returns just as we're leaving the control center, accompanied by a half-dozen soldiers from Squad Eight. Grimm directs them to the body and then helps me down the tunnel towards the garage. When we reach the fork, Keegan is standing there. He reaches out to me and pulls me into his arms, which causes me to wince since he hasn't noticed my injuries.

"Thank God you're all right. This never would've happened if she was still on Wavern's squad," he says, squeezing me.

I holler in agony.

"If you call getting shot all right then, yeah, she's fine," Grimm says as he shoves Keegan off me and reexamines the bandages.

"How the hell did that happen?" Keegan demands, pushing Grimm away and taking over the examination.

"Tennison," I mumble, starting to feel lightheaded. "Can we please have this argument somewhere else? I don't feel so well."

Keegan picks me up and carries me to the tunnel outside the garage. He places me in the seat beside him and presses down on the accelerator, leaving Grimm shouting obscenities at him as we leave him behind.

The drive back to the Rinku garage is a blur as I drift in and out of consciousness. Keegan radios ahead to have a medical team ready when we reach the compound, but I'm not sure if anyone hears him since he doesn't get a response. They're probably too busy preparing for Cody's arrival.

"I need to talk to Wavern," I mumble as we continue down the road.

"Sure, babe, whatever you need," Keegan says soothingly. "We're almost there, just hang on a few more minutes."

Words want to fumble out of my mouth, ones that'll only cause me trouble, so it takes what little strength I have left to try to prevent their escape.

I wince as the vehicle bounces as it enters the garage. Since there isn't anyone waiting for us, Keegan directs the ATV into the tunnel leading to the compound. Luckily we fit, with some room to spare. He turns left when we reach the intersection and nearly takes out a couple of display screens. He slams on the brakes when we hit the entrance to the medical ward, but again there's no one to greet us. He jumps out of the vehicle and begins shouting. Wavern steps out of an isolation room by the dividing wall and orders Keegan to keep his voice down.

"But Sara needs help! She's been shot!"

"Put her in the first isolation room," Wavern says.

Keegan picks me up and plops me onto the same bed I occupied only a few days ago. Brea, the other nurse for the compound, comes in to check my wounds. She has Keegan help me out of my wet clothes and into dry ones, hooks an IV into my left arm, and begins dosing me with antibiotics to kill any possible infection I may have contracted from being in the filthy water.

She apparently also gave me a dose of some kind of sleeping agent, because I'm having a hard time keeping my eyes open even with my strength returning. When I'm finally able to focus on the room around me again, Keegan is sitting beside my bed, his hand holding mine, and his head resting on the top of my blankets as he softly snores. My wounds have been cleaned, stitched, and wrapped in gauze. I glance around the room and catch Wavern standing at the foot of my bed, staring at me.

"What do you want?" I ask coldly.

"I just came to see how you were doing," he replies.

"Get out of my sight," I say, clenching my teeth.

"Let me explain," he begins as he steps around the bed.

"There's nothing to explain. Get the fuck away from me before I kill you."

"Sara, you need to know why," he protests.

I reach over Keegan's body, grab one of his guns, and aim it at Wavern. "Do you know what he did to me?" I ask, both my voice and body shaking. "He turned me into one of his slaves, Wavern. Is that what you really wanted him to do to me? To torture and rape me?" Tears flow down my cheeks, blurring my vision, but I don't relax my hold on the gun.

"I...I just wanted you to live," Wavern mumbles.

"I was never going to die until..." I lose my voice.

If Wavern hadn't made the request of the Arliss, I would've remained a victim of Andra's nuke. But the Arliss would still be in the Fomorian Plateau and not parading around as Cody.

"You mean the world to me, Sara," Wavern says, pulling me out of my head. "I couldn't live with myself if anything bad happened to you. You deserve immortality... you've earned it."

"What the hell does that mean?" I ask a little too loudly, and Keegan wakes up.

His eyes grow wide when he spots the weapon in my hand, but surprisingly he doesn't force me to lower it.

"What's going on?" Keegan asks, pushing his chair away from the bed slightly.

"Sara and I were just talking," Wavern says. "She's still a little groggy from the anesthesia."

I aim the gun a few inches above his head and fire off a round. "Does that make it seem like I'm groggy?" I ask angrily.

Nex and Macom rush into the room as Keegan wrests the gun away from me. Wavern looks terrified by what I've just done. I don't think he was expecting that kind of reaction from me.

"Keegan go secure your weapons with Squad Five," Nex orders. "Wavern, leave. You're not her squad leader any longer, so, technically, you shouldn't even be in her room."

Both men hesitate, but Nex threatens to report them both to Andra if they don't do as she commands. Macom retreats to the hallway just outside my door.

"I want to see Cody," I demand.

"You can't," she says, remaining at the foot of my bed. "He's in a coma and is fighting for his life right now."

"What?" I ask, puzzled but also slightly thrilled.

"He caught some sort of infection from the water you two were swimming in. His body is putting up one hell of a fight against whatever parasite is trying to take over. It'll be some time before he wakes up, if he does at all."

I want to smile, to laugh, but I'd never leave isolation since Nex would think I'd lost my mind, especially after shooting at Wavern. If Cody can keep struggling to stay alive, then it might give me an opportunity to find that portal into the plateau and destroy it and the stone, preventing the Arliss from ever returning.

And maybe take Keegan, too.

"Now that you're finally awake, I'll be releasing you to your quarters, so you can get some proper rest," Nex says.

"What day is it?"

"The memorial was yesterday. You've been out for almost twenty-four hours," she responds, then summons Macom back into the room. "Go over care instructions with Sara then send her on her way."

Nex leaves as Macom slips a sling around my shoulder to hold my arm before turning to the cabinet in the wall and removing a handful of ointment, gauze pads, and tape. She puts them all in a small bag, detaches my IV and removes the needle from my skin, closing the tiny hole with a small bandage.

"The stitches will naturally dissolve, so you'll only need to come back here if they give you any trouble. Try not to get the bandages wet. I would recommend bathing instead of showering, and use the sling as much as possible," Macom says as she hands me the bag and lowers the guardrail on the side of the bed. "I'll let Grimm know you've been discharged."

I thank her, exit my room, and stop briefly in front of Cody's, but the curtains are drawn and all I hear is subtle beeping from the other side. I approach the dividing wall and place my hand on the imager, but when it reads my palm it gives me a message that I'm not authorized to enter. I try again and get the same thing. Nex hurries over to me before I try a third time.

"Sorry about that," she says as she places her hand to be scanned, and the wall separates. "Andra had your biometrics suspended after your incident in Lymont, since she didn't want you repeating it. I'm not sure when she's going to have those reinstated."

I grumble as I leave the medical ward and make my way down to my quarters. When I enter, Wavern is sitting on the couch.

"Get out!" I shout, pointing out the door.

"Not until we discuss this," he says, putting his hands up in a defensive position.

"There's nothing to discuss. You're a fucking asshole and I fucking hate you!"

"I know about Keegan," he says quickly.

"What do you know?"

"Close the door so we can talk about it."

I want to slam the door shut but I know that will draw unwarranted attention, as it's now a rotation change throughout the entire compound, so there are a lot of people wandering about the tunnels and barracks. I gently shut the door instead.

"Talk," I say, still standing by the entrance.

"It took me some time to figure it out," he says. "I'd heard stories about the demon that once ruled our world – my mother told them to me – but I never truly believed it."

"Yet you bought the shit about the Arliss right away," I comment.

"He stopped the Pheles from destroying everything," Wavern snaps, jumping to his feet. "No one would exist if it wasn't for the Arliss."

"The Nathair lied to you," I say, seething as I finally step into the room. "The Pheles killed the Arliss, sending him back to the hell he comes from. The Levo are the ones who took care of the Pheles, isolating him in a tomb in the Kai Mountains."

"Who told you that bullshit?"

"The Arliss did."

Wavern clearly wasn't expecting that response. "He did?" he asks, stunned.

"Why do you sound so surprised? Did you actually think anything that was taught to you by a Nathair was the truth? You've been fed lies your whole life, Wavern—we all have."

"My mother would never have lied to me," he counters.

"How old was she when Keegan's grandfather took her into the mountains?"

"How do you know about that?"

"Just answer the question."

"She was five," he says, sinking back onto the couch. "She had me at seventeen. A lot of people back then had kids when they were young. My mother would tell me how the Nathair tried to save the world from dying, and that the Arliss was the only one who could do that. Especially if the

Pheles rose from his tomb." He lifts his eyes up to mine. "Keegan had a fit one day at the abandonment home and flashed a set of red eyes at me when I was called to deal with him, as I was the only leader available to help Haron at the time. That's one of the reasons I took him… to keep an eye on him."

"How did you determine he was the Pheles?"

"My mother wrote down all the stories she ever told me in a small notebook that I carry with me," he says, reaching into a pocket, removing a well-worn pad no bigger than a deck of cards, and handing it to me. "She made notes on everything anyone ever told her, hoping one day it would be of use. I want you to have it."

"Why?"

"It was meant for you," he says, then stands and places a hand on my left shoulder. "Everything I have is yours, Sara. I love you more than anything." He kisses me gently on the cheek. "You're the only one I trust, so please don't let me down." He hugs me then heads for the door.

"The Arliss is in Cody," I blurt out as I turn to face him.

"I know," he replies sorrowfully. "And I wish I could change that."

The minute he's gone, I head into the bathroom. I feel dirty, disgusting, and angry. I drop the bag on the counter and look for a place to stash the notebook, finally shoving it behind a loose board under the sink. I go to turn the faucet on in the tub when I catch my reflection in the mirror. It's one I don't recognize. I look tired, beaten, and old, and I feel the same way—which makes me wonder how much more my body can handle. I need to get back to the plateau, but how can I possibly do that if I can't even get out of the compound? I'll need help, but from whom? Wavern seems like my only logical choice but I don't trust him anymore, no matter what he says to justify what he did. You don't claim to love someone then feed them to the wolves, or in this case the Arliss.

Keegan's face joins mine in the mirror, and he wraps his arms around my waist. I try to fake a smile as he holds me tightly.

"How are you feeling?" he asks.

"Tired and sore. I was hoping to get cleaned up before I crashed for the day… or is it night now?"

"It's a few minutes past twenty-three-hundred, so it's definitely night-time," he replies before spinning me around. "As for showering you can't get the bandages wet, so I was thinking I'd assist in washing you and get to the places you might not be able to reach."

"Sounds great," I say, feigning delight.

He helps me undress and we step into the tub. He turns the faucet on and has me stand against the tile wall face first, with my right arm above my head so not to get it wet. I retreat into my mind as Keegan bathes my body with soap, separating myself from the world around me as a way to cope with the truth that punctures my heart. I close my eyes as an image of a world on fire floods my mind, every inch of dirt dissolving before me. Hundreds lay slaughtered at my feet, their blood thick around my ankles. I try to pull myself out of the delusion, but I'm only drawn in further. The air I breathe is filled with ash, the blood coursing through my veins is hot, and all I want to do is destroy it all. I glance down at my hands and notice they're covered in blood, dripping with the life of those I've just slaughtered. I'm no longer in the compound, but standing on the surface as entire cities fall before me. I know it's not real but when I try to regain control of my mind, I fall further and further into the rabbit hole.

"You're safe here," Keegan whispers in my ear. "Stay with me."

A sharp pain radiates down my neck, which pulls me into the moment. I'm still facing the wall, but Keegan has his naked body pressed against mine as his teeth sink into my flesh. A scream catches in my throat, and I feel my blood boiling. I push against the wall with my hands and wind up smashing the tile, which startles me.

"Stay," Keegan continues to whisper as he releases the pressure from my neck. "And we can rule together."

He turns me around just as I sense my eyes changing, turning red like his. He smiles with pleasure at the sight of them and forces himself inside me. Conflict rises within and a battle ensues with such ferocity that my scream shatters the glass enclosing the tub and the mirrors on the wall. Our bodies are nicked and bleeding, but Keegan won't let go.

"He tried to turn you, but he failed," Keegan says breathlessly. "The Arliss will die, as will all creatures on this earth, just leaving the two of us together… forever."

I stop speaking as he bites me again, this one lasting minutes. My blood washes down the drain with the water and I feel the Arliss' hold releasing.

"You knew?" I finally mutter.

Keegan brushes the hair from my face. "Who do you think put the idea into Wavern's head about marking you? Why else would you have run off into Lymont if not to fulfill the destiny I planned from the very moment we met? Andra knew you'd go through her things because I told her you would. She gave you the time you needed to find the monitors, just as I instructed her to. The Arliss thinks it was his idea to return to the surface when, in fact, it was mine," Keegan says. "How else do you kill a snake but by chasing it out of its hole."

"Why me?" I ask as he presses into me harder.

"The Pheles only has one love, and I chose you long before that bully of a child stumbled upon my tomb. But he made everything so much easier," Keegan says before covering my mouth with his.

I can't help but kiss him back and I grip his head, as it feels like he's too far away from me. He picks me up and carries me to the bedroom, leaving a trail of water and blood behind us. As he lays me on the bed I pray that the walls are soundproof as this is going to be a long night.

Twelve

"You're going to need to learn to hide those," Keegan says as he kisses me. He strokes my hair as he lies on top of me under damp covers. "Just close your eyes and pull them back slightly; the red will retract. When you want to show them, do the opposite, like this."

He closes his eyes and when they reopen the irises are as red as blood, but then he changes them back to their natural color. I do what he suggests and I can feel the color going back to green. When I reopen my eyes, Keegan is smiling.

"What do we do now?" I ask as I rub his back.

"We clean up and go kill the Arliss."

"You know where he is?" I ask, surprised.

"Of course."

"But he won't die," I mumble. "He'll simply go back to the Fomorian Plateau until he gets another host."

"So, that's where he's been hiding," Keegan says slyly.

"You know the place?"

"I was created there when the world first erupted into life. We both were. When we found our way to the surface we divided the world, but the Arliss got reckless and was murdered by those who feared him. After his death, word spread about my existence, so I was betrayed by those I called friends and sealed in the Kai Mountains."

"Why didn't you return to the plateau after the Levo entombed you?"

"Only those who die a violent death can get to the plateau. My host died of starvation, so I was trapped in the mountains until a viable one came along."

A pit forms in my stomach. "Do you know what he did to me down there?" I ask somberly.

"I know he has to bite you like I did for his poison to transfer. Why? What else happened?" Keegan asks with great concern.

"He tortured me," I say quietly. "In more ways than I care to remember."

Keegan's face turns to stone. "I'll make him pay for hurting you," he says harshly. "He's going to regret his entire existence when I'm done with him. We'll need to come up with a plan before we put Cody's body through hell, so the Arliss can suffer. Then we'll kill him so he can't return."

I was hoping he hadn't figured out who the Arliss' host was, but given that Cody and I are the only ones who've experienced trauma in the last twenty-four hours, he was the logical choice. I kiss Keegan deeply just as there's a knock on our bedroom door.

"Go away!" Keegan shouts.

"Andra is looking for you," Grimm says from the other side.

"Tell her I'm busy fucking my wife," Keegan says with sincerity.

"Now, Keegan. That's an order."

"It's the middle of the night—what could she possibly want?"

"How the hell would I know? She just told me to get you."

"Fine," he grumbles. "I'll be right out." He turns his attention to me. "You're going to want to hide that love bite, especially from asshole out there." He kisses me, gets up, dresses, and is in the process of leaving the room but stops because Grimm is blocking his path. "Why are you getting me and not Wavern? Or was I transferred to your squad unexpectedly?" Keegan's tone drips with hatred.

"Wavern is on his way to Demos with Jules and I'm the only squad leader up, so she had to use me," Grimm responds heatedly.

"Well, then, let's go," Keegan says, shooing Grimm away from the bedroom.

"Not until I check on Sara. You go ahead."

"What, you couldn't hear how happy she is?" Keegan smirks. "I'm sure the whole compound did."

"You're disgusting, you know that?" Grimm comments, scrunching up his face. "Get going before Andra wakes the entire compound with the intercom, searching for you."

Keegan shakes his head as he leaves the apartment but I remain under the covers while Grimm leans against the doorframe, his arms folded over his chest.

"As you can see, I'm fine," I say, gesturing down the length of the bed and its slightly red-stained sheets from additional bites Keegan bestowed upon me during our lovemaking.

"I'd hardly say you're fine. What's going on with you?"

"Nothing, except for being shot twice and nearly drowning. Otherwise, I'm good," I say as I slide off the bed, wrapping the sheet around me. "What?" I ask as I pass him and head towards the bathroom, the door to which is closed, thankfully. I dread the interrogation I'd get if Grimm saw the blood all over the floor and walls, as well as the shattered glass and mirror.

"Care to explain this?" he asks, pointing to the puddles of diluted red on the floor as well as the sheet.

"My sutures started seeping after the bandages got wet, so I'm taking care of that now," I say hastily, and show him my stained bandages.

"You're a horrible liar, Sara," he says, trying to follow me.

"It's nothing. I'll get it cleaned up," I respond, blocking him from seeing into the bathroom. "Now go away."

I slip into the bathroom and lock the door. I have to put on the clothes from the medical ward since I don't have anything clean, then I change my bandages and brush my hair so that it's covering my throat. When I open the door, Grimm is still standing there, so I have to quickly pull it shut behind me.

"Why are you still here?" I ask, annoyed.

"Because I'm concerned about you," he says.

"That would be a first," I mutter as I sidestep around him and make my way into the living room.

"Excuse me?" he snaps. "I've always had your back."

"Yeah, maybe eight years ago, but not since then," I say, sitting on the couch and flipping through the channels on the screen.

Grimm rips the remote from my hands and turns off the display. "You know that's not true," he says furiously. "Why are you acting like this?"

"Because I'm sick of pretending," I say as I push myself up off the couch. "I've finally realized after all these years that I've been fooling myself into believing that anyone actually gave a damn about me. I'd been holding out hope that maybe one day you'd see me as someone you could be with, but you never did. I was always your buddy, your friend, so when Keegan showed the slightest bit of interest in me I jumped at it." I get close to Grimm. "You asked me why I married Keegan. What I see in him. He's the only person who seems to care about me, even though he really doesn't. He only wants to control me." Tears fill my eyes. "I just couldn't wait for you any longer."

Grimm's mouth hangs open in shock. I'm also puzzled by my brazen comments. There's no way I would've openly admitted any of this before, especially to Grimm. What's the point of doing it now? Keegan has won, I'm his for all eternity, so what could my ramblings possibly accomplish except to stab Grimm in the heart. Maybe that's why I said it, to make him leave me for good, so I won't have to make that decision myself.

His tongue invading my mouth isn't the response I was expecting. He pulls me in closer as an intensity develops between us, almost to the point of combustion. Grimm pulls away as we both try to catch our breath, and he practically bolts for the door.

"Just so you know," he starts, his hand around the door knob, "you're the only person I ever cared about in this whole damn place. Leaving you in the abandonment home was the hardest thing I could've ever done, but now… seeing you with him… hearing you with him—I wish I'd never met you."

He slams the door as he leaves. I pick up the closest object I can find and hurl it at the plasma screen, smashing it to pieces. I sink onto the couch and cry like my best friend has just died, because in a way he has. I'm losing control of my life and I need to find a way to get it back. Can I undo what Keegan did, or is it permanent? He freed me from the Arliss, so there has to be a way to save me from being a Pheles. No matter what, though, I can't stay in the compound—I'll be too distracted by Keegan's happiness and Grimm's anger. But where do I go? And, more importantly, when? If I do it too soon it'll look suspicious, so I'll need to time it just right.

I decide I need to stop thinking about it all and get cleaning, so I start with the glass from the plasma screen. I'm in the middle of collecting the shards when Keegan enters, a scowl on his face. He pauses on his way to the bathroom when he notices the display.

"How'd that happen?" he asks curiously.

"I was aiming at Grimm's head and missed," I reply.

"Wow, you attacked Grimm? I'm impressed," he says, grinning.

"What did Andra want with you?"

"She's asked me to take her to Demos. We're leaving in about twenty minutes."

"Why do you have to take her?"

"Because Wavern, Jules, and the other squad leaders with the exception of Grimm, are already in the city. Andra doesn't have anyone to take her, as she needs Grimm to watch the compound while everyone else is away, and you're out of commission with your injuries, so I was the next logical choice."

"That still doesn't explain why she chose you specifically. Why not another sub-commander from a different squad?" I ask nervously.

Why am I afraid to be left alone? Keegan being away has never bothered me before, so why does it now? Is this one of the effects of him branding me a Pheles? If so, it'll make my escape that much more difficult.

"Don't sound so worried, babe," he says, kneeling beside me on the floor. "Remember, I've got Andra under my thumb so, of course, she'd ask me to escort her."

"Why is everyone in Demos?"

"Myr called an emergency meeting."

"Did she mention what the meeting is about?"

"Nope," he says as he gets back to his feet. "I'll be back before you know it." He kisses me and heads towards the bathroom.

I hear him cleaning up the glass before turning on the shower. I finish what I'm doing and take the debris out to a trash bin beside the laundry room. When I return, I gather all my dirty clothes and go back to the laundry room to start a load. Keegan hugs me before leaving and says he'll be back by tomorrow night at the latest. I spend a good part of the night scrubbing blood off the floor, mopping, straightening out the rest of the bathroom, and putting clean sheets on the bed. I'm bothered by the idea that Myr had to call this meeting, and that Andra delayed in attending.

My arm and shoulder start to throb, so I take some pain medication, finish my laundry, and head to the mess hall as breakfast is now being served. The room isn't as crowded as it normally would be so I ask someone about it, only to learn that Squads Nine and Ten were moved to the farms under the Factory yesterday morning to help control a supposed uprising that started the night of the memorial. Maybe that's why Myr is having the meeting this late at night; so she can have the leaders entering Demos when all its residents are asleep and not draw any attention to why so many leaders are in one place.

"There's a rumor going around that a body was discovered in one of the machines in the manufacturing section of the Factory," the woman says. "It was the greeter. He'd been practically cut in half. There's never been any type of incident like it before and some are questioning how the body actually got there, because his wounds don't correlate to what would be done by any of the machine blades."

I quickly lose my appetite as the image of the greeter coming out of the lake in the plateau floats into my mind, along with what he said as to how he wound up there. Wavern killed him, but why? Something about the old man screwing Wavern's girlfriend? I don't really recall Wavern ever getting violent, or having a girlfriend, but I haven't regained all my memories yet either, so anything is possible. There are security cameras all over that place, so surely something would've been noticed.

I toss out the rest of my food and return to the apartment, get under the covers, and try to get some sleep. But my mind is too restless. I get up and remove the notebook from under the sink to see if there's anything useful in it, but a lot of it is gibberish and difficult to read because of the faded ink. I hold up individual pages to the light on the nightstand to see if that helps. It does a little, but the only information I can read is what the Arliss has already told me about his resurrection and the imprisoning of the

Pheles. I catch a couple of references to the historian and something about Telus Mesa, but my eyes begin to hurt from the strain. I put the notebook back under the sink and am about to go return to bed when Nex's voice sounds over the speakers.

"Sara Gentry, please report to the medical ward," she says methodically.

I don't want to continue running around in hospital garb anymore, so I put on a pair of black pants and a hunter green shirt. Once I get my boots on, I head up the stairs and into the medical ward. Macom has the divider open for me when I get there and I'm directed to isolation, specifically Cody's room, but Nex stops me before I enter.

"He just woke up, and has been asking for you," she says as I glance into the room. The curtains are no longer blocking the door. "I've informed Grimm, who will be here once the rotation change is complete now that Andra is away. I can only let you stay for a few minutes, as Cody needs his rest."

I nod my head as she slides the door open. When I'm inside, she closes it behind me but stays there, watching us. I stand at the foot of the bed, partially to block Nex from witnessing our conversation, but I also don't dare get any closer in case the Arliss can sense what Keegan has done to me. The Arliss smiles, eyes tired and lips chapped. He signals for me to come closer, but I refuse to move.

"Scared of your master all of a sudden?" he asks in a weakened voice.

"No, I just don't want Nex to read our lips," I reply.

"Smart girl," he croaks. "How are you doing?"

"I've been better. You?"

"I wasn't expecting the kid to put up this much of a fight," he says, trying to snicker. "I give Cody credit for trying to stick around."

"Did you finally kill him?" I ask coldly.

"He's beaten back enough for the moment for me to gain the control I need, but I'm not sure how long that'll last since he's battling me something fierce."

"Why'd you ask for me?"

"I need a favor," he begins, then pauses as a coughing fit wracks his body.

Nex is about to bolt into the room when I move over to the Arliss' side and help him get a sip of water, which appears to help. She doesn't come in, but continues to linger on the other side of the glass.

"When do you not need a favor from me," I groan.

He's about to speak when his eyes narrow. "You're different," he hisses.

"I don't know what you're talking about," I say as my stomach tightens.

"He knows, doesn't he?" the Arliss asks, seizing my wrist. His strength is beyond immense and I can't break free.

"Who?" I ask, pain shooting up my left arm.

"Your husband," he replies through clenched teeth as he tightens his grip to the point where I hear my bones crack. "What did he do to you?"

"Let me go," I beg.

"He changed you… into one of his," the Arliss says, becoming furious. "How could you let him do that?" he screams, which draws Nex into the room. "I'll kill you, Sara! The moment I get out of here, you're fucking dead!"

"Macom, where's that shot?" Nex hollers.

The nurse rushes into the room and jams an injector into Cody's neck, knocking him out. When my wrist is free Nex checks for fractures, but it's badly bruised. I leave the ward just as Grimm enters, which allows me to exit through the divider. He glares at me as I hurry back to my quarters.

I pace in the living room, trying to figure out what to do. Since Andra is away and Grimm is probably still in the medical ward, I decide to head to the preparation room to snag a survival pack along with some surveillance equipment and cameras. I hurry up to the top level of the barracks then move quickly through the rec room and weapons bunker. Thankfully, everyone's at their stations or sleeping, so the tunnels are clear. I remove a pack from the wall and grab a small container of cameras that are the size of a pin, then I have to search for the matching tablet. I shove everything in the pack except the cameras, which I place along at the tops of the walls as I make my way back to the apartment.

I probably should've also snagged my weapons while I was in there but I'm sure they're on lockdown, meaning my code to call them up will be flagged, preventing Squad Five from sending them along with some extra ammunition. I settle on the couch and turn on the tablet to make sure the cameras I placed are working. Everything is functioning normally, so I take a few minutes to place a couple of them around the living room, bedroom, all open levels of the barracks, and inside the tunnel leading to the medical ward. I'll need to figure out a way to put one in the control room and the medical ward itself, since my access to both areas will be heavily monitored.

I set those aside and rummage through the survival pack, checking the contents: two flashlights – one of which will reveal the Mulgrim – dried food packets and nutrition bars, an empty water canister, a tightly rolled tarp, a large hunting knife, and several boxes of matches. I put everything back into the pack, adding the tablet and cameras. I'm about to hide it at the bottom of my locker when I decide to put Wavern's notebook in there as well. I dump my clean clothes on top, concealing the pack. The next thing I do is switch out the broken plasma screen, so I take one from an empty apartment and leave the broken one in its place. When I have it secured to the wall, I turn it on and look at the Daily Slate as I lay on the couch.

Sure enough, Squads Nine and Ten are listed as being in Demos, because the Factory is currently on lockdown. Squads One and Three are making adjustments to the Occlyn Ring for the Rodinea Expanse and security patrol; Squads Two, Four, and Six are in the control center, kitchen, and garage respectively; Squad Five is split between sleeping and working in the weapons bunker; Squad Seven is sleeping; and Squad Eight is in Demos. It's just past six in the morning, and since I've been up all night I'm finally starting to tire. I pull the blanket from the back of the couch over me and fall asleep.

A high-pitched beeping wakes me. I'm surprised to see it's coming from the Daily Slate. An emergency message scrolls in red along the top of the screen, followed by a mechanical voice stating that the leader of Demos will be making an announcement shortly. I've never known any type of message being broadcast from the Daily Slate before, so I'm concerned. This probably is in conjunction with the meeting everyone went to, but why is Myr giving the compounds the message instead of Andra or Demmer?

She's never addressed us before, with the exception of the memorial. Why the change? I take a quick look at the time and realize I've been asleep for over twelve hours; as it's now well past eighteen-hundred hours. I remain wrapped in the blanket as the Daily Slate disappears, the beeping ceases, and Myr fills the screen.

"Good morning citizens and soldiers," she starts, her voice trembling ever so slightly. "As many of you are aware, there was an incident in the Factory during the memorial service. One of our cherished citizens was brutally killed in what has been determined to be an accident with a cutting machine. This is the first type of incident to have befallen our community in all the time we've lived here in Demos. The farmers who live and work below the Factory saw this as an opportunity to escape their confines. Emergency measures were immediately taken, so the Factory is currently closed to all individuals. Soldiers from Rinku are working to control the growing unrest. It is imperative that we maintain order to secure our survival, so I'm enacting a curfew for all citizens of Demos until this situation is resolved." Myr takes a deep breath before continuing. "To enforce the curfew, squads from Rinku and Quarn will each be patrolling our streets and arresting anyone caught violating these orders."

"There's more that she's not mentioning," Keegan says as he closes the door and sits beside me on the couch.

"The meeting wasn't about the guy's death?"

"No, it was, but it was much more," he says, turning the volume down on the screen. "A small spider tattoo, much like yours, was discovered on Tennison's body when it was examined by the doctor in Quarn. It was also determined that the fatal bullet was fired from Cody's weapon. Myr was made aware of this during the meeting and Wavern made the mistake of mentioning that he'd given you Cody's guns before the memorial started. An inquest has been called and Demmer is waiting in Andra's apartment for you, so he can take you back to Quarn for questioning."

"What? You've got to be kidding me," I almost shout.

"I told Demmer I'd come get you, since you'd be more cooperative if your husband was the one to break the bad news."

"You know I didn't shoot Tennison on purpose. It was self-defense. Did you tell them that?"

"I did, babe, but Myr is still insisting that you be questioned by an impartial person, such as Demmer. Nex will be going with you as well, as she took care of your injuries from Virtus."

"But what about the tattoo on my wrist? He'll definitely be suspicious if he sees it."

"I thought of that," Keegan says, removing a hunting knife from a survival pack strapped to his back. "Give me your arm."

"Are you nuts? You're going to cut it off me?"

"Do you have any other ideas?" he snaps.

I hesitate, but do give him my arm. When he flips my hand over so it's palm up, he notices the bruises, which masks the tattoo, though not perfectly. Deep purple and blue fingerprints are embedded into my flesh. The bruises have grown in size and are more profound and sensitive since the Arliss gave them to me.

"Where'd you get these?" Keegan asks, putting the knife aside to examine my wrist.

"Cody," I say softly. "He woke up and asked to see me. Nex let me into his room but he noticed I'm no longer one of his slaves, so he gripped my arm tightly as he yelled. I thought he was going to break it. Macom gave him something to knock him out."

"He won't live to see another day," Keegan utters, his eyes turning red.

"You can't kill him, remember? The Arliss will simply return to the plateau and wait."

"I don't care—he has to pay for what he's done."

"Fine, but let me do it," I say. "I need to be the one to do it."

"Okay," he responds, changing his eyes back to normal. "Let's get you up to Andra's apartment before they grow suspicious."

Thirteen

Demmer is in a heated conversation with Wavern when Keegan and I enter Andra's apartment. Grimm is standing off in the corner, watching it all unfold.

"You're not her squad leader anymore," Demmer says, poking a finger in Wavern's face. "I don't need your permission to take her out of the compound. I only need Grimm's, which he's given."

I stare at Grimm, but he refuses to look at me.

"You need to get your squad ready for Demos," Andra chimes in. "I assure you, Sara is in good hands, Wavern. You're acting irrational about this whole inquest. If you don't back down I'll have you confined to quarters, and Jules can take command."

"If you won't let me go with her, then order Grimm to," Wavern demands. "She can't go by herself."

"Sara can handle herself just fine," Grimm comments in a sarcastic tone. "Besides, Nex will be going as well. No one else needs to be a part of this."

"Agreed," Andra says. "Wavern, this is your last warning. Return to your quarters and round up your squad for patrol. Am I understood?"

"Yes," Wavern answers sharply. "Come on, Keegan, we're not welcome here."

Keegan kisses me then disappears into the hallway with Wavern.

"Do you need anything else from me?" Grimm asks, sulking.

"No, Grimm, you may go," Andra replies.

Grimm gently closes the door as he leaves, still not meeting my gaze. I feel like he's abandoning me all over again, just like he did eight years ago. I don't care what Wavern said about Grimm not having a choice—he could've taken me with him, regardless.

"Now, Sara, I'm assuming Keegan explained everything to you," Andra says, taking a seat on one of her couches. "The inquest won't take long. Just answer Demmer's questions truthfully and you should be back by morning."

"Why can't I answer them here?" I ask.

"Myr has requested that the questioning take place in Quarn," Demmer says with clear contempt. "Now, I think we should get going."

"Nex will meet you in the garage," Andra says dismissively.

I follow Demmer as we make our way through the various sections of the compound before entering the tunnel that'll take us to the garage. I've never had much contact with Demmer before, so I don't know much about him. He's tall, perhaps around six-feet-five-inches, and medium build with graying hair. He has to be around Wavern's age, maybe slightly younger, but there's no way to tell for sure since his face is full of creases Wavern's is lacking. He doesn't say a word to me even as we climb into the ATV, with Nex taking the front seat beside him. It's going to be a long ride to Quarn, three hours if I calculate it correctly. I still don't see why Demmer has to take Nex and me to his compound. What exactly was Myr told? Was the Arliss even discussed, or just his marking?

"Do we really have to drive all the way to Quarn?" I ask after quite some time. "I mean, we're already an hour away from Rinku—couldn't we just do this now and get it over with?"

"You're as stubborn as Wavern," Demmer grumbles.

"I just don't see what the big deal is about Tennison's death. Everyone thought he died in the blast in Virtus and it happens they were wrong. But he's officially dead now, so what's the big deal about when his death took place?" I ask, seeing how far I can push Demmer before he snaps. I'm not sure why I want to push him, but something is telling me I need to in order to stop the interrogation that I know is coming.

"It's not how he died, but what was found on his wrist that has everyone greatly concerned," Demmer says, becoming hostile. "I don't give a damn that the motherfucker is dead."

"Well, that's good to know since you dropped a bomb on him a couple of years ago and that didn't kill him like you planned," I let slip on purpose.

Demmer hits the brakes with such force he nearly loses control of the vehicle.

"What's she talking about?" Nex asks, perplexed.

"You shut your fucking mouth," Demmer says, seething as he spins around to face me.

"Does Andra know what you've done? Do you know what she's done? I'm curious to see who's covering for whom."

Demmer reaches around and grabs my throat, squeezing it. "You have no idea what the hell you're talking about," he practically spits.

"I guess everyone forgot to mention to both of you that I've gotten most of my memories back, and that's not good for either of you," I squeak. "What's my silence worth to you?"

"Sara, what's going on?" Nex asks, becoming nervous.

"He and Andra are responsible for the bombings," I reply.

"This bitch doesn't know what the hell she's talking about," Demmer says, squeezing harder.

Spots fill my vision, and my hearing wanes. "You murdered Tennison a couple of years ago… just like Andra tried to kill me the other day." I suck in as much air as I can since I'm beginning to see black around the edges of my vision. "Whose idea was it to bomb the abandonment home? Yours or hers?"

"What?" Nex practically yells, glancing between the two of us.

"You don't know anything," Demmer says.

"I know more than you do! Why do you think Andra tried to kill me? Because I found out what the two of you had done," I retort.

Demmer loosens his hold.

"That's why you ran into Lymont?" Nex asks.

I nod. "Myr has no idea the two of you have nukes hidden in those precious satellites, does she?" I ask as I try to take in more air, which leads to a coughing fit. "Why'd you keep it from her?"

"She never asked," Demmer says, sitting back in his seat.

"That's a bullshit reason," I say. "You just didn't want to give your power over to someone with a Levo heritage. You and Andra are still trying to carry on a civil war that ended decades ago. I just can't figure out why."

"We're not," he blusters. "My father was a Levo, so there goes your theory."

"Then what is it? Why was Tennison chased from Virtus? So you could drop a bomb on him and kill him?"

"I have no fucking clue," Demmer says, turning back around and putting the vehicle into drive. "Myr knows about the bombs, by the way. Who do you think gave us the order to nuke anyone who's caught on the surface? There's been more bombings than just the two of you, but she's not about to admit to her citizens that she's authorized genocide. The one for the abandonment home couldn't be so readily covered up like the others."

"Why does she want you to kill her own people?" Nex asks.

"To prevent a specific person from returning," Demmer replies.

"So, murdering everyone was her answer?" I ask.

"She wanted to stop them from finding him, whether it was on purpose or accidental," Demmer answers.

"Who?" Nex asks.

"The Arliss," Demmer replies.

"But that's crazy. He was killed, which is how the war ended. Why would she think he could possibly return?" Nex asks.

"Well, considering his mark was found on Tennison's body, as well as on the guy in the Factory, I'd say she has a right to be concerned."

"But that's a Nathair tattoo—not anything from the Arliss," Nex says, sounding confused.

"You don't know your history very well, do you?" Demmer asks, glancing at her briefly.

She turns her attention to me and I know what she's going to say next, so I subtly shake my head, hoping she'll keep her mouth shut.

"No, I guess I don't," she replies after a few seconds.

"The Nathair worshipped the Arliss, so the mark was a way they could identify each other. Everyone knows that symbol is forbidden, so for it to show up after all these years on two people who weren't even alive during the war has Myr fearful."

"But not you or Andra, right?" I ask.

"We both believe it's someone trying to be funny," Demmer replies.

"Do you know when either of them could've gotten the marking?" I ask as a way to keep Nex silent.

"Our doctor examined it on both Tennison and the greeter, but only the greeter's seemed recent. Also, there wasn't any ink found in the symbol, so it technically can't be considered a tattoo, which means it wasn't obtained in Demos."

"What is it?" I ask.

"It's a change in pigmentation. No one can figure out how it occurred," Demmer says.

I glare at Nex, wondering if the test she supposedly ran on the scraping from mine came back with the same result. She's never mentioned it, and now I begin to wonder why.

"Grimm has that mark," Nex blurts out.

"Yes, but everyone knows how he obtained it," Demmer says, annoyed. "That fucking husband of yours, Sara. I swear, if he were in my compound he'd have been sent to the farms under the Factory a long time ago."

"I don't understand why Andra puts up with his crap," Nex says.

"Because he's a Comhar descendant," Demmer says mockingly, then stops the ATV once again. "How did you return from Lymont, Sara? Andra never told me."

"I found shelter before the bomb fell," I reply. "How did Tennison return if you nuked him?"

Demmer studies me carefully. "The same way, I imagine," he replies.

"Do you still need to conduct your little inquest, or have I satisfied your curiosity?" I ask, growing impatient.

"Does anyone in Rinku have the Arliss symbol, other than Grimm?" Demmer asks Nex.

"No," she responds confidently.

Demmer glances between the two of us. He probably knows we're holding something back, so to qualm any questions he may have I show him my left wrist.

"See, no Arliss marking," I say.

"Where'd you get the bruises?" he asks.

"Cody had a death grip on me when I tried pulling him back to the surface when we were in Virtus," I respond.

"Well, I guess that's better than being shot in the head," Demmer smirks.

"It was self-defense!" I yell.

"Yeah, Sara, I know. Calm down," he says before turning the vehicle around and heading back to Rinku.

"How did Myr manage to get the Rodinea Expanse cleaned if you and Andra are dropping bombs everywhere?"

"We're not dropping them everywhere—and that doesn't leave this vehicle," he says, sticking a finger in Nex's face. "The mountains act as a natural buffer, so none of the radiation penetrates the valley. The expanse dried up due to environmental reasons we've been working on correcting. Also, the satellites don't pass over that piece of terrain because when they were sent up both sides agreed to not spy on that section, as it had become neutral ground when the war with the Arliss started."

"What are you going to tell Myr?' I ask as we get closer to Rinku.

"The truth. Tennison and the guy from the Factory were isolated incidents. Nothing further needs to be discussed," Demmer answers, glaring at me in the rearview mirror.

When we're back in the garage, Nex and I barely manage to exit the vehicle before Demmer slams on the gas pedal, screeching away. As the two of us are making our way back to the compound, Nex pulls me off to the side.

"Was everything you said back there true?" she asks, worried.

"Yes, but you can't say anything to anyone about it." I'm about to step away, when she grabs my arm.

"Cody has the mark and so do you. Demmer isn't the sharpest tool in the shed when it comes to observing things, but the bruises didn't fool me. I want to know how you got that tattoo," she demands.

"I don't know how I got it."

"Yeah, right, Sara. You get killed in Lymont and come back with a Nathair symbol. Cody gets shot in the torso, nearly dying, and he gets pulled from Virtus with the same mark on his wrist in the same spot. Neither of you had them before, but now you do."

"I told you, Nex, I have no idea how I got mine or that Cody even has one," I say, feigning ignorance. "And besides, I thought you were running tests on skin cells taken from it. Why haven't you discussed the results with me?"

"Because Andra told me not to. She didn't want you to know," she responds. "Why was Cody threatening to kill you earlier?"

"He's crazy," I respond, shrugging.

She seizes my left arm and thrusts it up to my face. "You knew the bruises were covering up the mark, which is why you showed Demmer. Why would Cody do this to you? How was he able to inflict this amount of damage since he's nowhere near strong enough given his current condition?"

I simply stare at her.

"I want answers, Sara, or I go to Andra and tell her the entire conversation we just had with Demmer. If she killed you over you finding out about the bombs in the satellites, what do you think she'll do when she realizes you pieced together what happened to the abandonment home?"

"Why does it matter if you know?" I ask heatedly.

"Because I might be able to help you," she whispers.

"No one can help me," I say sorrowfully and then pull my arm out of her grasp.

"I lied to Demmer when I said I didn't know my history," she says as I begin to turn to leave. "My grandmother was the historian who brought the Arliss to the surface."

I spin around so fast I almost collide with her.

"My mother was already born at that time, and when my grandmother ran off…" she says, growing sad, "my grandfather had to raise my mom on his own in Demos when the war broke out. He refused to go with my grandmother into the Aslu Territory because he thought she was confused, that she'd interpreted those texts wrong just like most of the population had. She wouldn't listen to him and took off, starting the Nathair following, so I'm well aware of what that symbol on your wrist means. The Arliss destroyed my family, Sara, if he's trying to return then I want to know about it."

"He's dead."

"So were you, and yet here you are," she says in a tone that drips with derision.

"How do I know I can trust you?"

"Because if I really wanted to make trouble, I'd have told Demmer about the marking on you, Cody, and that idiot in the Factory commercials. The one Wavern keeps sneaking in and out of here."

"Casey is his girlfriend?"

"What, did you think you're the only one he has a hard-on for?"

"That's disgusting, Nex," I say, my gag reflex kicking in. "He sees me like a daughter."

"No, he doesn't," she blurts out. "Don't you remember anything from your time in the abandonment home? There's a reason those files were never transferred over when someone was moved to the compounds."

I try to recall anything from when I was younger, but only snippets of my studying and my relationship with Grimm during those years spring to mind. Nothing else. It's like my life really didn't start until I got to Rinku. "I only remember Grimm," I mumble.

"Really? You don't remember the abuse you all endured… the experiments that were conducted on you?"

"Do you remember?"

"I'm not from the home—I grew up in Demos."

"Then how do you know any of this?"

"My predecessor told me, but as part of me taking this job I had to agree never to discuss anything with the survivors."

"Survivors? What are you talking about?"

"Not here," she says. She takes my hand and directs us towards the medical ward.

Brea is sitting alone at the front station when we enter.

"You're back? You've only been gone a little over two hours. I thought you two weren't due back for at least another four," she says as we head towards the empty isolation room.

"Demmer got what he needed on the ride," Nex says, sliding the door open. "Don't bother us unless it's an emergency."

Nex pulls the curtain closed before shutting the door and locking it.

"Brea is a nosey piece of work, so if we keep our voices down she won't hear us," Nex says as she slides to the floor at the far end of the room by the shower.

"Okay, we're out of the hallway. Now talk," I say, growing impatient.

"Myr was desperate to get people back out onto the surface, so it was decided that those who had relatives who survived the apocalypse would make the best subjects to try experimental anti-radiation drugs on," Nex says, pulling her knees up to her chest. "Myr felt that since they were already predisposed to the contaminant, it would be easier. Plus, if anyone died from the tests, no one would think anything of it. They'd chalk it up to more post-war casualties."

"How long had that been going on?" I ask as I sit beside her.

"Not until your generation came along," she says weakly. "The governing body wanted to wait until they had a good supply of healthy candidates before they tried to poison them."

"And the compound leaders were aware of this?"

"Yes, as were the squad leaders. They're the ones who selected the kids for testing. If the child survived, when they reached eighteen they were transferred to that specific compound and squad, and their medical files from the abandonment home were erased or modified."

"Did this happen to all the kids? Keegan, Cody, and Grimm also?"

"Unfortunately yes. It's how the antitoxin Cymatilis was discovered."

"And Wavern?" I ask, leaning my head against the wall and looking towards the ceiling as tears start to flow at the lies that have been fed to all of us our entire lives.

"You were his favorite," she says. She starts to shake, but I can't tell if it's from emotion, stress, or guilt. "When it was his turn to conduct the testing, you were his one and only pick."

"But I thought Keegan had been experimented on too."

"He was, just not by Wavern. It wasn't until a year later that Wavern decided to take him. By that point Keegan had become almost uncontrollable. The squad leader who had originally selected him didn't want him anymore."

"How old were we when they started these experiments?"

"Thirteen," she says, swallowing hard.

I grow nauseated. "It wasn't just testing that was done on me, was it?"

She takes my hand and squeezes it. "No, Sara, there was more, and not just to you. Several others were abused—mainly the girls, though," she says, turning to look at me. "You're Wavern's favorite even to this day. He was so angry when you hooked up with Keegan, I thought he was going to kill you. That's when he began sneaking Casey into the compound. I think he uses her as a substitute for you since you're both the same age."

"I think I'm going to be sick."

"You'd been so cooperative at the home that he was under the impression you'd still be that way when you got here. He was shocked when you didn't comply."

"How do you know all this?" I ask, growing anxious.

"By the time you came to the compound I was the doctor in charge, so I had to know your history. All of it."

"I don't think I can hear any more of this," I say as I get to my feet.

Nex grabs my arm, halting my progress. "Haven't you always been curious as to why during all this time you've been sleeping with Keegan, you've never gotten pregnant?"

"Please stop," I beg, my heart sinking.

"He forced me to do it," she says. "He didn't want anyone finding out what he'd been doing to you all those years before you actually got here."

"Nex, please, no more," I plead, trembling. Nex ignores me.

"It was only the one time but he was terrified it would happen again, so he had me sterilize you."

My throat closes, and I collapse to my knees.

"You'd only been in the compound for two weeks when he found out you were pregnant with his child," Nex mutters. "No one else knew, not even Andra."

"Why don't I remember any of that?" I ask, my face soaked with tears.

"Because I made you forget. There's a procedure we can perform on the soldiers to alter or erase specific memories. We're given the option of doing this if the soldiers are severely traumatized and can no longer perform their duties. It allows them to go back to life as if nothing happened. They probably used this technique in the abandonment home, so none of you would recall the experiments or abuse."

I feel drained… and numb.

"When did you erase those memories?" I ask.

"A little over two years ago, when you started seeing Keegan."

I stumble over to the toilet and throw up. I don't have a lot in my stomach, so I mainly dry heave until the feeling passes.

"He said I earned my immortality," I mumble as I sit back and hang my head.

"Who said that?" Nex asks, coming over to me with a glass of water to rinse my mouth with.

"Wavern. He put a mark on my body here," I say, pushing my hair back and showing her the raised skin, "so that when I died I'd meet the Arliss, who would make me immortal. I'd always return to this world no matter what."

"So, that's how you really got the tattoo on your wrist? The Arliss gave it to you?"

I nod.

"And Cody?"

"Yes, only he's not Cody any longer."

She puts her hands to her mouth. "No," she gasps. "We have to kill him."

"Not yet," I say hurriedly. "There's something I need to take care of first."

"What?"

"You'll know when you hear about it."

I hand her the glass, wipe my face on a towel, and exit the isolation room. Brea opens the divider for me since Nex is still sitting on the floor, probably too emotionally exhausted to move. I know I am, but I have something that needs to be dealt with before I breakdown. I stand in front of Andra's door, hesitating. She'll question why I'm back already, but I think with the information I have to tell her she won't care. At least I hope she won't. Anything is possible with her. I take a deep breath before knocking on her door. It takes a few moments before she answers, and when she does she scowls at me. She opens her mouth to reprimand me but I hold up my hand, stopping her.

"I remember who branded me with the spider tattoo," I say.

She smiles and steps to the side so I can enter her apartment.

Fourteen

Andra paces her living room as she tries to locate Wavern, who's apparently not with his squad on patrol in Demos. I sit nervously on her couch, still shaking from the conversation I had with Nex. All I want to do at the moment is go to my quarters, but Andra is keeping me at her place until she's sure of Wavern's location. Andra was shocked to hear that Wavern is a child of a Nathair since she, as well as the rest of us, thought they'd been neutralized when the Arliss was killed.

Andra sat in stunned silence as I explained the markings to her, especially when I showed her the one that sent me to the plateau. I even told her how Cody received his. When I was done she asked about the Arliss, but I told her he was still trapped down there and how he was trying to figure out how to return to our world. She asks why he just doesn't come back like Cody and I did, so I explain to her that he needs a viable host in order for that to happen and he's never found one. She takes action immediately.

"I don't care what time it is!" Andra screams into her radio. "Wake the governing body! We have an emergency situation on our hands!" She flips channels, returning to the one she's using to talk to Jules. "Have you found him yet?"

"No. I have a couple from the team scouring hideouts in the Factory. Even though it's on lockdown there are still several ways to get inside," Jules replies.

"Call me the minute you find him!"

"Yes, ma'am."

Andra sits across from me. "And there isn't anything else you remember from that day? Like why you ran into Lymont?" she asks.

"No, I only recall what happened after the bomb dropped. Nothing from before."

"Yet you're certain Wavern marked you," she says, sounding skeptical.

"Yes, he told me he did. Also, Cody and I aren't the only ones he's done this to."

"Oh? Who else?"

"The woman from the Factory commercials—she has the spider on her left wrist as well. I caught it the other day while watching the display in my apartment when a commercial came on for the memorial."

"Does Demmer know about any of this?"

"No, just you."

"Good," she says, smiling. "Why don't you go back to your quarters, Sara? You look exhausted."

I nod, get up from the couch, and head down the two levels to get to my section of the barracks. I'm about to reach for the doorknob when I notice the door to the apartment next to mine is slightly ajar. It's the same residence I went into to swap out the screens, but I distinctly remember shutting the door. I step over to it and place my hand on the wood, forcing it open. Moans of pleasure fill the apartment, emanating from the master bedroom. I tiptoe over to the door, which is partially open. I hide along the wall with the bathroom so I'm not noticed, and that's when I see it… Wavern's hands on Casey's hips, guiding her movements up and down his member as they both sigh heavily.

I slip back into the hallway, making sure to pull the door completely shut before I go over to the communicator on the wall and call Andra directly. She tells me to go into my apartment as she'll send someone down shortly to arrest him. I hurry into my quarters and partially close the door, leaving it open far enough that I can see what happens. Moments later, Grimm rushes down the stairs with a few from his squad following right behind. He rams the door to the apartment, which causes Casey to shriek and Wavern to yell. Heated words are exchanged between Grimm and Wavern, followed by the sound of punches being thrown. I open my door the rest of the way and watch as Casey is escorted from the premises, half-naked and still fumbling to get her clothes on. Grimm has Wavern's hands bound behind his back, a sheet wrapped around his waist. Wavern has a bloody nose and an eye on the verge of swelling. Grimm is favoring his right hand and I notice his knuckles are scraped.

I glare at Wavern as he passes, our eyes locking. A vein in his neck bulges and he grinds his teeth. I want him to know I turned him in, to show him

I'm not afraid, and that he's going to pay dearly for what he's done. Grimm has one of his soldiers take over Wavern's escort as he stops by my door.

"Are you all right?" he asks softly.

"I'm fine," I respond, my gaze continuing to track Wavern as he climbs the stairs.

He continues to glare at me until he's out of view.

"Did you always suspect Wavern was the one responsible for the tattoo on your wrist?"

"No," I say as my eyes focus on Grimm. "I figured it out when Cody showed up with it after the incident in Virtus."

"Cody has it?"

I nod. "I noticed it when he tried to break my wrist," I say, showing Grimm the bruises.

I can tell he's about to ask more questions, so I abruptly turn and close the door on him. I enter the bathroom, crawl into the tub, and turn the shower on. I don't care that my clothes are going to be soaked or that my bandages will get wet, I just need to feel clean. After about a half hour I pull myself out, dry off, and put on dry bandages and clean clothes. I have to let the sling hang on the towel rod to dry so I can wear it again. The covers of the bed feel rough as I get under them, but I know it's simply my imagination. Sleep will evade me, so I lie in the dark and try not to dwell on what Nex disclosed to me, no matter how difficult that becomes.

Keegan brings me breakfast when he returns in the morning, as I refuse to leave the apartment. Word has traveled rapidly about Wavern's arrest, and the reason for it. Now everyone knows I'm marked with the Arliss symbol, but that was inevitable. Keegan tries to pump me for information on how it was determined that Wavern was the one responsible. Apparently Andra neglected to reveal to anyone that I was the person who turned him in, which she probably did as a way to protect me from any sympathizers he may have. I wonder why she's now watching out for me, when she had no qualms about murdering me only days ago.

Jules, who's now been placed in command of the squad, comes to collect Keegan after several hours. He goes reluctantly since they're working the control center for the afternoon, and being shorthanded will make the task a little difficult.

"He'll be in lookout number four in case you need him," Jules says before closing the door.

I curl up on the couch with the blanket tucked around me, watching the Daily Slate for a few minutes before changing channels only to turn the display off. There's a soft knock on the front door, but I don't bother getting up to answer it. Andra enters with a bleak look on her face. She sits on the edge of the coffee table and leans slightly forward.

"I thought you'd want to know what's been decided regarding Wavern and Casey," she says. "The governing body is taking this situation very seriously, and it's been determined that they'll receive the harshest punishment allowed." She swallows a lump in her throat before continuing. "At sundown tonight, they will be executed publicly in the plaza in Demos."

"Good," I utter.

"The traditional way is by firing squad, which will be made up of the squad leaders of Rinku," she says. "Everyone who isn't working will be required to attend. Myr wants to make sure their deaths are a lesson to all who try to bring the Arliss back."

"I want to see him first," I say as I push the blanket off.

"It's not normally allowed, but I'll have them make this one exception."

I turn the plasma back on to check the time: fourteen-hundred hours. Sundown is listed to occur just after eighteen-hundred hours, giving me four hours to pull myself together to face him.

"I'll call for you in an hour and we'll go together," she says as she stands. "I'll have Grimm drive us since he'll need to be there anyway." She pats my arm before leaving, then stops just as she's opening the door. "I don't think I need to tell you the importance of you remaining silent about all of this. I know the real reason you blame Wavern is because of what's been done to you and some of the others. Breathe a word of it to anyone and your fate will match his."

I feel violated all over again. I have no intention of bringing up my abuse to anyone, but being told that leaking such knowledge will get me executed sickens and saddens me. How can anyone live in a society where people treat each other this way? This is exactly why I ran in the first place. Was it always like this, or just after the war? Once Cody is dead, I'm leaving the compound and everything else behind me. I don't care if I have to traverse the entire planet to find a place far away from this life, but I'm not staying here any longer than I have to.

I'm still in my pajamas, so before Andra returns I change into a simple black tank top and pants, brush my hair, and pull it back into a ponytail. I no longer care if anyone sees the markings on my neck. I'll simply blame Wavern for them. I return to the bedroom and remove the hunting knife from the pack at the bottom of my locker. I don't plan on using it, but I no longer feel safe leaving unarmed. I slip it into my belt behind my back and hide it under the top. I then take a few cameras and stuff them in my pocket so I can place them on my way to the garage. This might be the only chance I get to pass through the control center for a long time. Who knows when I'll ever be allowed back to normal duties?

When Andra arrives, she informs me that Grimm will meet us in the garage, as he first needs to make sure his squad is taking care of things in the kitchen and mess hall. We take the tunnel from the barracks directly into the mess hall. I hadn't placed any cameras in here yet, so I slip one from my pocket and discreetly adhere it to the doorway for the tunnel into the control center. I manage to place a couple more on the satellite controls workstation in the center. Neither of us speaks as we make the journey to the garage. Grimm has the ATV waiting for us, so I climb in the back and Andra takes the front passenger seat.

They talk quietly as we go, while I contemplate exactly what I'm going to say to Wavern. Thankfully I've got several hours to figure it out. I catch Grimm glancing at me in the rearview mirror every so often, but I try to ignore him. Maybe this is another reason I hold leaving the abandonment home against him. He left me at the hands of Wavern, but he wouldn't have known what was going on. Even if he had, he doesn't remember—his squad leader would've made sure of that. There's no point in dwelling on my feelings for Grimm, as they were burnt away with his brutal, callous words to me.

The Demos parking pad is full of transports, making it almost impossible to fit all the vehicles into the spaces available. Grimm drops Andra and me at the entrance and decides to park the vehicle down a ways in the tunnel. Andra informs him before he leaves that he's to meet the other leaders, along with Myr and the rest of the governing body, in front of the meeting hall in Zone B. There, he'll be given instructions on how the execution is to progress and where he'll need to stand in the plaza.

Andra directs me through the dome entrance and then over to Zone B where we take one of the stone paths to the very back of the section, coming upon a small brick structure that's only feet away from the force field produced by the Occlyn Ring. The guard at the door steps aside and allows us entry, then takes his position in a small waiting room with a lone couch and plasma screen displaying the Daily Slate.

"Casey has already been moved to the plaza, so you'll be meeting Wavern alone. Now, are you sure you want to do this?" Andra asks before opening the door that'll take me to his cell.

"Yes. I need to," I reply, trying not to sound terrified.

She pulls open the door and I step into a small vestibule in front of the containment cells. Andra closes the door behind me while I cling to the wall beside it. Wavern is pacing the cell like a nervous animal, wringing his hands.

"Did you come alone?" he asks, without stopping his movements.

"Yes," I whisper.

"Does Keegan know you're here?"

"No, only Andra and Grimm know. Also, Keegan doesn't know anything about what you did to me other than the marking."

"I didn't do anything you didn't want me to," Wavern says, finally stopping and staring at me.

"I was a kid!" I scream.

"Not according to our laws. You came of age when you turned sixteen."

"You began raping me at thirteen!" I holler as I take a step closer to the cell. "How could you do that to me?"

"I wasn't the only one," he snaps. "There were several squad leaders taking advantage of a few of the kids, while the others beat the shit out of them."

"That didn't make it right," I say. "I looked up to you, Wavern. I trusted you and you do this to me?"

"We didn't know any better!" he yells. "Haron let us do whatever the hell we wanted. She didn't give a shit. She hated being there and held it against all of you, which made it easier for us to get away with it. The governing body didn't care either. They only wanted us to find the antitoxin that would allow us to return to the surface."

"Why me?" I ask, my eyes filling with tears.

"You're smart, tenacious, stubborn, and beautiful. Why wouldn't I pick you?"

"You're sick."

"No, just driven to have the best," he says, cocking his head. "Did Andra tell you all of this? Is that how it came up? You two conspiring against me?"

"No, someone else divulged your secret."

"Nex," he says, seething. "That bitch will pay for her wild mouth."

"I think she's paid enough with the guilt that's been eating at her all these years, especially when you had her get rid of my pregnancy."

"I had to!" he shouts. "Do you know what would've happened to me if people found out I knocked up a fifteen-year-old? I'd have been ostracized, made to live and work in the farms under the Factory like a criminal. Never able to see or be with you again. It wouldn't have been a big deal if you were sixteen but, no, you had to get pregnant at fifteen."

"Fuck you, Wavern! This is all your fault, not mine! You're no better than the Arliss! You do whatever you want and don't give a damn about what it does to other people."

He starts to laugh. "Yet no one will ever find out what I did to you, or what any of the other squad leaders did, whether it's the abuse or the testing, because you've been ordered to keep your trap shut, or your punishment will be the same as mine," he says, then slides up to the metal bars and wraps his hands around them. "I'm hoping you open your fucking mouth so we can be together in the Fomorian Plateau. Oh, the things I could get away with down there—and you'd never escape me. Never."

"The joke's on you, asshole," I say, taking another step closer and folding my arms over my chest. "With the Arliss topside there isn't a way into the plateau, so you'll be heading straight to hell where you belong."

"Who fed you that lie?" he asks, gripping the bars so tight his knuckles turn white.

"The Arliss mentioned it as a way to threaten me into obeying him, in case I had any ideas of self-destructing again." I turn around and head for the door. "Cody will be dead by tonight, hours after you of course, so you'll miss your chance to join the Arliss," I say, with a giggle that's mainly driven by my nerves. "You lose, Wavern."

He screams at me as I push the door open and rejoin Andra. We walk quietly towards the plaza where everyone has started to gather. She has me sit on a bench at the edge of Zone B near the square while she looks for Demmer and Myr. I smile to myself, knowing this nightmare might almost be over. I still have the Pheles inside me and Keegan to deal with, but one thing at a time. First the execution, then kill Cody and escape the compound to find the portal into the plateau, followed by destroying it and killing Keegan. Then I'll be free from it all. I'm sure if Keegan were to die now, just like the Arliss, he'd be sent to the plateau because his symbol is on the Degrem Stone, and I can't take them both on at once. The Arliss will be a lot easier to defeat on his home turf since Keegan changed me into one of his own, so one devil at a time it will have to be.

Trumpets ring out from the speakers attached to the light posts and buildings. Hundreds exit from the residential zones and I force myself through the crowds as they fill the square, blocking me. I need to be at the front to see Wavern die close up, and I'm hoping he dies as slowly as possible. A temporary fence has been erected around the pool, which has now been drained, the fountain turned off, and is currently descending into a subterranean level. A few moments after it's out of sight, a platform rises in its place, Wavern and Casey in the center, wearing white hospital garb. The two are bolted to a brick wall that rises at least two feet above their heads and which wraps partially around the platform. Casey is bawling as she tries to pull her hands free of the constraints. Wavern, however, is glaring right at me.

Heavy footsteps echo from the back of the wall as all ten squad leaders from Rinku, including Jules, move around the platform and into position. The trumpets stop and are replaced by Myr's voice, but I have no idea where she's speaking from.

"Citizens and soldiers, it's a dark day when two very prominent members of our community have been convicted of treason," she says, her voice not wavering. "Once again we've been placed in a position where our survival has been threatened by those who follow the Arliss. Let everyone here today bear witness that no one is above the law and that there are dire consequences for betraying the world that's raised, clothed, fed, and sheltered you. Leaders of Rinku, ready your weapons."

The ten remove guns from the holsters around their thighs.

"Aim…"

Casey screams in terror, her face going pale as she realizes she's about to die.

"Fire!"

Five bullets hit Casey in the head and chest, killing her instantly. The other five hit Wavern in the abdomen, leaving him alive.

"Cowards," Wavern tries to cry out as blood seeps from his wounds and pain paints his face. "If you really wanted me dead you would've aimed for my head. You're all pathetic."

Jules steps forward from the group. "Our aim was on purpose, asshole. There's someone here who deserves the right to take your life, and it's not us."

The leaders for Squads One and Six open a gap in the fence and wave for me to come over. I slowly move through the crowd, many of them parting to give me an unobstructed path. When I'm through the gap Jules takes my hand, helps me step up into the pool, leads me a few feet in front of Wavern, and places the gun in my left hand.

"He's all yours," Jules says.

"Wait, why?" I ask. I break out in a sweat from being so exposed in front of both compounds, especially since this entire ordeal is being broadcast on the Daily Slate for those who couldn't leave their posts, and the entire city, many of whom are here.

Jules leans in to whisper. "You earned it," he says before stepping back in line with the others.

A cold chill radiates down my spine since those are the same words Wavern used when he had the Arliss make me immortal. Is Jules another Nathair, or does he know what happened to me at the home? How'd he get the other leaders to go along with this?

Wavern starts laughing, which causes his muscles to spasm. "She doesn't have the guts," he mutters, then narrows his eyes. "Sara would never hurt me; she needs me too much."

I get to where I'm only inches away from him, close my eyes, and pull the Pheles forward. When I reveal it to him, his mouth falls open and his face grows white.

I place the gun against his forehead as I recall the red from my irises. "Goodbye, Wavern. I hope you enjoy Hell."

I pull the trigger and his blood spatter soaks me. Jules orders someone to bring me a towel. I clean myself up as best I can, hand the gun back to Jules, and step back into the crowd. No one says a word to me as I make my way to the parking pad. I want to hang my head in shame, but somehow I'm holding it higher than I've ever done before. However, when I enter the parking pad, I wander off to a corner as the weight of the day finally hits. I ball myself up against the stone of the mountain and cry.

Fifteen

It seems like I've been waiting for hours before Grimm finally emerges from the city to take us back to Rinku. Andra is staying behind since Myr has some questions that need answering, so it'll just be the two of us riding back. I lean my head against the doorframe as Grimm drives. He has a concerned look on his face when he glances at me, but I don't ask why— I'm too exhausted to care. After an hour, Jules' words return and I shiver.

"What's the matter?" Grimm asks when he notices.

"Why did you all decide to allow me to kill Wavern?" I ask, finally looking at him.

"Jules asked us to."

"Why? What did he say to convince you?"

"Does it matter now? Wavern's dead, so it's over." Grimm reaches over and tugs at my left arm, taking it out of my lap and flipping it palm up. "If you must know, that's why," he says, pointing to the spider hidden beneath the bruise.

"I don't believe you," I say, pulling my arm back.

"Why not?" he asks, sounding a little upset.

"Because of what Jules said to me… he said I earned it. I earned the right to kill Wavern."

"What's wrong with him saying that?"

"It's the way he said it," I say as I focus back on the road and adjust the sling on my shoulder since it's slipped down.

"What aren't you telling me?" Grimm asks, irritated.

"Nothing, just forget I asked."

I lean my head back against the doorframe and try to hide the tears that are filling my eyes.

"Jules told us that Wavern had been hurting you for years, violently at times," Grimm admits after quite a bit of time has passed.

"How'd he find out?" I ask, swallowing my emotions.

"He caught Wavern beating you a few years ago, around the time you began seeing Keegan. Your injuries were pretty severe, from what he told us. Jules threatened to go to Andra with what he saw if Wavern didn't back down and leave you alone, but Wavern didn't. When Jules caught him again, he had to break Wavern's arm to get him to stop. Andra got involved and the beatings ended," Grimm says. "That's what Jules told us, anyway."

If only it were that easy, I think to myself.

The memory of those two particularly violent incidents had hidden themselves very well but they finally reach out from the recesses of my mind. But there are plenty more in between where Wavern didn't hurt me as badly. He pounded on me as often as he could when he discovered I'd started seeing Keegan. I never knew why he reacted in such a way, so at the time I just chalked it up to stress, but now I know the real reason. He would've seen it as a betrayal, though my memories were altered by that time, so I still have little recollection of our sick relationship. I vaguely remember Jules walking in on us, him having to pull Wavern off me, and then taking me to the medical ward to be stitched up. He gave Nex the excuse that I'd fallen down the stairs. Since the sharp, grated metal covers the compound floor everywhere, it was believable, and so she bought it. Or at least she pretended to. I'm sure she suspected what had actually happened, but because of her position she couldn't disclose anything.

Maybe that's why I took to Keegan so readily. I saw him as a protector, someone who would stand up to anyone trying to hurt me. I'm kind of surprised I managed to block such horrid memories, but with the Arliss wiping them out earlier I'm glad they didn't resurface until now.

We pull into the garage and I get out while he parks, wanting to walk back to the compound alone, but Grimm hurries to catch up. He doesn't say anything, though the expression on his face tells me differently. When we get to the fork I go left, towards the medical ward.

"Why are you going that way?" Grimm asks.

"I need some pain medication," I say, and I gesture to my right arm.

He doesn't say anything as I keep walking, but I sense him watching. When I know he can no longer see me, I place a couple of cameras along the tunnel as I go as well as under the counter to the front desk Nex is standing at when I enter. She looks like how I feel: horrible.

"Ready?" she asks.

"Is he awake?"

"No, but I can have him woken up if you want."

I nod my head, so she calls Macom to meet us in the second isolation room. I'm surprised she wants a witness to what we're about to do, but I'm sure she has her reasons. Macom pulls the curtain and door closed before stepping over to Cody's side. I spot restraints on his wrists and ankles, anchored directly to the floor and not the bed.

"Remember what we discussed, Macom," Nex says sternly. "This is for the safety of everyone."

"I understand," she says confidently.

"Wake him," Nex orders.

Macom takes the injector she brought in with her and injects something into Cody's neck. His eyelids flicker before finally opening. He looks dazed as he glances around the room, noticing all our faces, but focusing on mine when he comes across it.

"Hello, Sara," he says darkly. "To what do I owe the pleasure of your company?"

I pull the knife from my waistband, gripping it tightly in front of me. "I have some questions for you," I say coolly.

"And is that little toy of yours supposed to intimidate me into answering?" he asks, glowering.

"No. It's purely for my amusement," I say, and I step towards the head of his bed.

Macom and Nex back away, but remain close enough in case I may need them.

"You can't kill me, you know," the Arliss says, gritting his teeth.

"Perhaps, but I can kill Cody," I reply, placing the blade against his cheek. "Which will send you back to the plateau. And without me there, you'll never find a viable host that'll allow you to resurface."

"I have my followers," he says. "They'll provide for me."

I slash him across the face, but it's not a deep cut. "And who would those be?"

"You already know," he utters.

"Casey and Wavern, correct?" I ask, and I take his hand and turn it until it's palm up as best I can before driving the knife into his wrist and cutting vertically.

He screams as blood soaks the sheets. I glance up and notice that Macom looks to be on the verge of collapse, so Nex hurries over and escorts her to the bathroom at the back of the room.

"Bitch!" he hollers, spit flying from his mouth. "You're going to pay for this."

"I already did," I say as I nick his neck.

"Where's Wavern? There's no way in hell he'd allow you to do this to me."

"He won't be joining us, considering he died several hours ago," I say, smiling. "Oh, and so did Casey."

Cody's eyes grow wide. "How's that possible?" he asks, startled.

I lean forward so our faces are close. "Wavern fucked with the wrong girl," I say, then plunge the knife into his chest.

The Arliss gurgles as blood flows down his lips, followed by his head lolling to the side and Cody's life expiring. I wipe the blood from the weapon onto my shirt just as Nex and Macom return.

"I'll take care of the body," Nex says. "Give Macom your clothes and I'll have you return to your quarters in hospital scrubs."

"What are you going to do with them?"

"The same thing I'll do with the body… burn them," Nex says before opening the door and stepping out.

Macom goes into the cabinet along the wall and hands me the scrubs. I quickly change, hand her my blood-spattered clothes after removing the few remaining cameras I have in the pocket, and tuck the bloody knife into my boot. Before going back to my quarters, I place the remaining cameras around the rest of the medical ward, making sure to leave one in Cody's room. I automatically go to the scanner before I remember they'd deactivated it, but am surprised to discover that my access has been reactivated. I guess killing my former leader proves I'm a trustworthy enough person now.

When I'm back in the apartment I wash the weapon in the bathroom sink, take a quick shower, and put on something to sleep in. I'm in the process of turning off the lights when Keegan comes in and rushes up to me, pulling me to his chest.

"How do you feel?" he asks as he rocks me.

"Vindicated," I reply.

He kisses the top of my head and squeezes me hard.

"Cody's dead," I mumble. "I killed him."

Keegan pulls away, but keeps holding onto my arms. "The Arliss has been sent back to the plateau?" he asks with glee.

I nod.

Keegan kisses me as he directs me towards the bedroom, stripping our clothes off as we go. Every touch of his skin against mine feels like a match trying to light, and when it does there's no stopping the inferno.

"All available personnel, please report to the medical ward," Andra's voice rings out, waking us up. "This is not a drill. All available personnel report to the medical ward immediately."

"What time is it?" I ask as Keegan and I throw on some clothes.

He runs into the living room. "Just after five in the morning," he calls out.

We head into the hallway, red lights flashing all around us. When we reach the top level, the entire floor is filled with smoke that fans embedded into the ceiling are venting out. The smell of charred flesh is heavy and gives me an instant headache. We push our way through the crowd and stop when we notice the smoke-covered dividing wall. The coat of grit from the smoke is so thick we can't see to the other side. I wouldn't have thought that Nex would burn Cody's body right here in the ward. Why would she do something so stupid?

"Open the door!" someone shouts. "The fire should be out now."

Keegan places his hand on the scanner and the wall opens. Clouds of smoke and ash rush towards us as we slowly make our way into the remains of the isolation section of the medical ward. I'm forced to cover my nose with my shirt so I can breathe, as the smell of burnt meat is overwhelming. The vents in the ceiling are turned up to full power to try to clear the lingering smoke. When it begins to subside, we see that the room Cody was in is nothing but melted glass, cinders, and a charcoal-black body lying on what remains of the bed. As I stumble around I notice that nothing is wet, even though each compartment has a series of sprinklers to keep any fire from consuming the entire compound.

"Why didn't the sprinklers go off?" someone behind me asks as more people filter into the ward.

"Better question for you," Keegan begins, "why are the hazmat doors closed?" He points to the sealed heavy metal door, which had been closed on Wavern and me upon my return from Lymont.

"They should've remained open," someone comments, "to allow escape."

"Over here," another person chimes in over by the nurses' station.

I run towards it and scream when I see what the discovery is.

Two more burnt bodies lie among the ruins, and I know immediately they're Nex and Macom.

"Stop her!" someone shouts as Brea bolts into the room.

I grab her just as she sees the remains, and her shriek almost shatters my eardrums. Jules takes her from me and has to drag her from the scene.

"I need everyone except the squad leaders to return to their quarters immediately," Andra says as she enters. "As of right now, this compound is on lockdown."

Keegan and I go back to our apartment as instructed, but it's not long until Jules comes to collect Keegan to assist with damage assessment and cleanup.

"Do they know how the fire started yet?" I ask, even though I assume it's too soon.

"No, but Andra is having us work on that as well while Squad Two removes the remains. The bodies will be transported to Quarn for examination. Grimm has taken lead on that," Jules replies. "Everyone else is confined to the barracks with the exception of Squads Nine and Ten, as they're still at the Factory, and Squad Three since they're handling the control center and lookouts for the day."

"I'll see you later, babe," Keegan says before kissing me and leaving with Jules.

I'm rattled by how Nex allowed that fire to get so out of control, but there's something bothering me about the whole thing. I go into the bedroom and remove the tablet from the pack, turning it on as I return to the living room and sit on the couch. The device automatically links to the additional cameras I spread throughout, but the ones for the medical ward are showing nothing but static. I spot a tab at the top of the images that appears to hold recordings of whatever the cameras picked up when the tablet was off. I tap on it and select the ones for the medical ward, but nothing shows; it's still only static. Those cameras should've at least picked up something, like me leaving the ward after placing them, but there isn't anything on here.

I check the recordings of the other cameras just before the fire, in case there was an issue with the entire connection, but they were all functioning normally. I tap on the camera for the tunnel between the medical ward and the barracks. I can't see what's happening inside the isolation section, only that it suddenly fills with smoke followed by a bright red flash as fire engulfs everything at once. I switch to the one I placed by the heavy metal door leading into isolation. It captures the door descending, but I can't see what's happening on the other side before being blocked off completely. I return to the live feed but the majority of the rooms are empty, with the exception of the control center since that still needs to function like normal.

I go back to the camera in the tunnel between the ward and barracks, but I turn time back to the moment the recordings started. When I select play I spot Nex going into the medical ward with several old texts in her hands nearly an hour after I put the camera into position. I pause the video and zoom in, noticing that the texts appear to be extremely old. It makes me wonder if these are the ones her grandmother used to bring the Arliss back to life. Why would she have them, and what's she going to do with them? I hit play and the video continues, but since I didn't have any cameras in the isolation section at the time I lose what she did with them when the divider closes. I wonder if they're still in the medical ward, or if they've been burnt to ash like everything else.

"Hello, Sara," a familiar voice says behind me.

I freeze in my seat, too terrified to move. Fingers brush the back of my neck, causing me to shiver.

"Oh, how I've missed you," he says, his hot breath touching my ear. "Where's your husband?"

"Why do you want to know?" I ask as my throat tenses up.

"Because I need to know if I'm going to be interrupted or not."

"He'll be back in a few minutes," I answer hastily.

"You're such a horrible liar. That's something we'll need to work on… together."

I close my eyes and hope I'm hallucinating, but when I open them Wavern is standing in front of me. He places a hand under my chin, lifting my face up to meet his.

"You don't look happy to see me," he says.

"How…how are you alive?"

"A dear friend of ours made sure my death looked real enough to fool everyone."

"That's not possible," I mumble, and start to shake.

"Anything is possible if you know the right people, and the right words. I assure you I was well protected from any actual harm."

"It was Nex, wasn't it? She used those texts of hers, didn't she?"

Wavern kneels in front of me. "And all it cost her was her life," he replies. "Such a waste of course, but she chose to save me and I did thank her for that. She didn't appreciate the gesture, though, so I made her suffer before incinerating her and Macom."

"How did she interpret the antiquated symbols? Her grandmother fucked those up, so how is she possibly an expert?"

"She had the Arliss translate it all. It's amazing what you can do to someone when they're under the influence of the right combination of drugs," he says, sliding his hands up my thighs. "He had no idea what was happening to him. The amount of information those texts contained was insurmountable."

"Where are they now?"

He taps his head. "In here, where no one else can obtain the knowledge—not even you."

"Where's the Arliss?"

"Trapped in hell where he belongs."

"He's dead?"

"Yes and no," Wavern says with a grin. "You see, Nex could only do so much with those texts of hers to assist in my survival. I needed the Arliss for the rest, and you provided him to me as planned." Wavern puts a hand to my cheek. "He's a part of me now, and gave me abilities I didn't think were possible. I can't wait to show you what I can do."

"What do you want with me?" I ask, trying to hold back the tears that are desperately trying to spring forth.

"All in good time," he says before leaning forward and kissing me, practically forcing his tongue down my throat. "But for now, I've other things to take care of." He snaps his fingers and vanishes.

I sit immobilized for a few minutes as I try to comprehend what just happened, but my mind can't process it all. How could Nex do this? I thought she hated Wavern as much as I did, so she must have just been pretending. I bet she told me all those things to get me to turn on Wavern so I would give him away. It was probably all planned like this from the beginning. What could the Arliss do that Wavern now has control over? Is there anything Keegan or I can do as a Pheles to stop him?

I toss the tablet aside and head into the hallway to call Andra from the communicator, but after several minutes she still doesn't answer. I dread the worst, so I head up to her apartment and pound on the door. Still no answer, and when I try the doorknob it's locked. I have to kick in the door, and when I enter I see why she didn't answer.

Andra is lying on her back on the floor, her eyes wide open, a look of horror frozen on her face. Wavern twisted Andra's neck around so she's facing her back. I rush over to her communicator and select the compound-wide broadcast.

"Medical emergency in Andra's apartment!" I holler as loud as possible. "Keegan, get up here!"

I hear doors fly open from the level below and feet rush up the stairs. A mob of people tries to gain access to the apartment, but I keep them at bay for as long as possible until Jules and Keegan arrive. The squad leaders order everyone back to the barracks so they can properly assess what happened. I'm the only one allowed to remain since I discovered her, but I insist that Keegan stay. I hold his hand tightly as Jules pulls me aside while the others examine and cover the body.

"What happened?" he asks.

"Wavern... he's alive," I say, my voice cracking with fright.

"Are you kidding me?" Jules asks.

I shake my head and squeeze Keegan's hand tighter.

"How?" Jules asks.

"Nex did it. She used the Arliss to bring Wavern back."

"The Arliss is dead, Sara."

"No, he wasn't," I say, dropping my head. "He was in Cody. The Arliss took possession of him while we were in Virtus."

"I don't understand," Jules says, confused.

I tell him everything that happened, including why I ran into Lymont, leaving out the abuse and experimentation from the home, and that Keegan is a Pheles. Jules has to step away for a few minutes, whether to be sick or punch something, or someone, I can't tell. He goes over to the other leaders and discusses Andra's death with them, along with Wavern's return. They decide that the leaders want everyone armed no matter where in the compound they are, and that there'll be increased security presence in all the tunnels including the one leading into the Aslu Territory.

"If a firing squad didn't kill him last time, what makes you think our weapons will work now?" one of the squad leaders asks.

"I don't know if they will, but at least it'll give everyone a chance to slow him down if nothing else," Jules says before turning to me. "Where are those monitors you found?"

"This way," I say, pointing towards the door between the screens showing the Daily Slate for Rinku and the one that once belonged to Virtus.

The door is locked, so Keegan has to force it open. I step over to the wall on the left and open it, revealing the monitors, all of which have been smashed.

"Do you know where she kept the controls for the satellites?" Keegan asks.

"No. She launched the nuke for the abandonment home from here, so I was assuming she did the same thing when she sent one after me."

"If Wavern did this, there's no telling if he managed to obtain the controls for the satellites from Andra before he killed her or not," Jules says.

"We need to alert Demmer," Keegan says.

"I'll handle that. You two get to the firing range. That's where Squad Five will be handing out all weapons," Jules says as we leave the office.

Since word hasn't spread about the order to collect our weapons, Keegan and I are practically the first in line at the counter down in the range. We're given two guns with holsters, and six extra clips, each holding thirty rounds of ammunition. I want to head back to our quarters to snag the pack I have hidden, but Keegan wants to get to the garage and take an ATV into Demos. We move to the preparation room to get out of the way of the growing crowds, so I leave him standing there while I run back to the apartment. I dig out the pack, stuff whatever else I can into it, and put it on my back. As I hit the metal grating for the floor around my level, I stop. I hadn't noticed it when I first got to the floor, but now there's a gaping hole in the stairwell leading down to the other levels. The sealant has been removed and the smell of gas wafts up from below.

I bolt up the stairs as quickly as possible and am able to reach the mess hall before an explosion rips the barracks apart. I'm thrown across several tables, cutting my forehead and slamming my already-wounded right arm onto the floor, but there isn't any time to worry about the pain shooting up my arm. I cut through the control center as Squad Three tries to seal off the gas that's started leaking in the life support level. I dart down the tunnel to the preparation room and nearly collide with Keegan as he's heading towards me.

"We have to get out of here," I say, grabbing his arm and pulling him along.

Another detonation rocks the compound, this one from the control center. Dust and debris rain down on us, but we keep moving. When we're back in the preparation room, Keegan snags a survival pack while I take a couple of radios, tossing him one and shoving a couple more into my pack. We take the tunnel leading to the exit into the Aslu Territory. Keegan places his hand on the scanner for the soft-seal door, and it opens. He's about to close it when I stop him.

"Leave it open in case anyone else is able to get out," I say.

"The other door won't open if this one still is," he says. "I have to close it if we want to live."

Another explosion erupts behind us, collapsing the tunnel just beyond the door. Keegan hits the button that'll shut the door while I run to the other one. Once the door is open, Keegan and I bolt towards the mouth of the cave, but we don't get far as several Mulgrim block our path. I pull out my gun when Keegan places his hand on the barrel, stopping me from firing.

"What are you doing?" I ask as he cautiously approaches the wolves.

"Just watch," he says.

He slowly walks towards them, exposing his palms. The Mulgrim growl so I raise my weapon again, readying to fire. The beasts howl loudly, which hurts my ears, but then sit down and pull back their ears in a submissive fashion.

"What the hell?" I mutter as I holster my weapon.

"The wolves that once roamed the Kai Mountains before the war were mine to command. They still remember their master even though we've both changed over the years," Keegan says. "Come on, they won't hurt you."

"How are we able to see them?" I blurt out. "And it's not nighttime, so why are they out?"

"The red in our eyes reveal them to us, even if we're not displaying it," Keegan explains. "It's also a myth that they only roam at night. They can be more aggressive during the night, but they're out at all times of the day."

I start my approach, but they quickly get to their feet and start growling again.

"You have to show them you mean them no harm, like this," Keegan says, flashing his palms.

I change my tactic and proceed like he had. The Mulgrim sit back down and one even allows me to gently stroke its coarse fur. We continue down the tunnel with the wolves following us as the sound of additional ruptures from the compound echoes around us. The sunshine penetrates several feet into the cave, but it's so hot and blinding that we can't leave the shelter of the mountain. The Mulgrim, on the other hand, continue their way onto the barren earth.

"How long do you think until the sun is on the other side?" I ask, squinting my eyes as I try to catch a glimpse of it.

"An hour or more," Keegan replies. "We'll have to wait in here until then."

"Where do we go?" I ask as I sit on the ground against the wall. "Demos is on the other side, Lymont is destroyed, and if we get too visible out in the open Demmer could launch a bomb at us."

"The abandonment home is about four hours south of here. There's a transportation tunnel that feeds into it from both sides of the mountain. We can go there."

"Did you grab any Cymatilis?"

"No. There wasn't any on the conveyor," he says, sitting beside me. "Anyway, we won't need it. The Arliss and Pheles are immune to the radiation. I only injected myself for show."

I lean my head on his shoulder. "Do you think anyone made it out?"

"I don't know," he responds sadly.

"The day Virtus was destroyed, you were supposed to have gone to the compound, not Wavern," I say after several minutes of silence. "Why did he go in your place?"

"I was suspicious of Tennison, had been for a long time. When he requested me that day I pretended to be too ill to go, so Wavern went instead of me."

"Why were you suspicious of Tennison?"

"I could tell there was something different about him. It was a sudden change I noticed one day, but I just couldn't put my finger on it. It was the same change I spotted in you when you came back from Lymont, which is how I knew you'd met the Arliss."

"You and Wavern had the same idea of making me immortal, but I don't know why you didn't just turn me into a Pheles years ago."

"Because I needed to know where the little bastard was hiding, and the only way I could do that was if you died and became one of his first. I knew about the mark behind your ear since I first felt it long ago, but I didn't know who put it on you. I honestly thought Grimm had done it. I never would've suspected Wavern. With that mark you were guaranteed to meet the Arliss, so I used you to find him."

"Thanks, babe," I say sarcastically, irritated by the deception.

"Look, I'm sorry, but I knew you'd come back and I'd have what I needed."

I push away from him and get to my feet. "You're unbelievable," I say, simmering. "Why did you brand Grimm when you were younger?"

"Because I saw how close the two of you were getting and as you know I'm a very jealous, possessive being. I wanted him marked as my enemy for life," he says, then laughs. "And I got away with it, too."

"That was a really shitty thing to do," I snap.

"Yeah, well, it worked, didn't it? You're *my* wife, not his."

"What would happen if I just shot you right now?" I ask, leaning on the wall across from him with my arms folded over my chest.

"That depends on where you hit me. If it's a fatal shot, then I'd be sent to the Fomorian Plateau, heal, and come back good as new as you see me now. But if it's non-life-threatening, then it would just need to be cared for like any other wound. Why? Do you plan on killing me now?"

"I was just wondering," I say. "Does that only work on the Pheles, or the Arliss as well?"

"The Pheles only," he says. "The Arliss would require a new host in order to return, whereas I don't if I die a violent death. Natural causes, on the other hand, are a different story for me."

"But the plateau has to exist in order for that to work, right?"

He abruptly stands. "Why? What are you getting at?"

"I'm just trying to think of ways to stop Wavern," I say with a forced grin.

"Uh-huh," he says, cocking his head. "You know it works the same for you as well. If the plateau ceases to exist and you die, there's no returning to this world. So I'd think very carefully about whatever is rambling around in that brain of yours."

Oh, babe, I am, I think to myself.

Sixteen

We have to wait for the sun to clear the mountain peaks before stepping outside. We heard the last explosion perhaps an hour ago, but since then everything has been silent. No one has met us in the tunnel, which leads me to believe either they managed to get out through the garage, or not at all. I wonder if Jules was ever able to contact Demmer before everything went to hell. If not, then no one will know what happened until those from Squad Two try to return from Quarn, if they even made it out to begin with.

We stick close to the base of the mountain as we make our way south. I let Keegan lead since he knows the terrain better than I do. We're forced to take a break after only an hour because the wound in my forehead has reopened and my shoulder is getting stiff. Keegan bandages my cut while I take off the sling and try to work the kinks out of my muscles. I toss the useless thing aside, as it's more of a hindrance. The sutures are holding pretty well, so I'm sure I won't even need the bandages much longer. I have to dry-swallow a couple of pain pills, which almost causes me to choke, but I do get them down… roughly.

We're both dehydrated, so I'm hoping when we reach the abandonment home there's something there to drink, regardless of what it is. We haven't come across any more Mulgrim, which I find troubling. Their numbers have always been known to be substantial, so where have they gone? Maybe because there aren't any populated settlements down here they've stopped roaming in this area. My mind drastically changes when we come upon two dead Mulgrim, their necks snapped.

"I thought we were the only ones who made it out," I remark as Keegan examines the carcasses.

"I thought so, too, but maybe I was mistaken," he says, standing.

"You weren't mistaken," Wavern says, appearing out of the shadows.

I go for my gun but I'm blindsided by a force that knocks me several feet away from the safety of the mountains, causing me to wrench my ankle when I land. Wavern seizes Keegan by the throat and lifts him off his feet. Keegan grapples with his gun with one hand and tries to free himself with the other.

I attempt to reach for my gun again, when searing pain radiates up my right arm. I look down at the bullet hole in my forearm and see the bandage is soaked with blood. I remove it and notice that the stitches have vanished and the wound is open. I hold my hand against the wound to slow the blood flow as I watch to see what Wavern will do next.

"Let… go," Keegan mutters as his face turns purple.

"Not until I get what's mine," Wavern says.

"You… can't… have… Sara," Keegan groans.

"That's not what I'm talking about," Wavern says.

A glowing pulse of energy surrounds the hand around Keegan's throat. His body goes whiter and whiter, he withers, and then crumbles into dust. I'm too shocked to move or scream. Wavern saunters over to me, kneels down and grips my left hand, pulling it off the wound. He closes his eyes and when they reopen the irises are red.

"And now we're the same," he says.

"Keegan will be back," I say through clenched teeth.

"I don't think so," Wavern replies. "You see, I absorbed him, just like I'm doing to the Arliss. He's a part of me now and can never return."

"Why are you doing this?" I ask, becoming hysterical.

"For you, Sara. This is all for you. I want everything to be perfect for the two of us. And now it almost is," he says, grazing my cheek with a bloody finger. "I'll let you keep going to wherever you're trying to hide, since it makes the game that much more fun." He snaps his fingers and disappears.

I struggle to get my pack off to get at the bandages, which are at the bottom, to stop the bleeding, so I wind up using a shirt I'd packed. After tightening it around my arm, I try to focus on getting to the abandonment home. I'll lose my shit when I'm someplace safe, but I can't afford to do that here in case Demmer is watching. How did Wavern find us? Does he have a device that allows him to view the images from the satellites? I doubt it, so then how did he locate us? I find myself feeling hysterical again, so I force myself to take some deep breaths to calm myself enough to move back to the shadows of the mountains, snagging Keegan's pack and weapons as I go since they didn't dissolve with him. It takes me several minutes because of my twisted ankle, so once I'm at the base I work on stemming the flow of blood in my arm even more and then wrapping it up tightly with bandages and tape. It takes me several tries since I only have one arm to work with.

I tuck Keegan's guns into his pack, leaving the holsters behind because they're too bulky to fit inside. I put one pack on my back and another across my chest, push myself off the rock I'd been leaning against, and continue hobbling south using the rock face for support. My heart races each time I replay Keegan's death in my head and I can't get myself to stop. I know I was planning on killing him, but after Wavern's return I changed my mind. I have to find that portal and destroy the plateau; only then can Wavern possibly be stopped. When he said the Arliss was in hell, I thought it meant he'd actually killed him, but he made it sound like the creature is still alive. If he is, then he has to be trapped in the plateau. So, what do I do? Kill the Arliss or bring him back to my world to halt Wavern's madness?

I'm not sure how much time has passed, but the air starts to cool as the sun falls further behind the range. I can't stop for a break no matter how much I hurt, as I need to get to the home. I finally come upon a tall, heavy metal entrance that's partially closed. I grunt as my muscles strain to pull it open. It does eventually give way to a long corridor filled with dust and chunks of rock. Once I close the door I'm in complete darkness, so I break out one of the flashlights. The tunnel I enter is narrow, maybe one vehicle's width at most, and long. When I get to the end of the space, it opens up to a parking pad, with a few transports still sitting in their spots. I swing the flashlight around and find a set of stairs ascending to the next level. They seem to be the only way up, so I grab the railing and haul my ass along.

When I reach the top I come to a hallway flanked by two large rooms. I don't have the time to check out what used to be in them, and instead, at the end of the hallway I take another set of stairs up. These are cracked and have chunks missing, but are still passable. Upon entering the third level I find myself in another hallway, this one much longer than the one on level two. Several doors stand open along the way, allowing me a peek inside. One of the rooms on the right has bunkbeds stacked three high and placed in every available space. Discarded clothes, overturned mattresses, and shreds of burnt cloth are scattered around the floor. The room across the way has only one entry, which appears to go into a separate hallway with smaller rooms encircling it.

The next set of stairs I get to is much more damaged, and littered with pieces of charred bone. I try not to look at the remains as I make my way up, keeping my eyes focused on the light above. Air whistles past when I enter the final hallway, which is small and empties into a massive room filled with table remnants, melted glass, bone fragments, overturned couches, and piles of ash. When the bomb landed, it must not have been a direct hit, otherwise there wouldn't be anything left. I'm sure the way the home was built into the western side of the mountain range had a lot to do with it, as it overlooks part of the valley. I make my way over to the far wall where windows that span the entire room have long since shattered. Only tiny bits of glass remain in the frames that stretch from floor to ceiling. I go up to one of the openings and look west, spotting the tip of the Demos force field gleaming in the setting sun.

I look into the valley below and am surprised at how lush the grasses are and how blue the water in the Rodinea Expanse is as it shines under its own dome. I retreat to a spot on the floor in front of a partially burnt couch, sit, and tend to my ankle. I'm forced to take off my boot to get a better look. The skin is starting to turn purple and is swollen. I dig through one of the packs to see if I have any more bandages and tape to at least brace it with, but I've used everything up on my arm, which has started seeping again. I toss the packs onto the floor, lean my head back, and bawl. But I don't get a chance to mourn long. A scuffing noise echoes behind me, so I pull a gun from one of my holsters, turn around, and aim the weapon at the intruder.

"Don't shoot," Grimm says, putting his hands up. He has a gun in one of them, along with two weapons in holsters around his thighs. He also has a pack on his back, but I don't recognize what type or what it might contain.

"Where'd you come from?" I ask, keeping my weapon aimed at his head.

"Rinku, or at least what's left of it," he replies.

"Where's your squad?"

"I sent the ones that were with me back to Quarn. Are you the only one who made it out?"

"No," I stammer. "Keegan made it, too, but… Wavern killed him."

"He's alive?" Grimm asks, startled.

"Yes, thanks to Nex and the Arliss," I say, then go on to explain everything that happened after the fire in the medical ward up until Andra's murder.

"Is he also responsible for what happened at the compound?"

I nod.

"Are you hurt?" he asks, still holding his hands in the air.

"My ankle, I think it's broken," I answer as I lower the gun.

Grimm comes around the couch, sits by my foot, and takes it gingerly in his hands to examine. I grimace in pain when he touches it.

"Can you move your toes?"

"Yes."

"Then it's not broken, probably just a bad sprain." He checks over the rest of me and finds the stitches gone from my forearm. "Did these come out in the attack?"

"No, Wavern did this. I don't know how, but he did."

Grimm checks the wound in my shoulder.

"How'd you get here?" I ask.

"Through the valley. The garage was hardly damaged and the door to the outside was wide open. I figured some of the survivors escaped that way so I sent my squad back to Quarn in the transport we'd used, took a four-seater ATV from the garage, and went searching."

"But what made you come here?"

"Because it's the only viable shelter around. You can't get into Demos from the valley but you can enter the parking pad for the abandonment home—which is how I assume you got in."

"Yes, but from the Aslu Territory side. We couldn't make it to the garage," I respond. "Did you find anyone on your way here?"

He averts his eyes. "Only what was left," he says coldly.

"How were they killed?"

"They were torn apart, probably by Mulgrim."

"But none roam in that valley. They're strictly on the east side of the Kai Mountains," I say, protesting his logic.

"I saw their tracks in the grass, caked in blood. What else could it have been?" he says with a shrug as he stands. "I'm going to look for something to wrap around your ankle for support."

"I want to come with you," I say as I try to push myself up.

"I won't be gone long," he says, irritated.

"That's not it."

"Then what is it?"

"Just help me," I say angrily because of his tone.

He rolls his eyes, puts an arm around my waist, and we make our way towards the back of the room to an area with four sets of doors, two on either side of the hallway. We start with the ones on the left since we're closer to them, but one is a boy's locker room, and the other a filthy kitchen with no running water, so neither are any use to us. We pass the hallway, and when we open the third set of doors, we discover dust-covered medical supplies, tilted file cabinets, bent examination tables, rusted equipment, and a battered nurses' station. Grimm helps me over to one of the tables and begins searching for a splint or wrap with my flashlight. He finds some material under a pile of debris by one of the busted cabinets and as he works on my ankle I look about the room, noticing that behind one of the file cabinets is a slit in the wall. I put my boot back on when he's done, slowly get down from the exam table, and make my way over to the cabinet.

"What are you doing?" Grimm asks when he notices me trying to push the heavy object aside.

"It looks like there's a door back here," I grunt as I topple the cabinet over, exposing the concealed entrance.

I touch the doorknob, an instant chill fills me, and my stomach falls. I push the door open and lights immediately turn on as I hear a generator kick in from somewhere off to my left. Grimm comes up behind me and gasps at the sight.

Grungy blue tiles cling to the walls and discolored concrete makes up the floor. To the right and left are two workstations, but the horror is what's in front of us that has us in fright. Twenty hospital beds line the back wall, each with fluid pumps attached, and some still containing liquids of various colors. Ragged curtains hang between each bed, but all are pushed up against the wall. I take another step into the room and see three mummified bodies of young children accidentally, or purposefully, forgotten after the bombing still strapped to their beds and left behind to die from starvation.

"What is this place?" Grimm asks, fully entering the room.

"This has to be the testing room," I mumble.

"The what?" he asks as he maneuvers around the pieces of debris that had fallen from the ceiling.

"What do you remember of your childhood?"

He turns to look at me. "Our training… school… you. Why?"

"Nex told me that our medical records from the home weren't transferred to the compounds when we moved," I say as I hobble over to the workstation on the right. "The data in the compounds' computers were about when we started in our squads. There's nothing from before then."

"So?" Grimm asks, shrugging.

I spot a cracked plasma screen on the floor by the entrance as well as a computer console underneath the station. I turn the computer on as well as its screen, then I switch on the plasma from the computer itself. Static fills the frame, so I scroll through the thousands of video files that appear on the monitor before me so I can find something to play. I have to use the search function to find Grimm's files, select one labeled *GT751*, then hit play.

The scene is of a young Grimm wearing a green hospital gown, and strapped to one of the beds. His eyes are listless, hair uncombed, and demeanor sluggish. The curtain is around him cutting him off from the others. I can hear screaming and moaning in the background.

"Experiment 751. Subject is Grimm Thomas, age sixteen," a voice I don't recognize says from behind the camera.

Grimm kneels in front of the screen and grazes the glass with his fingertips.

"Go ahead and start the flow," the man tells a young woman standing next to the bed.

She turns on the fluid pump, and a light orange liquid begins coursing through Grimm's veins. His muscles tighten and his eyes roll back in his head as he goes into a seizure. Neither the nurse nor the man behind the camera move to help Grimm.

"Give him the other drug," the man says calmly.

The nurse stops the flow of the light orange liquid and replaces the container with a clear solution, which is immediately released into Grimm's body. After what seems like minutes, the seizure passes and Grimm opens his eyes, fully alert.

"Is it over?" he asks.

The man finally comes into frame, which causes the young Grimm to recoil in fear.

"Yes, son, you did fine," the man says as the nurse unhooks the pump.

"Do I have to do this again?" Grimm asks as he puts on some clothes that were piled on the floor.

"Of course, but not for a few days. You need time to recuperate," the man says.

Grimm hurries away, the curtain falling back into place behind him, but the glimpse of the background is enough to reveal a couple of the squad leaders from Rinku and Virtus stomping around just outside. The man turns to the nurse as he pulls a tablet out from under his coat.

"Will those two drugs be useful?" she asks as she comes up to his side.

"The first one, no. According to the readouts it nearly killed Grimm, but the second drug freed him from the virus, so we should report that one as successful," the man says, smiling.

I pause the recording and glance at Grimm, who looks to be in shock, so I step over and sit beside him.

"Who's that man?" I ask, pointing to the screen.

"My former squad leader from Virtus," he replies. "I…I don't understand. What is this?"

"There was a reason our medical files from the home were kept here," I say as I pull my knees up to my chest. "The leaders experimented on us, since we were expendable. Nex told me that's how they discovered Cymatilis, but I guess they were trying to create more than just the antitoxin."

"All the leaders knew? Even the compound leaders?"

I nod. "It was a direct order from Myr herself," I reply. "Each squad leader got to choose their victim. If you survived to the age of eighteen, your memories of the testing and abuse was wiped clean, while everything else was left intact before you were placed into your squad."

"Abuse? What kind of abuse?"

"Beatings, and probably torture, but who really knows what all they did."

"And Nex told you this?"

"Yes, but now I know it was only a ploy to get me to turn Wavern in to Andra," I say, burying my head in my knees.

Grimm stands and goes over to the nurses' station. "Are there more files?" he asks eagerly.

"Thousands from what I can tell," I say, still sitting on my spot on the floor.

I hear him scrolling through the list for a minute before finally stopping.

"Here's one labeled *GTSR4*," he says.

The image on the plasma changes to an even younger Grimm, probably around thirteen, judging by the fact that Nex said that was the age we were when all of this started. Grimm is cowering on a heavily stained floor, but it's not the testing room. His arms are covered in bruises, some of them fresh.

"Why do I have to keep doing this to you, Grimm?" the squad leader asks harshly.

"Leave me alone," Grimm whimpers.

A small metal ball comes sweeping in on a chain and hits Grimm on the arms. He hollers in pain, but doesn't move.

"I'll say it again, son—you're mine and there isn't anyone here to help you," the man says sternly. "So stop pretending that your life is yours because it's not. It's mine… forever. You got that?"

"No!" Grimm shouts.

The leader grabs Grimm's wrists, hauls him to his feet, and secures him to chains attached to the wall. He goes over to a rack filled with torture implements, takes one, and begins whipping Grimm until he passes out. The leader then leaves, so we fast forward the video until someone else appears on screen. I look at the timestamp and notice several hours have passed before a nurse comes down to collect him.

Grimm pauses the video, and when I look over at him his eyes are filled with tears. His cheeks are red with anger.

"Did they do this to everyone?" he asks.

"Yes," I reply.

"Even you?"

I close my eyes. "Yes."

"No wonder Keegan got away with everything he did," Grimm says furiously. "He was just as bad as they were."

I abruptly stand and leave the room, heading back to the main space where I take my seat behind the couch. I can't stomach hearing Keegan's name, especially when it's spoken by Grimm. It hurts too much because of what he did to Grimm and how Wavern killed him. I did love Keegan in a weird, sick kind of way, and I miss him… badly.

Through the open doors I hear Grimm start another video, so I busy myself with sorting through the two packs to see if I can combine any of it to make it easier to carry. A short time later I hear him going through cabinets in the medical room as the recordings keep playing, probably looking for some Cymatilis which suggests he didn't bring any. A sigh of relief escapes his lips, and he comes over to me with a small case of injectors loaded with the antitoxin.

"Put this in your pack and give yourself an injection," he says before returning to the testing room, closing the door behind him.

I put what I can in Keegan's pack since mine is filled with other stuff. Several hours pass and Grimm is still in the testing room, so I dig through the pack with the food, and eat one of the nutrition bars as I watch the sun finally sink and the stars begin to shine.

"Sara," Grimm says solemnly behind me.

I hadn't even heard him approach.

"What?" I ask without turning around.

"There's something you need to see," he responds.

I begin to feel sick because I assume he's found my recordings. I hang my head and try to disappear.

"Sara," he says again, this time almost in a whisper. "You know, don't you?"

"Did you watch them?" I ask, as I swallow bile.

"Only a few minutes of one. I couldn't stomach any more than that."

"How bad is it?"

Grimm comes around the couch and sits in front of me. "Pretty bad," he says. "Do you know how many girls Wavern did that to?"

"Just me. Nex told me that I was his favorite, and I guess I still am since he claims he's doing all of this for me."

"Did it continue when you got to Rinku?"

I nod. "It got worse from what I've been told." I still refuse to look at Grimm as I speak because I'm too mortified by the truth. "Wavern got me pregnant while I was still in the home, shortly before I was transferred to the compound. Right after I got to Rinku he had Nex terminate the pregnancy. He said he couldn't risk anyone finding out what he'd done because I wasn't of age. He had me sterilized and continued raping me up until a few years ago, when I began seeing Keegan. My memory was altered again, this time by Nex, but it still didn't end. He started beating the shit out of me because I'd replaced him with Keegan, or at least that's how he viewed my new relationship." I glance up into Grimm's sorrowful eyes. "He only stopped because Jules turned him in to Andra. Otherwise I'd probably be dead by now."

"And no one else knew about him doing this to you?"

"He's always been good at hiding things, so this wouldn't have been any different. No one knew about the sexual assaults, except for Nex, and she kept her fucking mouth shut. Now I know why."

I can tell Grimm wants to hug me, but he's afraid I'll probably break. He's right, I will.

"It's been a long day," I say when the silence becomes awkward. "I'm tired and we probably should get some sleep."

"Okay," he says quietly.

I use my pack as a pillow and lie down where I'm sitting. Grimm digs around for a suitable cushion to use and sleeps a few feet away, but he keeps his eyes on me. I can't sleep, but I need Grimm to if I'm going to hunt for that other room, the one in his torture video. I know I'm just going to make myself sick, or worse, but I need to see it to make it real. I don't understand why I want to, it's just an overwhelming sensation I have. Maybe I'm hoping it'll trigger some type of recollection in me, but who would want to remember that part of their life?

The moment I hear Grimm snoring, I get up and return to the testing room.

The plasma screen is off, as is the computer, so at least I'm not walking into that. I scour the walls for another door, as something in the back of my mind is saying to look carefully around the room. I notice a storage closet set behind the nurses' station, but when I open the door the closet is empty with the exception of another door set into the back wall. I open it to find a staircase that descends into darkness. The moment my foot touches the top step, lights shine from the walls and the dim glow radiates all the way down into a room below to reveal a door slightly ajar. I take my time going down, as my ankle is still throbbing. When I reach the room, I push the door open the remainder of the way as lights embedded in the ceiling turn on.

The floor and walls are so heavily stained with blood and other fluids that I can't tell what their original colors were. Across from the door is a rack filled with rusted torture devices, just like the ones I saw in Grimm's recording. To the left of that is a series of chains attached to the wall, and on my right is a large circular bed with what looks to be freshly laundered sheets on the mattress.

"What the hell?" I utter as my hand rises to my mouth.

"Welcome home, Sara," Wavern says behind me. "I was hoping you were coming here."

I spin around with one of my guns aimed at his head.

"I wouldn't do that if I were you," he says then flicks his wrist which causes something to pull the weapon out of my grasp and send it under the bed.

I dive for it, but Wavern snatches my hair and pulls me back to my feet. As I struggle to reach the other weapon, Grimm comes bolting down the stairs with his gun drawn.

"Let her go!" he demands.

Wavern grins. "Sorry, Grimm, but she's still out of your reach," he says, holding up his hand and stretching his fingers.

Grimm freezes in place, but his one arm is moving, placing the barrel of the gun against his temple.

"No!" I scream.

"Too late," Wavern says and with a flick of his wrist Grimm pulls the trigger, shooting himself. Wavern then waves his hand and Grimm's body disintegrates right before my eyes. He closes the door as the dust coats the stairs.

"You fucking bastard!" I shriek as I try to kick him.

He lifts me up and throws me hard onto the mattress, causing me to bounce and hit my head on the wall beside it. I'm dazed as Wavern climbs on top of me, one hand stroking my face while the other moves up under my shirt.

"No," I whimper as I try to push him off, but I'm in too much pain from the impact with the wall and my right arm to get a decent hold or any real strength behind it.

"Don't worry, my love, I'll be gentle like always," he says just as his mouth covers mine.

I continue to fight him off, but his hand slides from my face to my neck and he starts to choke me. I struggle to breathe as he begins to undress, and I pass out just as the real nightmare begins.

Seventeen

I'm slow to open my eyes since I sense Wavern staring at me, which makes me want to remain secluded under the darkness of unconsciousness. I feel his hand brush my face then his mouth over mine, prying it open.

"Wake up, beautiful," he whispers. "I have something for you."

"Leave me alone," I moan as I try to roll over.

He seizes my right arm, removes the bandage from my shoulder, and jams a needle directly into the wound. I scream as he presses the plunger, injecting me with a clear liquid that burns as it enters. A few seconds after the needle is removed, my wound heals perfectly without leaving a scar.

"What did you give me?" I ask, startled.

"A serum that we'd been perfecting before the home was destroyed. It rebuilds your cells at a molecular level, fixing whatever needs to be repaired," he answers.

"Does it spread throughout the entire body? I mean, will it heal my ankle too?" I ask as a plan begins to formulate.

"No," he says, removing the bandage around my forearm. "It has to be injected directly into each wound." He tosses the used needle aside, removes another one from a small pouch in his lap and plunges it into the open wound, which elicits another cry from me. "No one's had a chance to retrieve it until now." He scrapes the needle across my ankle to open up tiny pinpricks in my skin before dropping the remaining serum into the scratches. The bruises disappear as the swelling goes down.

"Now what?" I ask, even though I'm dreading the answer.

"Well, we could stay here, but I have a feeling Demmer has soldiers out looking for me. They may not think to look in the abandonment home at first, but it will eventually come to them," he says, tossing me my clothes.

I quickly get dressed as I think of ways to get away from Wavern, who's putting his shirt and boots on since he was already wearing his pants. I reach for my holsters, but Wavern takes possession of them before I can, then he retrieves my gun that's still under the bed, securing it in one of the holsters. He reaches for the door and as he opens it bullets fly past, several striking him in the chest, killing him.

"Come on, let's go!" Grimm calls as I huddle on the floor to get out of the line of fire.

"What? How?" I ask, as I pull the guns out of Wavern's hands.

"Not now, we have to go," Grimm orders.

I snag the pouch with the serum just before Grimm can start shoving me up the stairs. When we reach the main room, we take our packs and put them on as we bolt down the back stairs to the lower levels. I stick the pouch with the serum into the bag containing the Cymatilis for safe-keeping.

"He won't stay dead," I say, my lungs burning as I vault down the stairs two at a time.

"I know, that's why we've got to move," Grimm says, pushing on my back.

We hit the first level, leap into the four-seater ATV Grimm had used to get to the home, and exit into the Aslu Territory after opening the door wide enough for the vehicle to pass through. When we're about a mile away he stops the vehicle, removes the hunting knife from my pack, takes my left arm, and slices through the spider.

"What are you doing?" I ask fearfully as he creates a deep cross over the image.

"Hiding you," he says as he does the same thing to his burn. "This is how he keeps finding you. There's more to the image than just identification purposes."

I take the blade from him and cut the mark behind my ear, making sure all my bases are covered. Grimm slams on the gas and we shoot south while I rip a shirt of mine into strips to use as bandages for our cuts. I have to wrap his piece around his wrist since he's driving, as well as my own, and I take the rest to apply pressure to the wound behind my ear.

"Now, do you care to explain what the hell just happened?" I practically shout as I strap the holsters to my legs.

"Let's get out of the sun first," he says, maneuvering the vehicle away from the mountains.

I hadn't even noticed the sun had risen. Didn't it just set? I wonder how long I lay unconscious in that room with Wavern, not knowing all the things he could've possibly done to me.

"Won't Demmer see us on the satellites?" I ask as the mountains rapidly disappear behind us.

"No. He can only control the ones over the Ulun Territory, just like Andra could only control the ones over the Aslu Territory," he says.

"How do you know this?"

"I'll tell you everything when we get someplace safe."

He drives for another hour before we come to a small group of brick buildings, half of which have disintegrated into little more than rust-colored dunes. Grimm parks the vehicle at one end of the complex, grabs his pack, and we run to the end unit which still has a partial roof supported by two and a half walls. Grimm tosses his pack into the corner where it's the darkest and sits, but instead of joining him, I aim a gun at his head.

"Who are you?" I ask, keeping several feet between us.

"I'm me, Sara," he says. "Sit down and I'll explain."

"Talk now," I demand.

He lets out a sigh. "All right, but would you mind lowering the weapon?"

"Not until I can be sure you're still Grimm."

"I am. Mostly," he says as he leans his head back and rests it against the wall. "I guess I should really thank Keegan for the shit thing he did when we were kids. It's what saved my life."

"You went to the plateau?" I ask.

He nods. "At first I had no clue where I was, especially when I floated to the surface of that lake. The sun was shining brightly in the sky, but I knew I was dead. I was so confused about everything that it took me quite some time to realize what was happening. While I sat on the edge of the lake, trying to figure out where I was, a low moan echoed from a group of boulders so I followed it. I wasn't expecting what I saw," he says before taking a deep breath. "This *thing* was strapped to a long metal table, clearly in immense pain. Something in the back of my mind told me I knew exactly what it was."

"The Arliss."

He nods. "Only, it was a lot weaker than I ever thought it could be. I knew his form resembled that of a man from what they taught us at the home during our lessons, but this thing barely looked human. It was pale, shriveled, and so deformed that I found myself feeling sorry for it."

"Did he say anything to you?"

"Not at first as he didn't have a mouth, but he began speaking in my head."

"What did he tell you?"

Grimm lifts his head off the wall and gazes at me. "He said that Andra killed you on purpose; that Wavern asked him to turn you into an Arliss slave so you'd be more compliant; that Keegan was a demon known as the Pheles and that he'd turned you into one as well after you returned; that Nex tricked him into deciphering some old texts, which allowed Wavern to be protected from dying and transition him to the plateau with ease if anything were to happen; and that if I promised to help defeat Wavern I could come back to our world."

"He's a part of you?"

"What little there was of him, yes."

"How could you bring him here?" I say, tensing up. "Did he tell you what he did to me down there? That he's just as abusive as Wavern in every sense of the word?"

"I guessed that for myself," he says coolly as he stands and walks over to me. "The Arliss isn't the same as he once was. Wavern's made sure of that by draining whatever life he had left. Now that the creature is no longer in the plateau Wavern can't draw any more power from him, meaning he can't get any stronger."

"How were you able to channel him into you? I thought he needed a follower to assist with that."

"He lied to you about that, in a way. He needed an able-bodied person to perform the merging, but since Cody was unconscious he had you do it."

"How do you know about that?" I ask, startled.

Grimm taps his temple. "The Arliss is in here, remember? I have all his knowledge, thoughts, and memories. Many of which I could do without," he adds.

"What happens to you if the Arliss regains his strength?"

"Nothing," Grimm says, placing his hand on the muzzle of the gun. "I wouldn't agree to help him unless he promised I could stay myself. It took a long time to convince him, weeks at best—at least down there, but he finally agreed. It was either that or fade off into oblivion forever. I guess he really didn't want to die."

"And the satellites?"

"Demmer confessed it to me right before my team returned to Rinku. He was terrified of something, but he wouldn't tell me what. He didn't trust anyone in his compound, so he spoke to me privately. It wasn't until we were back in Rinku that I realized what frightened him so much."

"How do we stop Wavern?" I ask, lowering my weapon.

"We get the Degrem Stone. It's the only thing that can strip Wavern of his abilities."

"And how exactly do we do that since we can't get into the plateau without the marking?" I ask as I hold up my wrist.

"We find the portal, the one that brought the Arliss up here to begin with, and enter that way."

"But we don't even know where to begin looking for it."

"We'll think of something," he says, stepping back.

I holster my weapon and take a seat beside him.

"Did Wavern give you those marks around your neck? They look new," Grimm asks, glancing at me.

"Yes," I respond, hanging my head. "It was so he could… well, you know." I can't bring myself to say it, especially in front of Grimm, as I'm too embarrassed and ashamed that I allowed it to happen. Grimm will think I'm weak if I can't defend myself against a man like Wavern, and I can't handle it if he believes so little of me. "He's going to find out, you know, that the Arliss is no longer in the conversion room," I say after a few moments' thought.

"I know."

"He'll know it was you."

"Yeah, I know that too."

"Do you have any of the Arliss' abilities?"

"Very few. Wavern had almost sucked him dry by the time he agreed to my terms," Grimm replies. "Is it true that Keegan turned you into a Pheles?"

"Unfortunately, but I don't think I'm as powerful as he was."

"Do you know how Keegan became one?"

I tell Grimm what Keegan recounted to me about finding the demon trapped and how it took him over at a young age.

"I guess the real Keegan was still an asshole anyway," Grimm mumbles.

"Can we please not talk about him?" I ask, becoming uncomfortable.

"Sure," he says, slightly bewildered at my tone.

I'm not sure how much time has passed when we hear something moving around just outside. We draw our weapons, aiming them at the hole in the wall we used to enter the structure. A Mulgrim wanders in, followed closely by another one. I hesitate to lower my weapon until the first one sits down and drops its ears. I stand, holster the gun, and begin walking over to it.

"Sara, what the hell are you doing? You don't know what's out there," Grimm says, alarmed.

I forgot that he can't see the wolves. "Get out the specialized flashlight from my pack," I tell him as I approach the animal the way Keegan taught me.

It takes Grimm a minute to find it since it's buried at the bottom of my pack. When he turns it on, I hear the click of his weapon being cocked.

"Don't," I say, spinning around. "It won't hurt me."

"Are you fucking crazy?" he practically shouts, startling the wolf. "How are you able to see that thing?"

It starts to growl, so I stand perfectly still and continue to show my palms.

"The red in my irises from being a Pheles works the same as those flashlights. Now, put the damn gun down," I instruct.

He does and the Mulgrim relaxes, so I begin my approach again. I slowly reach my hand out when I get closer, and the wolf allows me to touch the top of its head. The second Mulgrim approaches and rubs against my legs.

"Follow the wolves," I whisper, Haron's words rushing back to me.

"What?" Grimm asks.

"This is how we get in. The Mulgrim—we need to follow them," I say a little louder. "Haron mentioned to me the last time I was on the plateau that if I ever wanted to return I just needed to follow the wolves."

"You mean right now? That sun will burn us."

"Yes, right now," I say, stepping back over to him and grabbing my packs. "Are you coming or not?"

"I'm coming, just wait," he says, getting to his feet and slinging his pack over his shoulders.

We follow the Mulgrim from the building, hop into the ATV, and pace ourselves behind them as they lead us deeper into the deserted world. Grimm has me drive since I can see them and he can't without having to hold the flashlight. They take us several hours southeast of where we were and pick up speed when we hit smoother terrain. I wish I knew how much longer this was going to be—the seat is becoming very uncomfortable.

"What's that?" Grimm asks, sitting up and pointing to a dark area surround by sunlight.

"That has to be it," I say as I slow down, then slam on the brakes when a sign half-buried in the sand catches my attention. It's created out of thin metal covered in fading paint, with a cheery-looking sun sticking out of the top.

"Welcome to Telus Mesa," Grimm says, reading it out loud.

"I've heard that name before. It's the area where the historian was said to have emerged with the Arliss. I wonder what used to be here," I say as I look around, but the only thing showing that life once existed is the sign.

I turn off the engine and we exit the vehicle just as a pack of Mulgrim crosses into the dark space, disappearing from view. I decide to only take the pack containing the drugs because we might need them. Grimm turns on the specialized flashlight and shines it into the void we now stand in front of, revealing a group of wolves congregating by the entrance, that move away when I begin to cross over.

Darkness immediately envelops me though the stars shine brightly overhead. I smell the crisp lake air and know I'm back on the plateau. Grimm steps in behind me and removes one of his weapons, holding it out front as a precaution.

"Do you know how far we need to go?" Grimm asks as we begin our journey.

I squint my eyes and spot two small buildings in the distance. From their outline they look to be the ones the Arliss kept Cody and me in.

"It's over there," I respond, gesturing to the horizon.

I take out the regular flashlight I'd left in this pack before we get too far away from the portal and shine it on the ground before us. Bones, tattered rags, and what looks like dried meat has the shape of human limbs as I get close enough to see. Grimm keeps his flashlight trained on the Mulgrim, which are leaving us alone for the moment, while I lead the way. The wall separating the two sections isn't as high as I thought, so we climb over it and make our way to the conversion room. I have Grimm take over so he can open the alcove with the stone while I stand guard, even though there isn't anyone else here. He opens the small niche in the wall, removes the green-colored stone, and slips it into his pack. As he does so, I catch a glimpse of at least several dozen or so small metallic spheres inside the pack.

"What are those?" I ask, gesturing to the items.

"Demmer gave me these," Grimm says, pulling one out. "It's a transportable Occlyn Ring. If you put a couple of these together you can form a useable force field to protect yourself."

"Why'd he give them to you?"

"To use, of course. If you have the Occlyn Ring rotating clockwise it produces a force field, but counterclockwise and you get an explosive," he says, holding the device gingerly in his hands.

"And he just voluntarily gave them to you?" I ask, slightly taken aback.

Grimm let's out a nervous laugh. "Not exactly," he says, putting the sphere back into the pack. "I swiped them from the garage in Quarn before we headed back to Rinku. I saw a couple of soldiers configuring them to operate around a transport, so I inquired about them and took some when they weren't looking. We never had tech like this at our compound, so I was curious. This is probably how they were able to stay on the surface long enough to clean up the Rodinea Expanse."

"So much for sharing resources," I retort. "Can we use them to destroy the plateau?"

"It can't be destroyed," Grimm replies harshly.

"Why not?"

"Because it's connected to our world," he says defensively. "You can't destroy one without destroying the other. We'll just have to close the portal."

"But Wavern will know how to reopen it," I protest as Grimm starts heading back to the wall.

"He'd have to be alive to do that and, besides, once he's drained of the Arliss and Pheles' powers he won't be able to return to the plateau. Both will be killed when we demolish the stone and he needs them to get down here."

"He didn't before, so how can you be so sure of that now?" I ask as I run to catch up.

Grimm spins around to face me. "Because the Arliss told me so," he says bitterly. "The incantation Nex performed bound Wavern to the Arliss before he died, which is how he was able to get to the plateau and then return. Without the Arliss, Wavern is screwed."

We make our way back to the portal, but stay on the plateau side until the sun has moved behind the Kai Mountains. I'm surprised all the wolves that had been congregating at the entrance are no longer here, but I'm also glad. We spend the time trying to figure out the best way to destroy the portal and settle on using the small Occlyn Rings, but we need to test them first since we have no idea what kind of detonation they'll create.

"How do you turn these things on?" I ask, holding one as carefully as possible.

"You need to turn the top half of the sphere in the direction you desire and it'll turn on from there," Grimm says. "It'll take about a minute or so for the device to reach the critical mass needed to either produce the force field or explode." He hands me the pack after removing a sphere. "Hold these, I'll be right back."

He runs towards the wall and I lose sight of him. Several minutes pass and his return is illuminated by an immense eruption at or near the conversion room. The ground shakes as a shockwave races across the terrain, rocks and flames shooting high into the sky. I get knocked over and covered in dust, but otherwise no injuries. When Grimm makes it back, he has a cut on the back of his arm from debris and is just as filthy as I am.

"I suggest we place a couple on each side of the portal," he says, sitting down. "Just to make sure it closes."

I nod in agreement.

Another hour passes before the sun has moved enough for us to leave the plateau. We each take three spheres, spin their tops, and then drop them on either side of the portal. We rush back to the vehicle and Grimm floors it to get us a good distance away from the detonation, which causes the ground around the portal to partially collapse, burying any evidence that it once existed. The shockwave hits the ATV and nearly causes it to turn over, but Grimm manages to get the vehicle under control and we continue heading towards the mountains.

"Where do we go now?" I ask.

"We need to find Wavern, so we'll return to the abandonment home."

"Any ideas on how we're going to subdue him so we can plant the stone against his chest?"

"No clue."

"Don't you think we should discuss that before heading into the lion's den?"

"Fine, we'll shoot him like before. That should give us enough time," he says, annoyed.

"Why does it sound like you're not taking this seriously anymore?" I ask, worried.

"I am," Grimm gripes. "I just don't know why you're trying to make this more complicated than it needs to be."

I keep my mouth shut for the remainder of the ride, mainly because I'm trying to assess if the Arliss is having more of an influence over Grimm than he's willing to admit.

We left the bay door into the tunnel for the home open, so it makes our reentry a lot easier. We pull into the parking pad and Grimm is on the verge of turning off the engine when I reach out and stop him.

"He's not here," I say.

"What makes you think that?"

I reach for the specialized flashlight, which Grimm had placed on the dashboard after we got back into the vehicle, and shine it on several dead Mulgrim heaped into the corner of the massive room. The bodies weren't here before, so Wavern had to have killed them when he was leaving. From the looks of it, he used a gun.

"I wonder where he got the weapon from," I state as I hand the flashlight over to Grimm.

"I'm sure there's a weapons cache in this place somewhere," Grimm replies as he tosses the flashlight back onto the dashboard and heads the vehicle towards the other entrance.

We're halfway through the valley as the sun begins to set, only it doesn't look quite right. I keep an eye to our west while Grimm navigates around the expanse's force field. A bright flash radiates upward, causing the sun to appear ten times brighter before diminishing.

"Holy shit!" escapes my lips.

"What is it?" Grimm asks, his eyes glancing over at me briefly.

"Wavern is in Quarn. He's trying to nuke Demos," I say, pointing at the small mushroom cloud slowly dissipating.

"The Occlyn Ring will protect them since that's what it's designed for," Grimm says casually.

"But it can't take a constant barrage of the bombs. It'll eventually fail," I say as disbelief washes over me.

"He can't launch them continuously," Grimm says. "The satellites have to recalibrate when a bomb is deployed and the interval lasts five minutes, so there's at least some pause between each bomb."

"How can you be so calm about this?" I ask, horrified. This isn't the Grimm I know. "If that dome does break, there won't be anyone left in this world but Wavern. He'll have killed everyone!"

"Except us," Grimm says with a sly smile.

"What the hell is wrong with you?" I yell.

He shakes his head as if trying to clear it. "Sorry, I don't know what came over me," he replies, sounding slightly scared.

"It's the Arliss—he's trying to gain control of you."

"I guess Wavern won't be the only person we'll be using the Degrem Stone on," Grimm says as he maneuvers the vehicle into the garage for Rinku.

He makes a sharp left, steers the vehicle down into the tunnel that'll take us to the city, and presses the gas pedal to the floor. Even at our current speed it'll take us a few hours to get there. I'm hoping the Occlyn Ring can hold out that long and that Myr has taken precautions to keep her people safe.

Eighteen

The parking pad for Demos is deserted when we arrive, but the bombing hasn't stopped. We park the ATV and run through the double doors after they open. All the streets are quiet, but I feel eyes staring at us from the residential housing in Zones A and E. We hustle to the center of the city, but no one is there. Raised voices from Zone B attract our attention, so we follow them and come upon a group of people arguing in front of the meeting hall. Myr is standing on the top step, so she can see over everyone screaming in front of her.

"Why hasn't anyone been sent to Quarn to stop this?" an elderly gentleman demands.

"We can't get into the compound," a familiar voice replies. "The garage has been sealed with the same substance we use to cut off the levels in the barracks that aren't being used, and there's no getting around it."

I crane my neck to get a glimpse of who it is and practically cry with excitement when I notice Jules standing in front of the crowd.

"Jules!" I call out, and I push my way through with Grimm following.

"Sara?" he responds, before throwing his arms around me. "Oh my God, I didn't think you made it out. Where's Keegan?"

"Gone," I say solemnly.

Jules frowns, which causes the cut by his eye to bleed a little. His body is covered in dried blood and sweat, and his clothes have holes with corresponding wounds behind them. I know he's in pain and has probably internal injuries, but he's got a job to do, so that'll take priority over his own health.

"Then how do we get into the compound?" another person asks.

"We won't need to," Myr says confidently. "The Arliss is wasting his efforts. The force field is impenetrable."

"It's not the Arliss doing this," Grimm says. "It's Wavern; he's a Nathair descendant."

"What?" Myr asks, turning pale.

"I tried telling you that," Jules snaps.

"It doesn't matter who's doing it, we're still safe under the dome," she says stubbornly.

"That's only if he keeps aiming directly at it," the leader of Squad Nine says. "If he's able to readjust those satellites' alignment, he could point the bombs to the base where the ring is embedded in the mountain. Several strikes there and the ring becomes too damaged to operate."

"She's right," an elderly man says. "We need to evacuate the city."

"And go where?" another person chimes in. "The farms under the Factory? Those criminals would just love that."

"There's a shelter under the pool for the fountain," Myr says, sounding defeated. "It'll hold everyone until this is over."

"We'll secure the farms," the leader of Squad Ten remarks.

"That still doesn't answer how we stop this whole thing," someone says.

"Sara and I will take care of that," Grimm says.

"Fine, then let's get everyone underground as quickly as possible," Myr says, dismissing us.

"What are you going to do?" Jules asks while the others hurry away.

"You don't want to know," I answer. I remove the two packs and hand them both to him after first removing the hunting knife and several syringes containing the serum, which I place into the pockets of my pants. "There's Cymatilis in this one as well as a healing agent. The other has Keegan's weapons. You'll need all the ammunition possible if this goes south."

Jules gives me a hug then runs off towards the center of Demos.

"How do you want to do this?" Grimm asks.

"I draw him to us," I reply as I look down at the spider on my wrist.

"Let me do it," Grimm says, placing his hand on my arm, covering the tattoo. "You'll know what Wavern will do the minute he sees you."

"I know, but it has to be me. Otherwise I don't think he'll come."

An evacuation announcement sings out from the speakers attached to the lampposts, giving instructions to meet at the pool in the center of the square. Grimm and I head in that direction, but mainly to make sure everyone gets there safely. We help Jules go through the apartment buildings, clearing them out. The pool has been drained, the fountain lowered, and a staircase set in its place, leading several stories down.

"I'm staying with you," Jules says as we assist people onto the stairs so they don't crowd each other, all while bombs continue to explode over our heads.

"No, you need to go with them," I say, pointing to the crowd of terrified individuals around us. "You're the only soldier here, Jules, so you have to go with them. It's your job."

He grumbles, but as soon as the last person has been sent below he follows and a heavy steel door slides into place. The city now has an eerie, abandoned air about it and it's quite unsettling.

"Where do you want me?" Grimm asks.

"Go into the ice cream parlor and ready your weapons. When Wavern appears, start shooting."

"What about the stone?"

"Give it to me."

He opens his pack, removes the stone, and places it into my hand.

"Are you sure this is how you want to do it?" Grimm asks, his hand still on the stone.

"I'm not sure about anything anymore," I utter. "I just know this all needs to end, one way or another."

He hesitates, almost as if he's waiting for something between the two of us to happen. I would love to kiss him right now and tell him we'll be better when this is over, but I can't. Knowing the Arliss is lurking inside him and trying to come out has me sickened. Also, his words from the other day still sting, and I doubt that'll ever go away.

Grimm finally turns and heads into the parlor, ducking behind some tables but still in a position to be able to see out of the bay windows. I tuck the stone under my arm, remove a syringe from my pocket, and take off the safety cap. I force myself to take several deep breaths before plunging it into the spider, and then grit my teeth as the serum burns through my wrist and hand. I toss the syringe away and wait, but I don't have to wait long.

"What are you trying to pull, Sara?" Wavern asks as he appears before me. "You hid yourself from me and now, just like that, I'm able to find you again."

"I'm not trying to pull anything," I say, shaking a little. "I just wanted you to stop bombing Demos."

"Well, this is only a pause. I'll resume as soon as you and me—" he pauses when he notices the Degrem stone under my arm. "Where'd you get that?"

I pull it out and hold it firmly in my hand. "I visited the Fomorian Plateau," I say coolly. "And came home with a prize."

"You found the portal," he states.

I nod. "But it no longer exists, I made sure of that," I comment.

"What do you intend on doing with the stone?"

"Using it… on myself," I reply. "I figure if the Arliss and Pheles are both gone from inside me, then when I die I won't be able to return and I can finally move on from this world."

"Your marking will prevent that from happening," Wavern says, seething. "You'll be drawn back to the plateau, where you'll be stuck until I decide when to let you out."

"That's only if the tattoo is still on me," I say as I remove the hunting knife from under my belt. "The Arliss told me once that the spider is only superficial, so I'm guessing that if I were to cut down a few layers I could properly remove it and be free—from all of you."

I set the tip of the knife against my skin and am in the process of driving it in, when a searing pain rips through my shoulder in the same spot Tennison shot me. I drop the knife as another bullet strikes my calf, knocking me to the ground and causing me to release the stone. I roll over and try crawling to it as a foot stomps on the wound in my leg causing searing pain to race up my body and me to scream.

"That was a horrible idea, Sara," Grimm says, flipping me onto my back and standing over me. "If I'd known what your true intentions were, I never would've given you the stone."

Wavern pulls two guns from under his shirt and aims them at Grimm's head. "What the hell do you think you're doing, boy?" Wavern asks, his mouth curled up into a snarl.

"Fixing this," Grimm responds as he shoots Wavern in the head.

Grimm reaches for the stone, places it on Wavern's chest, and holds down the spider and pentagram symbols simultaneously. The stone glows white instead of green and absorbs the Pheles and everything Wavern took from the Arliss into its coarse surface. When the stone is no longer glowing, Grimm removes it and shoots Wavern in the head again to ensure he's dead before bending down next to me.

"Now, my dear Sara, for your punishment," Grimm says, straddling me and placing the muzzle of his gun against my head.

"Fight him, Grimm," I plead as tears rain down my face. "The Arliss doesn't have you, not if you keep fighting."

Grimm's face contorts. "He's too strong," Grimm utters.

"No, he's not. He needs you to live which makes him weak, but you don't need him," I say as I fumble with the holster on my left leg and work to get the gun out.

I hear the click of the chamber for his gun loading as he places the stone on my chest. "Before I send you back to the plateau that Pheles inside you has to come out, as does whatever of me still remains," he says, pressing the symbols on the stone.

I feel as if I'm being ripped in two and I holler from the agony. I'm struggling to get air into my lungs and become lightheaded as small dots fill my vision. He releases the stone and the pain ends, but I'm still dazed and having difficulty focusing on what I need to do.

"My love, this is for betraying me," Grimm says.

As he readies to fire, I manage to put the muzzle of my pistol against his side and fire. The bullet pierces him all the way through, and he falls off me onto the ground. I move slowly as I wrench the stone from his hand, press the spider symbol, and watch Grimm suffer as I suck the Arliss from his body. Once the transfer is complete, I take a syringe and inject the serum directly into his wound, hoping it reaches his vital organs before the life drains from his body. I apply the serum to each of my wounds, pick up several spheres that have scattered across the ground from Grimm's pack bursting open upon his collapse, and make my way to the parking pad. The Degrem Stone grows hot as I feel the Arliss and Pheles battling for their freedom. I climb into the ATV, turn it around, and head down the tunnel towards Rinku with the stone warbling in the passenger seat.

I'm just past the tunnel towards Quarn when the stone starts glowing green and violently vibrating. I stop the vehicle, turn on all but one of the spheres, and bolt back towards the city. I turn the last sphere I have clockwise and create a force field around me knowing that I'm not going to make it a safe distance in time. The explosion that follows hits the force field and sends me flying several feet down the tunnel, landing hard on my shoulder. Debris rains down, cutting me off from the vehicle and burying me under the shield. I start panicking after some time has passed because I don't know if anyone will know what happened or know to even look for me.

Debris slides down around the dome, opening up a hole for me to see out of. Jules and several other soldiers are frantically pulling chunks of concrete off the shield. I don't turn the sphere off until I know I won't be crushed to death. Jules reaches for me, but unfortunately, grabs my damaged arm, which causes me to scream.

"Get a medic!" he shouts as several members of Squad Nine hurry towards us.

"Where's Grimm?" I ask as I stumble around, trying to get my footing.

"He's being looked at by a doctor," Jules says, helping me down the tunnel.

A stretcher arrives and I'm gently placed onto it. "If no one minds, I think I'll pass out now," I say, then close my eyes and fade.

It's been several weeks since everything happened, and Jules is the only visitor I've had the entire time I've been in the hospital. I stopped asking about Grimm after my second day in intensive care. He's never going to come see me as I lie in my hospital bed, nursing a newly repaired shoulder. I wound up shattering the bones when I landed after the explosion, so before I can be released I have to have a few weeks of physical therapy, but I'm almost done. Jules has told me I've been offered a squad leader position in Quarn, a job he himself recommended me for now that he's been made compound leader. If I decide not to take it, Myr has an apartment set up for me in Zone E, so I'll have someplace to go no matter what I decide.

The casualties in Quarn were extensive, so any former soldiers who were sentenced to work in the farms due to any infraction have been given another opportunity to prove themselves worthy of redemption. Personally, I don't think I can go back to that kind of life. I'm sick of it, plus I'd be getting nothing but stares and weird looks from the others in the compound since everyone has been well versed on the events that led up to the showdown with Wavern… and the Arliss, though much has still been kept from them. I don't need that kind of stress in my life. Having the memories of it is punishment enough.

"Hey," Jules says as he enters my room. "You're being released today, so Myr needs your decision."

"I can't, Jules," I say sadly. "I can't go back to that life. I'm too damaged to be of use to anyone."

"Don't say that," Jules says, sitting on the edge of my bed.

"Well, it's obviously true. There has to be a reason why you're the only one I've seen outside of the hospital staff," I say, getting choked up. Knowing Grimm is avoiding me is more painful than any physical injury could be.

Jules knows who I'm talking about, even if I don't mention his name. "I told you before, Grimm is still having a hard time dealing with what he almost did to you. It's eating him alive, Sara. The guy is crazy about you, we've all known that for years, even before he moved to Rinku. Just give him some more time. He'll come around," Jules says, patting my hand.

"I wouldn't be too sure about that," I say.

"Well, I need to head back to Quarn but I'll check on you as often as I can," he says as he stands, then kisses me on the forehead, and leaves.

When the door closes I feel more alone than ever. If I had my way, I'd live out my days in the Aslu Territory. It wouldn't take long for me to die since I'm no longer immune to the radiation. But that would be a painful way to go and I'm tired of hurting. A few minutes after Jules leaves, a nurse comes in to give me my discharge orders, clean clothes, and an escort to my new home. I'm not surprised Myr isn't handling this herself. From what Jules has told me, she barely leaves her apartment above the meeting hall. She's too ashamed of her actions, even though very few know the truth about everything she's done.

I'm placed on the third floor of an apartment building situated in the center of Zone E. It's clean, well furnished, and lonely. The days pass quietly and uneventfully. I keep to myself mostly, only venturing out on days where I can tolerate being around others, which isn't often. I go to the library every now and then to check out a book since I refuse to watch anything, afraid I'll see familiar faces that are long gone.

A month later, Myr is found dead in her home. Rumors start that it was the Arliss exacting his revenge, but I hear from hospital staff it was just a heart attack due to her age. A new leader is quickly selected, and life continues as normal. Today I'm feeling somewhat social, so I pick a spot under a tree in the park to sit and watch as children chase each other. A few soldiers stop to say hello, but it's mainly those who were in Rinku. I close my eyes and rest my head against the tree trunk, when I sense someone watching me. I try to ignore the person, but they sit beside me and I can tell they're scared to talk to me. That tells me who it is before the person even speaks.

"What do you want, Grimm?" I ask without having to open my eyes.

"I came to see how you're doing," he answers.

"I'm alive, so that pretty much sums it all up," I say sarcastically.

"Look, Sara—"

"No, you look, Grimm," I say as I open my eyes and stare at him. "I thought, of all people, you would always have my back. I'm recovering in the hospital for weeks and the only one who visits is Jules. I ask him why and he tells me you're too embarrassed to see me, which is utter bullshit.

After everything we've been through, I thought maybe my best friend would have the decency to see me. You were all I had left at the time, but now... I don't even have that." I abruptly stand as I choke back tears. "Please leave me alone."

"Sara, wait," he says, standing and grabbing my arm. "Let me explain."

I pull out of his grasp. "Your inaction has said enough," I say, dropping my head and walking away.

When I get back to my apartment I slam the door and fall onto the couch, shaking from the exchange. I can't handle seeing him, not now anyway, but maybe eventually. I'm almost calm, when there's a knock on the door.

"Go away," I call out, but my voice has very little effort behind it.

The door opens and then closes.

"Not until you hear me out," Grimm says, coming around to face me. "I needed time... time to adjust to what had just happened. I never thought myself vulnerable like I was when the Arliss tried to control me. There's only been one other time when I felt that weak, and it was when I met you. I couldn't deal with almost killing you. It tore me up inside, knowing I was capable of doing such a thing. Of everything I've witnessed in my life that was the hardest, and I can't shake it from my mind."

"Try," I mutter.

"That's why I came to see you," he says, kneeling in front of me. "I need you to help me with this. I can't do it on my own."

"That's bullshit, Grimm. You've never needed my help with anything. You made your thoughts very clear to me back in Rinku."

"I was angry," he says, bolting to his feet. "I was so mad at you for being with Keegan that I wanted to hurt you like I was hurting. I didn't mean any of it—you have to believe me."

"I loved you so much," I mumble as I hang my head.

"Then why marry Keegan?" he asks as he returns to his knees and places his hands on the couch alongside me.

"For protection," I reply. "When I was with him I knew I was safe from Wavern, that he wouldn't dare hit me again because Keegan would've killed him."

"But you married him after I moved to Rinku. Why, when you knew I could help you?"

"To protect myself from you," I answer. "I figured that if I was married then I wouldn't have to worry about my feelings when it came to you. I'd be free from it all. But it only made things worse."

"Then let me fix it," he says, placing his hand on my cheek.

"I don't think it can be," I reply, putting my hand on top of his.

He pulls me to him, taking my lips with his. We take it slow at first, easing our way into each other. Once we find our rhythm the loneliness melts away, and I finally feel happy.

The End

Lightning Source UK Ltd.
Milton Keynes UK
UKHW020651170621
385673UK00010B/714